SOUTH PACIFIC MARINE

A Novel of World War II and Korea

Paul Nickerson

HERITAGE BOOKS
2010

HERITAGE BOOKS

AN IMPRINT OF HERITAGE BOOKS, INC.

Books, CDs, and more—Worldwide

For our listing of thousands of titles see our website
at
www.HeritageBooks.com

Published 2010 by
HERITAGE BOOKS, INC.
Publishing Division
100 Railroad Ave. #104
Westminster, Maryland 21157

Copyright © 2010 Paul Nickerson

Other books by the author:
Marine Raiders: A Novel of World War II

International Standard Book Numbers
Paperbound: 978-0-7884-5150-8
Clothbound: 978-0-7884-8327-1

Dedication

I dedicate this book to the generation of American men and women who fought and struggled through World War II to save the world from slavery, tyranny and genocide. I especially remember the South Pacific Marines and Sailors who gave their all for God and country.

Table of Contents

Background- Jungle Hell   3

Chapter One -Respite   7

Chapter Two- Home   13

*Chapter Three-*Reunion   21

Chapter Four- Camp Pendleton   43

Chapter Five- Bloody Iwo   63

Chapter Six- O.S.S. and M.I.6   95

Chapter Seven- Back to the Corps. 117

Chapter Eight- Survival 143

Chapter Nine- Home Alive in Forty Five 163

Chapter Ten- Korea. 195

Chapter Eleven- Inchon to Chosin 219

Chapter Twelve- Recovery 251

Epilogue 260

Acknowledgements

I truly appreciate the consideration and support of Leslie Wolfinger, Publishing Division Director of Heritage Books, Inc.,

I also wish to recognize with thanks my Editor of Research & Formatting, Ruth Nickerson. Her continued help throughout the development of this book is appreciated.

I give special thanks to the U.S. Marine Corps and U.S. Navy Archives for the historical information in this book and the U.S. Marine Raiders Association for their help and support.

Especially helpful was Ervin Kaplan, M.D., Second Marine Raider Regiment, for his support. Marines like these are why we live free today. Semper Phi. They gave us their tomorrows so we could have today.

SOUTH PACIFIC MARINE

PAUL NICKERSON

Background

JUNGLE HELL

Guadalcanal Island - August 1942

Edson's Bloody Ridge, adjacent to Henderson Airfield, 0300 hours. The Japanese Sendie Division was storming the ridge, two battalions in battle order, bayonets fixed.

The First Marine Raider Regiment under Colonel Red Mike Edson and the First Marine Parachute Regiment, attached on their right flank, two companies of each Regiment were all that could be spared to hold the ridge.

Henderson Field, the only U.S. Airfield in the Solomon Islands, was the prize. The Americans held it. The Japanese wanted it. It was the whole reason for the Guadalcanal Campaign.

Screaming, opium influenced Japanese attacked by the hundreds in an all out banzai charge.

* * * * *

Sgt. Rawlins Thompson sub machine gun had grown hot from firing; mowing down the enemy at close range.

The machine gun sections Browning L1A1 30 cal L.M.G. had begun cooking off rounds due to an over-heated barrel. It had to be changed or melt-down could occur.

Marines had thrown grenades and riddled the enemy with shrapnel. Still the horde came on, screaming like demons.

Mortars, both 60mm and 81mm, had thinned their ranks, cutting huge swaths from their line of advance. Then the living climbed over their dead and dying comrades, still charging the Marines. There were so many that the Marines could not kill them all. The enemy was overwhelming the defenders. Rifle butts, bayonets, knives, rocks, fists were the order of battle during that night in hell for the Marines.

Rawlins Tommy gun had run dry so he fought with his 45 cal pistol and Ka-Bar knife. Japs were all around him, trying to kill him any way possible. He shot one in the face as the enemy tried to bayonet him. Then another in the chest, that had nearly shot him from six feet away. The B.A.R. Team was over-run, clubbed and bayoneted. Three more Marines that wouldn't make it home. The whole line was fighting hand to hand.

English and Japanese oaths and curses could be heard over the din of battle, up close and personal. This was a preview of what was to come. The Japanese, a ruthless enemy, were famous for closing with their enemy and fighting this way, the way of Bushido and Samurai.

The Marines, too brave and stubborn to give up, fought to the death on that bloody ridge and many other places like it.

* * * * *

Corporal Russo from Chicago drove his bayonet into a Jap's gut as the enemy tried to stab his Sgt. in the back. The surprised son of Nippon grunted, dropped to his knees and tried to get up, clutching the muzzle of the Springfield rifle and bayonet that had impaled him. Russo ripped it out of his gut and drove it in his throat. End of problem. One dead Jap and one live Sgt.

* * * * *

The Airborne Marines held the flank as the Japs hit them hard, trying to break through to the airfield. If the Marines had retreated that night and failed to hold the Raiders flank, Australia would surely have been invaded.

* * * * *

Private Heys, alias the Joker, strangled a Jap killer after the enemy had relieved the Marine of his rifle. The hook on Japanese bayonets worked well for this. An unwary enemy's rifle could be ripped from his hands with a twist of the bayonet hook when in contact with an opposing rifle muzzle. A nasty surprise in a close fight.

The tide was turned. The fanatical enemy was driven back for the third time on that night in hell. They left piles of dead comrades for the Marines to bury. Sadly, more than a few Marines had suffered the same fate.

Bougainville Island - November 1943

The horror of jungle warfare continued as the battle for Piva Trail became critical if the island of Bougainville was to be held. Piva Trail was the only way through the jungle so events centered on holding it. The Raiders, along with the 9th Marines, set up a road block and held the enemy during a three day encounter. It ended with 550 Japanese dead, 19 Marines dead and 32 wounded. Gunnery Sgt. Rawlins was one of the wounded and Joker, who had been with Rawlins since Bloody Ridge on the Canal, was one of the dead. Russo had made it out of that shit hole and had made Squad Leader when Rawlins was hit.

6   South Pacific Marine

Chapter One

RESPITE

Gunnery Sgt. Rawlins awoke with a start, *the nightmare still fresh in his mind. The image of ghostly white light from parachute flares and long shadows of bayonet brandishing ghouls charging him had returned once again. The impulse to run for his life, away from these evil minions of hell, was strong. But Marines don't run, especially stubborn old sea dogs like him. This same dream visited him almost nightly, and probably would for the rest of his life.*

* * * * *

"Where the hell am I?"

"Honolulu Naval Hospital, Sgt."

"Why?"

"You were shot. Remember?"

"Oh, yeah, that's right. Bougainville. The Nip officer with the Nambu."

"Yes, Sgt."

"That's Gunnery Sgt., Nurse."

"Yes, I know, Sgt. And I'm Lieutenant, not Nurse."

"Sorry, Sir."

"You Marines are all the same. Big muscles, big mouth."

"And that ain't all, Lieutenant Nurse."

"That will be all, Gunnery Sgt."

"Yes, Sir."

* * * * *

Rawlins thought of his ex-wife, Susan.

I wonder where she is now, and with whom? I guess my last

letter didn't interest her. I guess you can't expect a queen to stay with a Marine.

Nurse Trumbolt had made him think about women. She would be going home shortly after she fulfilled her obligation to the Service. He had been very surprised to learn that she lived in Niagara Falls, NY only a few miles from his home in Buffalo, NY. Might be interesting to look her up when he got state-side.

* * * * *

He began to think of his Raider Squad, back on Guadalcanal by now, waiting for re-deployment orders. The Canal that had been secured long ago was now a forward base for operations in the Solomon Islands. He still found it hard to believe that Joker was dead. He had stepped on a mine on Bougainville, on the Piva Trail. Instead of paying attention to business, he had been pining over a "Dear John" letter he had gotten from his wife. Just like a boot at Parris Island. Some guys just couldn't take it.

Now that they're breaking up the Raiders I wonder what will happen to us.

Rawlins had heard rumors of a new Marine Division being formed for upcoming large scale operations.

That's probably where we'll go; or replacements for the First and Second Divisions. After Tarawa and Peleliu they were depleted. Both ops suffered real slaughter.

Both atolls were held by bad ass Rikusentai (Japanese Special Naval Landing Force Troops (Marines).

All I know is that in a week or so I'm outta this lash up and home for ten days. First time since Pearl got hit. Been a long time.

The wounded Marine drifted back to sleep and the nightmares returned.

The long patrol, a thirty day deep recon patrol on Guadalcanal. The First Raiders drew the mission. Heavy swampy jungle full of snakes, crocodiles, clouds of insects, malaria, dengue fever, and Japs. Hundreds of them. The Raiders set up ambushes, destroyed supply dumps, and raised hell with the enemy. They learned some things from the enemy about how to use the jungle to their advantage.

Rawlins remembered the nights on the Canal. Hot. Always hot or rainy and bugs and leeches by the millions. Rats as big as small dogs. Bats that would bite you. And the Jap. The terror by night. They would infiltrate the Marine N.D.P. (night defense position) and try to kill you with a knife, or drop a grenade in your hole.

He recalled Junior, the big farm kid from Idaho. After being stabbed in the shoulder he beat in the attacker's head with his steel helmet. In the morning there were three dead Japs lying around the farm boy's hole. When asked what happened the big Marine replied:

"They kept trying to stick me with them long skinny knives all night. That made me mad, so I smashed 'um to death. They shouldn't a made me mad."

This brought some strange looks from fellow Raiders but no one said a word. No one dared. This nineteen year old Raider was the biggest Marine anyone had even seen. Rawlins remembered he was the biggest anything he had ever seen.

He recalled the kunai grass fields and the booby traps and hidden bunkers. One Raider lost his legs to a Bouncing Betty mine designed for that purpose. As the Navy Chaplain sat by his side he quietly smoked a cigarette and died. No fuss, no big deal. Didn't want to make a scene.

Tough bastard, thought Rawlins.

And the machine guns. The enemy would wait until the point element was on top of them as they hid in the grass. Then they would open up and mow down as many Marines as possible until they themselves were killed. A grenade or two usually did the job. The Japs had no problem spending the lives of their men as they tried to kill the Marines. Seemed like a hell of a waste of good infantry to Rawlins.

The caves were another problem. The little buggers would dig in so deep that air, arty, and Naval guns couldn't reach them. This was a standard tactic of the Japanese throughout the Pacific War. And they always sacrificed to the last man. Sometimes they were even chained to their machine guns. Rawlins hated this. Satchel charges, grenades, even gasoline were the only way to silence these fanatics.

The night raids during the Toulabong operation often entered the Marine's dream shattered sleep. He remembered the submarine that took his Raider platoon there. It had seemed to him like a steel coffin just looking for a place to sink. Rawlins detested these underwater craft. It was surely unnatural to sink a perfectly good boat intentionally. He recalled the sound of water rushing past the pressure hull as he wondered when it would collapse the thin iron shell that kept out the Pacific Ocean. He recalled the old Chief of the boat trying to cheer up the gloomy passenger.

"Don't worry, Gunny. If we go down you won't have time to drown. The pressure will kill you first."

Gunny had responded:

"Gee thanks, Chief. I feel so much better now."

During this job Corporal Ramirez from San Antonio found out how sneaky the Jap was. While trying to help a wounded Japanese soldier, one of the men in his squad was stabbed by a half dead enemy. Another wounded enemy threw a grenade at his own people while they were trying to help the wounded. After these experiences Ramirez and company always killed the enemy twice. Just to make sure.

After Toulabong another long campaign on another big island like the Canal. They would us a P.T. boat to infiltrate this time. The mission was to recon the island for the upcoming invasion, and raise as much hell as possible for a diversion.

They met with a whole division of Jap regular Army, recently deployed after four years of war in Manchuria and China. These boys were pros. This battle had been a tough fight with battle hardened, combat ready soldiers.

The jungle itself became their enemy. It was so thick that an enemy could be ten feet away and not be seen. The dense, hot, wet weather caused equipment and weapons to rust and rot constantly. Also, the jungle took its toll on the men's bodies. They had ongoing problems with jungle rot and malaria. Screeching, howling monkeys and gibbons jangled nerves, squawking birds or no birds at all were a worry. Leeches and insects attached to any skin found bare and accessible. Snake bite wounds and rat bite wounds contributed to the jungle hell.

In the mornings the thick mist would cling to them and chill them to the bone and in the afternoon it would be so hot they would sweat until they passed out.

The Japs loved it all. It was their playground. They would use it to help kill the weak, soft Americans.

* * * * *

Rawlins recalled all too clearly being blown off the deck of a P.T. boat and into the sea. He and three sailors had lived through the explosion. This experience began an ordeal of surviving on an island in enemy territory. After twelve hours in the water they had come upon an island and had gone ashore. Living off fish, wild pig and fruit they had stayed alive, ducking enemy patrols until finally stealing a Japanese boat and making their escape. They would eventually be picked up by an American submarine.

* * * * *

Rawlins drifted back to sleep, remembering dead friends. He was glad to be out of it, at least for now.

For the first time since his wife had left him for the Navy officer slob he was interested in living. Until meeting Nurse Trumbolt he hadn't cared what happened. His stay on the hospital ship off Bougainville had changed everything. Much to his surprise someone seemed to care whether he lived or died.

The islands and the Japs would have to wait. He was going home. For the first time since the war started Gunnery Sgt. Rawlins was going home.

Chapter Two

Home

Rawlins left the hospital with a new issue, service dress green uniform. The starched uniform felt strange after months of worn dungarees and the fore and aft cover felt much lighter than the steel G.I. helmet he was used to.

Boarding a C47 Dakota transport, the Marine settled in for the hop to San Francisco. There he boarded a troop transport and headed east. The train was full of service men coming from or going to one theater of war or another. Many, like him, were wounded and going home on furlough or for good; their war over. A one-armed Sailor sat next to Rawlins and stared out the window.

"Where you been, Gunny?"

"Everywhere."

"Yeah, me too. Get hit?"

"Yeah. Pistol bullet and shrapnel. Bougainville."

"I heard that was a bad one."

"Bad enough. But the Canal was worse. How about you?"

"Leyte Gulf. My destroyer got the hell shelled out of it while on picket duty at night in the slot. Jap battle cruiser. Eight inch guns. We had nowhere to go. Just took it. In the morning the bridge was blown away. Just gone. Captain and Exec. were both dead. All guns were out of action and we were all out of torpedoes. The ship was taking on water, thirty degree list, so we abandoned her. That is the few that were left. Two days in the water. Sharks hit us the first night. Smelled the blood I guess. Men screaming all night. Hell of a note. Finally a PBY Recon Flying Boat found us, and the rest is history."

"Hell of a war, ain't it?"

"Yeah, Gunny, hell of a war."

* * * * *

Rawlins recalled the savage night attacks by the Japanese

Marines. Screaming like banshees from hell. Rifles, swords and bayonets wielded by hoards of crazy men. They attacked straight into the Marine line. In the open. No cover. Suicide. The Marines mowed them down by the hundreds and they still came. It was almost like they wanted to die. Crazy sons of bitches.

And the bunkers. Japs chained to their guns. The Marines roasted them alive with flame throwers. Rawlins never got used to that. The screams and the smell of burning Japs. He never got used to it.

Hell of a way to fight, he thought.

Pushing those images of horror from his mind he thought of home. He hadn't written in so long or got any mail that he didn't know what to expect. Getting wounded always messed up the mail. No one knew where you were. The old man was probably at the VA Hospital on Bailey Ave. playing checkers and telling war stories to some captured, unfortunate patient.

Mother would be cooking something. She was always cooking something. His sister would be in school, some college or other. Probably Niagara University. That's where her boyfriend got his Army commission. R.O.T.C. Another sad letter home. Operation Torch. Invasion of Libya. Objective - remove or destroy Vichy French and Nazi government from Libya and Morocco. Second Lieutenant Theodore Jarvis was killed in action by German machine gun fire while leading a combat patrol. Hell of a note. It broke his sister's heart. It's a real shame when a twenty year old kid gets it.

Then there was Evelyn Trumbolt, or as Rawlins preferred, Turnbolt, like the Springfield rifle. The little nurse from Niagara Falls. They had grown up within twenty miles of each other and never met until he got hit on Bougainville. She was his nurse on the hospital ship. She had big blue eyes, long reddish brown hair, and was only five foot two. She would fuss over the hard ass Marine almost constantly, like he was her personal property. He had discovered something in her that he hadn't noticed in women before. Something more than their physical attributes, something strangely attractive to the Raider that he had never felt before. Not her body. It was something new and different and very appealing. He found himself thinking about her often. Too often. That kind of thinking could get a

Marine dead. He was confused and he didn't understand these weird feelings. They made him uncomfortable. What really bothered him was he had never felt this way about Susan, his ex-wife. Strange.

* * * * *

The train ride was long and boring. Rawlins sat by a window and watched the scenery. Herds of antelope and an occasional mule deer caught his attention occasionally but not much of anything else. Finally the desert landscape turned into prairie; a sea of grass swaying in the wind like ocean waves. It had a calming effect like the ocean at night.

For a while he forgot the horror of killing men he didn't know a thing about and watching old friends blown to pieces or machine gunned. He left the war behind. It was a long way off now in a strange, alien place far away. Now he understood why his father had the thousand yard stare and the nightmares and the drinking binges when it all got to be too much for him. When he was younger he had thought the old man was crazy. Now he understood and it was time to tell his father so. Make things right between them before one or the other of them was gone. Too much time had been wasted because of a young man's egotistical conclusions. The Marine would not make that mistake again.

And Susan. Should he look her up or forget her. After all they were divorced. Maybe it was time to move on. Like all the other poor slobs that got the "Dear John" letter, sometimes you gotta let go. You can't make a woman want you if she doesn't. It's just a waste of time. And the friend routine is even worse, especially when you get to meet the new husband or boyfriend. Better to walk away and start something new.

He remembered a Marine who was wounded on the Canal and got the letter while in hospital at Pearl. The story went through the whole regiment.

The guy gets a furlough and meets the old lady in Frisco to discuss their new lives. His little girl is along for the ride. So is the 4F Joby that's riding his wife. According to her they're all supposed to hold hands and sing songs and do other shit together. One big happy mess. So he meets the broad and the kid and everything is OK. The next day they meet for dinner. This time wifey brings Jobey with her. So far so good. The Marine keeps his cool, not wanting to do brig bread and water. But he's thinking the whole time.

How the hell can she do this to me? I'm fightin' the war and she's playing with this 4F slob and my kid is in the middle of it. Son of a bitch. Rotten bastard. I got more respect for the Japs. At least they fight like men. This asshole thinks he can move in and just take over. Doesn't he know I was killing people a month ago? Lowlife shitbird. He better watch his civilian ass.

Then the comments began.

"I hear you Marines are real killers. Too bad you don't take care of your families. Good thing I stepped in to take over and do what's right."

"Don't you think fighting the war is right, slacker?"

"Now wait a minute, Jarhead. I'm university material, not cannon fodder."

"Then why aren't you an officer in the Military?"

"Because I'm not dumb enough to get shot for the politicians."

"Don't you remember that we were attacked and twenty five hundred Americans died at Pearl Harbor?"

"Yes, I know. But if we had left the Japanese alone in China it would not have happened."

"You mean when they were murdering thousands of people and using babies and their mothers for bayonet practice?"

"Those are unfounded rumors. Not according to the news reels I saw. You're just a capitalist bully."

"What the hell are you? A communist, a coward, a traitor? Or all three?"

"I won't stand for this abuse from this ruffian, Margaret. We're leaving."

"What's the matter, pansy? Can't take the heat? Gonna run home to Momma?"

"Sit down, Kermit. I told you he was a brute. Not sensitive like you. Just ignore his outbursts. He's been in the jungle too long."

"Yeah, Kermit. Sit down and have a drink with the old

hubby. Like we're good buddies."

Then it happened. The ultimate slap in the face for the Marine.

"Daddy, can I go to the bathroom?"

And Kermit replied,

"Yes, if you must. But make it snappy. We won't be here much longer."

Then the Marine:

"Wait a minute. Who you calling Daddy?"

"Mommy told me to call Kermit, Daddy from now on and call you Bill."

That did it. Kermit was lifted by his throat and hair across the table and dragged outside onto the pier above Frisco Bay. New Daddy emitted squeals and curses but to no avail. While the combat vet was polishing the pier railing with Kermit's face someone called the cops. Just as Kermit was launched over the railing into the Bay the M.P.s arrived. The jilted Marine was beaten to the deck and hauled to the Frisco Navy brig. Kermit was recovered by the Coast Guard. The Marine got life in Miramar Naval prison. Mommy married Kermit's brother two years later.

Better to walk away.

* * * * *

Rawlins remembered New Orleans where he met Susan. He was working with the Higgins Boat Works helping design a landing craft for the Navy. Her father, a Navy Captain, was in command. Rawlins was the top NCO of the project and the two became friends. The Marine filled a gap left in the Captain's life when his son died on the Arizona on December 7th.

The old man encouraged the relationship that developed between the Gunnery Sgt. and the Captain's daughter. Then the old man died and the daughter slipped away like the tide rushing out to sea. It was like a dream. Cloudy memories from long ago.

* * * * *

Rawlins decided to keep his promise to Joker when the train reached Pittsburgh. He had promised the dying Corporal that he would visit his wife and tell her how he died.

He found Mrs. Heys living in the tenement house the Joker had described. He knew he wasn't welcome right away.

"What do you want, Marine?

"Can I come in?"

"Well, I guess. If you must. Is this visit about my husband?"

"Yes. We were in the same Raider squad. He asked me to stop and see you when I got home."

"Why?"

"To tell you he still loves you and will wait for you on the other side."

"Why did he bother? He didn't love me when he was here."

"He was dying, Ma'm. It was his last request."

"How did he die?"

"Stepped on a land mine."

"Did he suffer?"

"No. It was over pretty fast. We gave him morphine. He went out quick."

"Damn fool. I told him this would happen if he joined the Marines. I told him it was dangerous. But he wouldn't listen. Oh, no, not him. Now I'm stuck raising his brat alone. And everybody says I should be proud. He was a hero. Big deal. Another dead hero and I'm alone."

Rawlins spoke up:

"I thought you met someone else."

"I did. He took off after hubby's letter got here and he read it. It explained in great detail how he was going to gut Alvin like a fish and give him a taste of the war he missed. He claimed I would be the last woman he would ever steal from a Marine. Alvin got scared and left me, saying he wasn't prepared to face a crazy Marine. Do you think he meant what he wrote, Sgt.?"

"Yes. I was with him when he read your letter. He told me the same thing he put in the letter to you."

"I told you he was crazy. Like all you Marines."

With this insult Rawlins left the Joker's medals and wedding ring on the kitchen table and left.

 Damn shame, he thought. *Another destroyed family from this shitty war. And there's no end in sight.*

* * * * *

 The ex-Raider boarded the train for Buffalo. A Navy Steward gave him a sandwich and coffee and a pack of Luckies someone had donated at the last stop. He ate the sandwich and drank the Navy coffee. The best in the world. He fired up a Lucky and glanced out the window. And there was something he thought he would never see again. Lake Erie, the inland sea that would be by his side all the way to Buffalo. The playground where he had fished and duck hunted years ago. And the Niagara River, which flowed from the Lake at Buffalo to Niagara Falls and beyond. Right past Nurse Turnbolt's parent's house. A bungalow right on the shore of the upper Niagara. The woman he had met off Bougainville Island, a million miles away, grew up just downstream from his home. How strange.

Chapter Three

REUNION

Rawlins took a cab from the Buffalo Train Depot to his parent's home. Opening the front door he entered the familiar abode and dropped his sea bag on the deck. From the kitchen his mother called out:

"Ken, is that you? You're early."

"Yeah, Ma. It's me and I ain't early."

SILENCE.

Then the Marine's mother looked around the corner from the kitchen.

"Kenny. Oh, my God, it's you. You're home."

Mom ran to her son and threw herself on him and began to cry.

"Mom, what's the matter. Why you crying."

"You're home and alive."

"That upsets you?"

"Oh, shut up and hug me."

Women. Rawlins would never understand them.

Mother and son went into the kitchen and had coffee.

"What happened to you? We heard that you were wounded but nothing since."

"I picked up some grenade fragments and a Jap officer shot me with his pistol."

"Does it hurt much?"

"No. No big deal."

"You're so skinny and tanned and your hair is so blond.

You look different."

"The tropics will do that to you."

And so will malaria which he didn't mention.

"How's Sis?"

"She's fine. Working and going to school. She's sleeping upstairs. It's her day off."

"And Dad?"

"OK. Down to the VA like always."

"I'll have to go see him and let his buddies gawk at me. After all they did write to me a couple of times. I'm sure they would love some new war stories. Dad's are kind of worn out. They all know how he and James Cagney won the war in France in 1918."

"Oh, Kenny. You're being nasty."

"Just kidding, Mom. I know he was above and beyond over there."

"Kenny!"

Sis entered the room and embraced her older brother.

"You're home! Why didn't you call?"

"Couldn't find a phone booth in the jungle."

"Same old Kenny. A laugh a minute. We heard you were shot."

"Just a little bit. No big deal."

"How do you get shot a little bit?"

"Same as gettin' shot a lot but less."

"Oh, you. Always the joker. How are you feeling? So skinny, so brown. And your hair. You were never that blond before."

"I had it dyed. Thought I would become a movie star while I'm home."

"You did not. You're a Marine forever, unfortunately. You were a Marine before you became one. Lost cause, you and Dad. The Corps this, the Corps that. Boring."

"Now you sound like Susan. She hated the Corps."

"Well, of course, silly. She was afraid you would get killed."

"Is that why she left me? In case I got killed?"

"That's was part of it. After her brother died at Pearl Harbor she couldn't take any more stress."

"Is that so?"

"That's what she told me."

"How nice. Try to kill a man before he gets killed."

"It's not like that, Ken. After I lost Howard I couldn't be with anyone for a long time. Even now it's hard."

Yeah, thought Rawlins. *Susan didn't find it too difficult to play with the Navy slob Airedale. Until he got greased over Truk Lagoon, that is.*

"*She called, Ken.*"

"Why? Did she want to throw a party if I was K.I.A.?"

"That's not fair and you know it."

"Yeah, I know. I'm the big mean son of a bitch. I don't understand the poor dear's feelings. All I know is that when it was play time at the Officer's Club in D.C., when Susan and Lieutenant shitbird were playing tennis and hide the mouse, I was getting shot at on some snake and Jap infested island.. Poor wifey. Just couldn't handle the stress of being a wife and not a slut."

"Ken, that's enough. I won't have this barracks talk in my house any longer."

"OK, Ma. Sorry. I get carried away sometimes."

"Yes, I've noticed. Someone else called too. A woman named Evelyn. Said she was your nurse on the hospital ship. She wanted to know if we had any news about you."

"Well. Imagine that. The little nurse from Niagara Falls calling about me. Ain't that something. Maybe I should look her up and say hello."

"Yes, Ken, you should. She seemed very concerned."
"She did on the ship too. Imagine that."

* * * * *

Rawlins took a cab to the VA Hospital. Thought he would surprise the old man. Walking in the entrance foyer gave him the creeps. He hated hospitals. He had spent too much time in them since the war began. Taking the elevator, he got off on the third floor. The rec room for patients and visitors. He knew this is where his father would be. He asked for him at the entrance desk.

"I'm looking for Ken Rawlins. Is he here?"
"Yeah, Marine. I'll find him."

The orderly entered the room where patients and friends played checkers and cards or listened to the radio.

"There's a big ass Marine out here looking for Ken Rawlins. You want to see him?"

The old man was startled at this. Afraid it might be bad news about his son.

"What's his name?"
"He didn't say."
"What's he look like?"
"Tall, blonde hair, blue eyes, Gunnery Sgt. Enough ribbons to start his own parade."

"Sounds like my son."
"It is, Dad. I'm home."

The Marine let himself into the room.

The old Marine didn't say a word. Just got out of his chair and embraced his son and held him for a long time. Then he wept like a child. No one said a word. They just looked away. They all understood.

Finally a Navy Senior Chief Petty officer with one leg

and one arm grabbed the Senior Rawlins by the shoulder.

"C'mon, Gunner, you owe me a game of checkers. This time I'm gonna kick your Marine ass so your kid can see that you ain't invincible after all."

"OK, Chief, you're on."

Then the questions from fellow warriors.

"Where you been, Gunny?"

"The Canal, Toulabong, Ruwawa, Enogay, Enewetok, Bougainville, and a hundred other no name shit holes. Lots a jungle and Japs."

"No shit. Solomons. Right?"

"Yeah, that's right. Bad ass place. Lost a lot of good Joes to the little bastards."

"I thought those cross eyed monkeys couldn't shoot."

"Like hell. We suffered more sniper wounds than any other kind."

"You going back, Gunny?"

"Not for a while. Got ten days and a wake up on deck. Then I gotta go to Pendleton for re-assignment. They're breaking up the Raiders."

"You get hit, Gunny?"

"Yeah. Nip officer got me with a pistol. Didn't see the son of a bitch. Picked up some grenade fragments too."

"Tough break, Marine."

"Not so bad. Lotta guys got worse."

The old man just finished off the Chief.

"Why you old sea dog. Got me again. Showin' off for your kid. And of course I let you win in front of him. I'll whip your Marine ass next time."

The young Marine looked at the old Chief and nodded, silently thanking him for helping his father save face. The Chief nodded back and smiled.

"Give 'um hell, Gunny."

"Aye, Senior Chief."

As the two Rawlins' left the room a young Marine Corporal yelled at the two:

"Semper phi, Gunny."

And Rawlins replied:

"See you in hell, Corporal."

* * * * *

O'Malley's Bar and Grill. The two Marines stopped for a drink. As they walked in everyone in the place stared at them.

"That must be Ken's kid. Big son of a bitch. Look at them ribbons. Damn. He's seen some heavy shit. Lucky he made it back."

"What are you drinking, Marine"

"Johnny Walker and a beer."

"Same for me, Todd."

"Is this that kid that used to bring me the paper?"

"Yeah, that's him."

"Damn, he got big."

The bar owner brought the drinks and Rawlins tried to pay.

"Put your money away, Marine. It's no good here. I hope you got a lot of Japs. A lot of guys from Buffalo ain't coming home."

"Thanks, Mr. O'Malley."

His shoulder was hurting like hell and Rawlins hoped the booze would help. He pulled out his free pack of Luckies and gave the old man one and lit one for himself.

"I didn't know you smoked, Ken."

"You ever see a Marine who didn't? Helps with the nerves."

"Yeah. I remember. Where do you think you will be

assigned?"

"Either Fourth or Fifth Division, I think. That's why Pendleton." There's some big ops coming up. Maybe Japan itself. They need lots of combat NCOs. That's why they broke up the Raiders. They need our experience."

"Makes sense, I guess."

The elder Rawlins speaks up.

"Wild Bill Donovan is in town. He called the house asking about you. Said he had to talk to you about an incident in New Zealand."

"No shit. I'm surprised he heard about it. The Brits must have informed him."

"What happened, Ken?"

"A Kraut Abvere agent tried to whack me in my hotel room. I got him instead. British M16 Intelligence interviewed me about it. They must have passed it on to the O.S.S. Figured I'd be an easy target, I guess."

"Figured wrong, didn't they?"

"Yeah."

"And your forty five did the rest. Good weapon, that forty five. Glad you had it with you."

"Yeah, me too, but the Kraut didn't care for it."

Rawlins was feeling better now. The pain was gone and he was relaxed. Something he hadn't been in a long time.

"I gotta tell you something else, Dad, before it's too late."

"What is it, Son?"

"I'm sorry."

"For what?"

"For being an asshole when I was young. For bitching and moaning when you were having a rough run and for running to Mom behind your back. For talking like a punk when you were trying to advise me."

"Don't worry about it, Son. I was the same way. We're all that way when we're young. When I was eighteen I knew everything. Now I don't know shit."

"Yeah, Dad. Me too. Like this lousy war. What's it all about? Thousands of guys dying and for what. It's a bunch of bullshit."

"Yeah. Just like my war. Same shit."

The two men got drunk together and cleared the air. Never again would there be a rift between them. They both knew how precious life is and how quick it can end. Both men now and both combat Marines. Twenty-five years apart but the same mind and the same inner battles. They staggered home and left the thirty eight Chevy at the bar, too drunk to drive. As they hung on to each other they sang barracks and marching songs. Marine Corps tradition. Get drunk and celebrate being alive. You may not get another chance.

* * * * *

The next day Rawlins called Bill Donavan's Buffalo office. The O.S.S. Director wanted to debrief the Marine/Operative about his run-in with the German Abvere agent in New Zealand. They met for lunch at the Hilton Hotel.

"How have you been, Ken?"

"OK, Sir. Only problem is I keep getting shot."

"Yes. I know how that is. What happened in New Zealand?"

"The Kraut they called the Adlar (eagle) was laying for me in my hotel room one night. When I returned, after having been out, I noticed that the door had been opened. The match in the door jamb trick. The dummy didn't see it. I knew something was wrong so I pulled my forty five and got ready. I pushed the door open and hit the deck. Total darkness. He fired at me and I fired at his muzzle flash. Unfortunately, he was hit in the chest. Didn't last long enough to give up any Intel."

"How did you know it was the Adlar?"

"The Brits identified him. They knew all about him. I guess he was Hitler Youth, SS, Gestapo, and Abvar. Real nasty son of a bitch."

"Yes. The Brits informed me of the incident. That's why I called your father. Wanted to hear it for myself."

"Why do you think he was in New Zealand, Sir?"

"The Abvar is working with Japanese Intelligence. They're trying to eliminate O.S.S. and British M16 operatives in the South Pacific area and you are a prime target after your escapades in Norway."

"I thought that might be the connection."

"Yes, Rawlins. You and your friends really upset the German High Command when you blew up their heavy water facility."

"Gee, imagine that. Me upsetting the top Krauts. Yes, indeed."

"So where to now, Ken?"

"Camp Pendleton and the Fifth Marine Division. Then back to the war. I heard rumors that we might hit mainland Japan. I hope they're wrong. We're gonna lose a lot of good men if we do."

"Rumors are rumors, Ken. Don't worry about it. In the political circles I move in I'm hearing the opposite. America is sick of war. Too many losses. The last thing the politicians want is a large scale, very costly operation. Germany is pretty well finished and the Russians will be in Berlin in a month or so. The end is in sight. When Japan is on its own and every one gangs up on them they will sue for peace."

"I don't know, Bill. You don't know the Jap. They don't give up ever. They prefer to die with honor. That bullshit

Bushido of theirs is nuts. And they really believe it. Die with honor. Kill the enemy and yourself. Nuts. Even Jap broads and kids. Fight to the death. If we invade the home island we're in for a major shit storm. They won't give up. They will fight to the last asshole."

Rawlins and Wild Bill parted company. The Director would look up his operative when they needed him again.

* * * * *

Now the Marine's thoughts turned to Nurse Turnbolt in Niagara Falls. When he got home he borrowed the thirty eight Chevy from his father for the weekend, then packed his sea bag and headed down stairs to leave. Mom grabbed him and dragged him into the dining room. His father and sis were at the large table. All of his favorites from long ago were laid out like a king's feast. His mother had cooked all day to prepare for the home coming meal. Roast beef, turkey, clams, spaghetti, macaroni salad and all the trimmings. The Marine sat down with his family. The people he was fighting this horrible war for. And they knew it.

"Dig in, Ken. You earned it. "

The food was like heaven. He hadn't seen food like this in years. Sadly, he could barely eat. Months of C rations or nothing at all had shrunk his stomach.

"Ken. What's wrong? Don't you like it?"

"It's great, Mom, I just can't eat. Been on short rations so long I got no stomach. Sorry, Mom, but thanks for the effort. Been a long time."

And out the door he went to see if Evelyn Trumbolt really did give a shit about him.

* * * * *

Rawlins found the small house on the Niagara River very easily. He followed River Road, which ran parallel to the River, from Buffalo to Niagara Falls. One left turn and right to the house. He could have come by water if he had had a boat. Parking Dad's Chevy in front of the cottage, he got out and headed for the door. The door opened and an older woman asked:

"Can I help you?"

"Is Evelyn in?"

"Yes. I'll get her."

"Ken. My God, it's you. Mom, it's Ken!! It's really him. He's alive."

"Hi, Turnbolt. Happy to see me"

"You dummy. What do you think."

"I dunno. You might be tired of me."

"You silly Marine."

The little nurse dragged the big Marine into the house.

"Dad. Come and meet Ken."

"Hi, Ken, good to finally meet you."

"Pleased to meet you, Sir."

"How are you feeling, Ken?"

"OK, Nurse."

"I'm not your nurse."

"Then who are you? Did I find the wrong house and the wrong woman?"

"No, silly. I'm more than your nurse."

"Really?"

"Yes, really."

"What are you?"

"You know."

"Know what?"

"What I am."

"Then why am I asking?"

"I don't know. You're silly."

Finally, the questions.

"Looks like you have seen a lot of action, Ken."

"Yes, Sir. From Guadalcanal to Bougainville where I was wounded. That's where I met Evelyn."

"Yes. She told us all about you. The stubborn Marine from Buffalo. Our neighbor's son is in the First Marine Division. He was on Guadalcanal and Peleliu. Now we don't know where he is."

"Hope he makes it, Sir."

"He's a tough kid."

"They're all tough kids and getting younger all the time. We're running out of men, Sir. I've seen them as young as seventeen in the Raiders."

"That's awfully young to fight a war, Ken."

"Yes, Sir, but they're doing a hell of a job. After their first fight with the Japs they ain't kids anymore."

"I can well imagine, Ken. It's a shame it has to be that way. War should be up to men to fight."

"Yes, Sir."

* * * * *

Evelyn was tired of war and talk of war.

"Ken. Let's go to the Dance Hall. My friends will be there."

Before Rawlins could reply he was dragged out to the old Chevy.

"C'mon, Ken, let's go."

As he drove to the Dance Hall Evelyn talked non-stop.

"I didn't really think you would come to the house."

"Why?"

"Well, the big Marine Raider war hero. I thought you

were too important to spend time with us little civilians."

"You know better than that, Turnbolt."

"How can I be sure?"

The Marine stopped the car, grabbed the girl and gave her a big kiss.

"Well, I guess you are interested in little old me. I was beginning to wonder."

Then she kissed him back.

"Let's go, Ken. It's getting late. The place will close. Have you heard from your wife?"

"I don't have one of those."

"You know. Susan."

"Who?"

"The woman you were calling for when you were delirious on the ship."

"Oh. That's my pet cat, Susan."

"I take that to mean there's been no contact with her."

"No, I'm afraid not. Just as well. We weren't right for each other."

"Why not?"

"She was used to Naval hierarchy. High ranking officers and the life style that goes with it. Not a mud Marine like me. All I had to offer was far off duty stations, damn little money, lots of loneliness and not much else. Can't blame her for leaving, I guess. I should have known better. No queen stays with a Marine."

"You mean no spoiled brat, don't you?"

"Never thought of it that way, Turnbolt. Always thought it was my fault."

"Ever think of leaving the Marines?"

"Maybe some day. If I live that long. Right now I can't see the end of this shit I'm in."

"It will end, Ken, and you will survive. I just know it."

"How?"

"Women know these things. I knew you would come to the house too, It's our destiny."

"Well, imagine that. A Marine with destiny. Sounds like a movie title."

"There you go again with the jokes. Are you ever serious?"

"Yeah, Turnbolt. When people are trying to kill me. That's serious."

"Sorry, Ken. All I know is that we were meant to be together. I knew it the first time I saw you."

"Really, Turnbolt?"

"Yes. Really."

"You don't even know me."

"Yes, I do."

"No, you don't."

"Don't argue with me. I know I'm right."

"How do you know you're right?"

"Just because."

"OK. Turnbolt."

"Why do you call me that?"

"Because you remind me of my favorite rifle."

"How nice. I guess that's a compliment, coming from a Marine."

"That's right, Turnbolt. Not everyone gets to be a rifle."

"You're weird, Ken."

"I know, but that's why you love me."

Rawlins took a chance with the big word. Evelyn began to cry.

Shit, thought Rawlins, *did it again. Never could talk to women.*

"Whatsamatter?"

"You're making jokes about my feelings."

"No, I'm not."

"Yes, you are. You men are all the same. Everything is funny."

Shit, thought Rawlins. *Here we go. So much for this romance.* The Marine got quiet. Didn't know what to say. Just drove the Chevy to the Dance Hall. Then Evelyn grabbed his hand and held it.

"I'm sorry, Ken. I didn't mean to snap at you. It's just that my feelings for you are serious."

Shit, thought the Marine. *I ain't ready for this. She's looking for a permanent lash-up. I'm not over the last one yet.*

Finally, they arrived at the Dance Hall.

"C.mon, Ken, my friends are here."

Rawlins felt out of place. Now he had to tolerate these civilians. Pain in the ass.

Oh, well, duty calls. Be a nice Marine and let the babies interrogate you. I'd rather be in the jungle. At least there's no bull shit there. And the Japs don't bore me with meaningless conversation.

"Hi, Evelyn. Who is this?"

"This is Ken. The Marine I met at Bougainville."

"Really?"

"Yes. It's him."

"My. So big and handsome. When you're done with him give him to me."

"Hi, Marine. I'm Jim."

Rawlins shook his hand.

"Just got back from Italy. Thirty Sixth Texas Division. Kraut mortar shell landed next to my hole. Broke some ribs, caught some steel."

"Pleased to meet you, Soldier. I got the same on Bougainville."

"Yeah. Evelyn's told us about you. Glad you made it

out."

"Yeah. Likewise, Troop. Hell of a war."

"You know it, Marine."

The Soldier ordered a pitcher of beer and he and Rawlins shared it and a pack of Luckies.

Evelyn was up dancing with some college kid. Finally, they returned to the table, the bebop tunes finished.

"Ken. This is John. We grew up together and he's in O.C.S. (Officer Candidate School) at Niagara U."

"Good for you, kid. What are you going for?"

"I'm gonna be a pilot. As soon as I get my commission the Army is sending me to flight school."

"Well, ain't that something. No mud and blood for you. Gonna be special."

"That's right, Marine. I'm gonna fight the gentleman's war."

"Well, imagine that. Good luck, kid."

The two buddies got up to dance again. Rawlins spoke up:

"That kid reminds me of a Navy Lieutenant I knew. Same bull shit. He was a gentleman. Now he's fish food in Truk Lagoon. Dumb bastard. Got his ass shot off in a T.B.F. Avenger dive bomber."

"How did you know him," asked the Soldier.

"He was the guy that stole my ex-wife."

"Good for the prick then. Lousy officers. They think they're God. Can take a man's wife or anything else they want."

"Amen to that, brother."

"Hey, Rawlins. You notice those two swabbies at the bar?"

"Yeah. I've been watchin um."

"They're staring at your girl."

"Yeah. I see. As long as that's all they do the hell with

'um. I've done too much brig time over this kinda shit. That swab officer cost me my stripes for the same shit. Didn't realize at the time it takes two to dance."

"Yeah, Rawlins. I know what you mean. Seen a lot of Joes get the letter."

"Yeah. Hell of a not, ain't it?"

"Sure as hell is, Marine."

The dancers returned.

"Do you want to dance, Ken?"

"Naw. No good at it. Me and the Sarge here are devising strategies to win the war."

"Oh, I see. Very important."

Just then the band began to play the classic, "In the Mood." The little nurse grabbed the big Marine and dragged him to the dance floor.

"I thought you couldn't dance."

"I can't."

"Well, you're doing a great impression."

Half way through the song Evelyn whispered in Rawlins ear, "I love you."

Rawlins didn't know what to say or do. She had caught him off guard with this. He figured the best defense sometimes is to do nothing, so he complied with that thought. Finally the song ended and the pair returned to their table. Rawlins noticed the two Sailors were still staring and it was beginning to piss him off.

"I got to hit the head, Evelyn"

"What does that mean?"

"The bathroom, Sorry. Forgot my manners."

As the Marine walked by the starrers, they exchanged menacing looks. When Rawlins left the head the two predators were talking to Evelyn at their table.

Well, I'll be a son of a bitch. Here we go again. Lousy

swabs. Gotta have all the broads.

Rawlins addressed the two adversaries.

"Shove off, Navy. This table is taken."

"Well, look at a jarhead and a dogface holding hands. How cute. They must be in love. We'll leave, mud brain, but the dame goes with us."

The big Petty Officer grabbed Evelyn by the arm.

"C'mon, honey. We'll show you what real men can do."

Rawlins hit him between the eyes hard. Said "real man" dropped like a stone. Laid out across a table like he was dead. His partner pulled a switchblade.

"I'm gonna cut you deep, jarhead."

"Go ahead and try, deck ape. I haven't seen any action lately."

The Sailor lunged at the Marine, trying to stab him. Rawlins side stepped him, grabbed his arm and elbowed him in the face with his free arm. Then he collapsed the attacker's elbow and reversed the knife until the weapon was at the attacker's throat. The Sailor bucked and squealed, thinking he was about to die. Then the combat Marine administered a savate strike just behind the bad guy's ear, sending him off to dream land. Rawlins took the knife and gave it to the barkeep.

"Give this to the cops when they show. Let's go, Evelyn. Time to shove off. Take care, Sarge."

"You too, Marine. Good luck."

The pair left in a hurry. Rawlins didn't want a run-in with the law.

"Ken. Are you all right?'

"Yeah. No big deal."

"Are you sure."

"Yeah, I'm OK."

Rawlins was hurting like hell but he wasn't going to admit it. Marines don't whine.

"Where did you learn to fight like that. I've never seen anything like it. My God. I thought he was going to kill you."

"That dumb swabbie. He didn't know shit about a knife fight. Raider School taught all forms of hand to hand combat. And so did the Japs. It's their favorite way to fight."

The nurse began to cry again.

What's wrong? What did I say this time?"

"You're going to get killed if you go back to the war. You're crazy. You don't fear anything."

"I got to go back. There's no choice."

"Yes, there is. Run away with me. We'll go to South America where there is no war."

"And do what? Pick bananas? Live on love? I have to go back and take my chances like everybody else."

"Then I don't want to see you anymore. I already lost someone in this war and I'm not going through it again."

"OK, Evelyn, suit yourself."

Silence now; all the way home. Then at the house:

"Goodbye, Ken. I hope you enjoy your war."

And out of the car she went.

"Well, I'll be a sad son of a bitch.

* * * * *

Rawlins stopped at a liquor store on Hertel Avenue back in Buffalo where he purchased a supply of both he and his father's favorite drinks.

"What will you have, Marine?"

"A six pack of Black Label and a fifth of Johnny Walker."

After pouring drinks for his dad and himself, he had a conversation with the old man.

"Well, how did the visit go? She remember you?"

"Yeah, she remembered."

"Well, what happened? Did you get your ashes hauled?"

"Shit."

"Didn't go so good. Why not?"

"I got in a rumble with two swabbies. One of 'um had a knife, so I put him to sleep."

"No shit. You didn't kill him, did you?"

"Naw, nothin' like that. Just put out his lights."

"Did that piss her off?"

"Boy, I'll say. All of a sudden I became the bad guy. And I was protecting her."

"Did she know them?"

"Naw. Just a couple deck apes passing through. Looking for some action. They tried to leave with her and I stopped it."

"Where?"

"In some dance joint on the River. She was sashaying her all important ass all over the floor with some ninety day wonder shave tail she grew up with and they were watching from the bar. As soon as I hit the head they moved in. The Army kid wasn't up to it so I took over. After we left she got kinda funny. The she told me I was nuts and said I shouldn't know how to fight like that. Too dangerous, I guess."

"What the hell did she think. You're in the Boy Scouts or something?"

"I don't know, Dad. Damn mystery to me. Like all dames. Anyway, she told me to beat it and go enjoy my war."

"She'll be back. You scared her, that's all. Probably never saw a real skirmish. Used to watchin' those college kids play with each other."

"Aw, shit. Don't matter. Any port in a storm. Don't mean shit. After Susan I don't really give a shit."

"Yeah. I can see why."

Rawlins poured another round.

"Where do you know Wild Bill Donovan from?"

"France. Nineteen seventeen."

"No shit."

"We were bivouacked near the same town for a while. He was with the Fightin' Sixty Ninth New York infantry. I was with First Division Expeditionary. We kept runnin' into each other, hittin' the same joints. Finally started talking and found out we were both from Buffalo. Got to be friends. His outfit moved up to the Marne River. We devil dogs, as the Heinies called us, headed for Belleau Wood and relieved the frogs. After the war I saw him at one of his political rallies. He was runnin' for Senator or Dog Catcher or something. He spotted me and came over."

"Hey, you old jarhead. Good to see you made it back."

"And have been friends ever since. That's why when he started the O.S.S. I recommended you. I figured once you get tired of the mud and blood you might like the Intel life. It's a good racket. And this war ain't gonna last forever. By the way; what did he want when he called?"

"I had a run in with a Kraut Abvar agent in New Zealand. Laid for me in my hotel room. Lucky for me I had your 45 with me. The Kraut missed; I didn't. Tried to make him talk but he kicked off on me. The Brits knew all about him and they reported it to Bill."

"Why were the Germans after you?"

"Because a squad of Raiders and a company of British Commando blew up their Heavy Water facility in Norway. I guess it really pissed off the German High Command."

"Yeah. I heard about that. You and your boys did one hell of a job."

"We were lucky. They didn't expect us."

Father and son finished their booze and went to bed. Rawlins drifted off to sleep, thinking about the little nurse, wondering if he would ever see her again. Then the smell of rotting vegetation and rotting flesh invaded his dreams. Screaming Japanese Soldiers in the stark white light of trip flares. Black and orange flashes from artillery shells tearing the enemy to pieces. Another night in Marine hell.

* * * * *

At 0400 hours Rawlins slipped out the door and hailed a cab on Hertel Avenue. He took it to the train station and headed for Camp Pendleton, California.

Chapter Four

CAMP PENDLETON

Camp Pendleton, California - Amphibious Warfare Training Center

"Gunnery Sergeant Rawlins, Second Raider Regiment reporting for re-assignment, Sir."

"At ease, Gunny. Let's see here. Got it. K. Rawlins, Gunnery Sergeant, Service Number 997038. That you, Gunny?"

"Yes, Sir."

"You're on the Fifth Division list. Twenty Seventh Marines, Second Battalion, Baker Company, First Platoon. Report to Lieut. Pruitt."

"Aye, Sir."

Rawlins left the office and asked the Desk Sergeant:

"Hey, Mac. Where's the Twenty Seventh Marines, Second Battalion?"

"Head down this road until the second intersection. Swing to starboard, head down that stretch until the first crossing and you're there."

"Thanks, Mac."

"OK, Gunny."

The Sergeant thought to himself, *man, I feel sorry for the boots that draw that salty son of a bitch. Pure lifer."*

Rawlins headed down the muddy road in his Class A uniform. The Marines he passed stared at him like he was from another planet, especially when they saw his Raider patch and ribbons. Wow, a real live hero. He had been to places very few Marines at this camp had seen. And lived to tell about it.

Finally, Rawlins found the C.P.

"Gunnery Sergeant Rawlins reporting as ordered."

"Gimme your papers, Gunny. Take a seat."

After some paper shuffling the Corporal told him that the officer on deck would see him.

"OK, Mac."

Rawlins went into the next room.

"Gunny Rawlins, you old sea dog. Come in and sit down."

"Lieut. Pruitt."

"Well, I'll be a sad Sailor in a cheap whorehouse."

"Good to see you, Sir."

The Platoon Leader gave Rawlins a glass half full of Johnny Walker.

"Thanks, Lieut. I can use it. Too many mud bunnies around this place. Too crowded."

"Not like the jungle where we're from, Gunny."

"That's for sure, Sir. So what's the deal, Sir?"

"I'm Second Platoon Leader and you're my Gunny."

"Well, imagine that. Just like old times. What are we working with?"

"I managed to get you Russo, Ramirez and Junior from the Second Raiders. The rest are all boots."

"Well, at least there's a few old salts to tell the kids what not to do."

"Aye, Gunny. See the tent with the sign in front? That's NCO quarters. Stow your gear there and grab a rack. The head and showers are behind it and get out of those Class As. Dismissed."

"Aye, Sir."

The ex-Raider left the C.P. and headed for NCO country, not relishing the thought of training a bunch of baby boots for the next slaughter in the Pacific. He was tired of teaching men how to kill the enemy, only to watch many of them die in the process. Lousy war.

His old mates from the Raiders were in the large tent

waiting for something to happen.

"Well, I'll be a sea dog's sister. It lives."

"What lives, Russo?"

"Gunny Rawlins. And here he comes."

"Get off your asses. you lazy bunch a misfits. What is this? A five start hotel? Where's the broads and booze?"

Rawlins dressed down his mates just for fun.

"Just because you've been playin' footsies with the Japs don't mean shit. You ain't Raiders any more. Now you're real mud Marines. No more Hollywood bull shit. Time to earn your pay. Move, move, move. Get your asses outside. Grab a formation if you still know how. Alright. Form up, ladies. C'mon. I ain't gonna hold your hand or wipe your asses. You're in the real Corps. now. Playtime is over. I am the big son of a bitch your mother warned you about. I wanna see a shine on your shoes and brass that will make Tojo cross-eyed."

Young Marine boots looked on in terror at the new monster in town dressing down the squad leaders.

"Your weapons and gear better be cleaner than a baby's ass or there will be hell to pay."

"Gunnery Sgt. What is the meaning of this? Why are you harassing these combat vets?"

"I'm not, Sir."

"Then what the hell are you doing? These men have been through hell while you were no doubt riding a desk in some state side barracks, nice and safe."

Rawlins mates were trying not to laugh but it wasn't easy.

"Well, Mister. I'm waiting."

"Well Sir. It's like this, Lieutenant. I was saying hello."

"Saying hello?"

"Yes, Sir."

"Oh, I see. The Hollywood heroes. Well, Gunnery Sgt.

you will discover there are no favorites here. We all do our part. Is that understood, Gunnery Sgt?"

"Yes, Sir."

"All right then. Try to use a bit better judgment from now on. You have been in the Corps. long enough to know how to handle men. If you need a lesson come and see me."

"Aye, aye, Sir."

"You Raiders carry on. And try to forgive this dinosaur. He is out of touch I'm afraid."

Rawlins was burning into the deck as the nineteen year old junior officer walked away. He lost it.

"Shave tail, moron son of a bitch. I was killin' Japs when his mother was wipin' his ass. He goes into combat he will get it before his boots are muddy. Cocky shit bird, no nothin' son of a bitch."

This was too much for the ex-Raiders. They all laughed so hard they couldn't speak. Onlookers thought they were all crazy. Too much time in the jungle.

"C'mon, Gunny, let's have a drink. We got a bottle stashed here somewhere. Unless you would rather go see the new Second Luey and get some instruction on how to be a good Marine."

"Stow the bull shit, Russo. Break out that bottle."

* * * * *

In the morning Rawlins introduced himself to his new men.

"My name is Gunnery Sgt. Rawlins. I am your Assistant Platoon Leader. I will teach you how to kill the Jap. I will teach you what they did not teach you in boot camp."

"I have met the Jap and learned his ways. You will also learn his ways. He is a formidable enemy and will not give up.

He will kill you any way he can, then kill himself if need be to avoid capture. His one goal in life is to die for the emperor. I will show you how to help him realize his dream. You have become spit and polish Marines. I will teach you to become jungle killers."

"You have ten minutes to form up in two ranks with full field gear and rifle. Dismissed."

* * * * *

Rawlins went into his tent and hit the bottle from the night before. He reasoned that it helped with the pain from his wounds; both external and internal. He was drinking more and more, trying to deal with his life and the war. The two had become one. Ironically, when he was in combat was the only time he felt safe. No judgment of his actions, no people trying to gain his trust only to leave him behind. Combat was his element. No bull shit. The ultimate truth. Kill or be killed.

Time to go. The combat Marine mounted his ruck and grabbed his Thompson. Not the 1928 A1 Model with fifty round drum magazine, Cutts muzzle compensator, and rear tangent elevator sight. This was the new 1942 cheaper model he had drawn from ordnance the night before. The amenities were gone. No tangent sight or Cutts comp. Just a peep sight and short barrel, a twenty round stick magazine in place of the fifty round drum. *Lotsa luck in a banzai charge*, he reasoned. The walnut stock replaced with birch wood and the operating bolt handle had been moved from the top of the receiver to the side. The weapon felt odd in his hands. No balance with the short barrel.

Son of a bitch. They couldn't even leave my Tommy gun alone. Not too many banzai charges at the Ordnance Dept. in Maryland, Rawlins speculated. *This stubby damn thing is no better than my 45 pistol. Oh, well, semper phi.*

* * * * *

The Squad Leaders were outside forming up the young Marines.

"Aw right. Line up, people. Column of twos. Move when I say move. Get your asses in gear. If you ladies are finally ready our Gunnery Sgt. is taking us on a nice twenty mile hike just to get acquainted."

Rawlins was now standing before the platoon.

"All right, people. Now that we're finally ready."

Rawlins bellowed in his best Gunnery Sgt. tone.

"Right shoulder arms, left face, forward, march."

And into the hills of Camp Pendleton they marched with the Squad Leaders calling cadence.

"You're left, you're left, you're left right left."

Russo started the marching song he had learned as a Raider.

"Your Momma don't want you no more."

And the Marines answered:

"You're right," remembering this from boot camp.

"Jobies at the door,"

"You're right."

"Your girl forgot your name."

"You're right."

"To joby we're all the same."

"You're right."

"Sound off."

"One, two."

"Sound off."

"Three four."

"One, two, three, four."

"One, two, three, four."
"The Marine Corps gave you a home,"
"So you're never really alone."
"You're right."
"Gunny Rawlins is back and he's gonna kick your ass."
"You're right."
"The Jap is waitin' for you."
"You're right."
"To see what you can do."
"You're right."
"Sound off."
"One, two."
"Sound off."
"Three four."
"One two, three four."
"One two, three four."

And so it went as the Marines marched into the hills of sunny California to prepare for their journey into hell.

* * * * *

Iwo Jima. A steamy, smelly Japanese infested rock and sand island known by the Japanese as Sulfur Island. Twenty thousand Japanese waited for the Marines on this island of death.

The enemy was entrenched so deep that air strikes and Naval bombardment had little effect on the inhabitants.

Additionally, General Kuribayashi has his artillery and heavy mortars zeroed in on every inch of the island. He had pre-registered the preparations for the assault he knew was coming. His island held three air fields and the Americans wanted them.

* * * * *

Bivouac. The Marines halted for the day in some low hills overlooking the ocean.

"Dig in, people. Nice and deep."

"But, Sarge. There ain't no Japs here and we're tired."

"You see that ocean, boot?"

"Yeah, Sarge."

"What's out there?"

"Water."

"And what's in that water?"

"Fish?"

"No, dummy. Submarines. And Jap subs carry Jap commandos and Jap commandos love to sneak in at night to kill people real quiet like so they don't know they're dead until the next morning."

"Really, Sarge?"

"Really. I saw it happen on the Canal. Sneaky little bastards. So dig in deep and stay awake. One man up at all times. Two men to a hole."

As the night passed the men were extremely bored. It became difficult for the exhausted riflemen to maintain their alertness. At 0400 hours Gunny Rawlins threw a live grenade behind a low hill. After the detonation he fired a full magazine from his Thompson into the air. The whole platoon began firing at nothing. Fire discipline was non-existent. That's what Rawlins had wanted to find out. He had done so by playing a Japanese trick on them. Get the enemy to fire their weapons to give away their positions. Then the mortars and artillery would pour in on target followed by banzai charges while the enemy was stunned.

The next morning the platoon got a collective ass chewing.

"What the hell is wrong with you people? Do you realize you are all dead right now? Who told you to fire? You brought enemy artillery right down our throats. Fire again without orders and I'll beat out your brains with your rifle. If you're gonna get us killed you're going first. Now form a column of twos. See if you can manage that. How the hell did you dummies graduate from boot camp. The Japs are gonna eat you alive."

Rawlins marched the raw riflemen to a firing range two miles inland.

"All right, people. Let's see if you can intentionally hit anything with your weapon. First squad in the target pits. Change targets. Second squad assume the prone position on line. Fire on my order. Lock and load rifles. Ready on the right. Ready on the left. Fire."

The sound of M1 Garand rifles firing in unison was deafening. Some with deadly accuracy, others not so good.

"Cease fire. Private. What's the problem? You didn't hit the target."

"This rifle is junk, Gunny. No good."

"Gimme that weapon, Private."

Rawlins shouldered the M1 and fired five rounds into the target from a standing position, all in the X ring.

"Private, there is nothing wrong with this rifle. Reload and remount."

"Aye, Gunny."

"Now listen to me. Get you head down tight on the stock and don't close your eyes. Squeeze the trigger nice and slow. Don't jerk it. Keep your feet wide apart and elbows on the ground. Put the front blade in the middle of the ring and center the target. Now fire three rounds nice and slow. Now look at that, Son. Right in there. That's three dead Japs. Good man."

"Thanks, Gunny."

"That's OK. We all gotta learn somehow."

Rawlins thought to himself, *what the hell are they doing with these kids in boot. That boy didn't know shit about rifle fire. They must be pumping them through fast because of the upcoming big operations. Poor bastards. They're gonna get slaughtered.*

* * * * *

That evening the field kitchens brought up hot chow. Rawlins let the boots bivouac in their shelter halves instead of diggin' in. He posted guards around the perimeter. He knew that things happened that could not be anticipated. These kids were so green it wouldn't take much to wipe them out and the Japs shelled the coast from submarines on occasion. A commando raid was possible. Those sneaky bastards were capable of anything.

He recalled hearing about a thwarted attempt by the Japs to blow up the Panama Canal with subs and commandos. You just never knew what to expect.

The next morning the men started with bayonet drill, then more range time. They did much better with their veteran Squad Leaders instructing them.

Then hand to hand combat drills. Instruction in the use of the Ka-Bar knife, entrenching tool, and steel helmet as a weapon. All valuable and deadly in a close fight. Also, the rifle butt. The bayonet and rifle butt used in unison worked very well in dispatching an attacker.

* * * * *

That evening the men cleaned their weapons and gear for inspection, then went on a night navigation problem. At 0300 hours they broke camp and marched for home, arriving at

At 0700 hours Rawlins dismissed them for a much needed rest.

* * * * *

Then the rhetoric began.

"Man. That Gunny is one tough son of a bitch. Never gets tired and mean as hell."

"That guy could chew up nails and spit out battle ships."

"You see that tattoo on his forearm? Mom with a heart. That son of a bitch don't have a mother. He's too damn mean and ugly."

"And the Squad Leaders. Where the hell did they come from" They're like smaller versions of him. Shit. We got all the luck."

"At least when we're in combat we won't have to worry."

"Why not?"

"Cause that big son of a bitch will scare the Japs to death."

"Did you see the ribbons on his Class A's? Must have been in every war for the last hundred years."

"Some guys you just can't kill. The perfect Marine. Big, ugly, and unkillable."

* * * * *

The next day the platoon took a bus ride to San Diego and loaded on L.S.T. (landing ship tank) transports. This began two days of amphibious landings on the shore of Pendleton.

"Alright. ladies. Climb down the cargo net into the L.C.V.P. (landing craft vehicle personnel) by twos and threes."

After the landing craft was loaded Rawlins pointed out a

few things.

"Alright. Listen up. Undo your chin strap and loosen your web gear and pack straps. If you wind up in the water your gear will drag you down like a stone. So leave it loose so you can shake it off. As soon as you hit the beach you will drop your pack anyway. You won't carry it in combat. It will slow you down too much and make you a target. Forget what they told you in boot camp. You're in the real world now. All you need is your ammo, two canteens, a C ration or two, and a dry pair of socks. That's it. Take your bayonet off your pack and put it on your belt. Put your Ka-Bar on your leg just above your boondocker. That way if you lose your gear you will still have your knife and that can save your life."

"Don't look over the gunnel of this barge. When the artillery and machine gun fire come in you may get your face removed; or your head. And that hurts like hell. You will see what's happening soon enough. Don't be a dummy and get killed right away. Better to die killing the enemy."

Oh, great, thought the young Marines. *This guy is nuts and we gotta follow him around some Jap infested island. Shit. We'll all be dead in a week.*

Rawlins did what he could to convert the new cannon fodder into combat Marines. He hoped what he had told them would save some lives but he knew the operations coming up were going to be very costly. For the first time they would take on the Jap on his home turf. The battles so far were only the warm-up for what was to come. This was going to be slaughter on a whole new level and many of those kids were going to pay the ultimate price.

* * * * *

For a week the Twenty Seventh Marines practiced

landings on Pendleton's beaches. Then back to San Diego where they boarded troop transports bound for Camp Tarawa on the big island of Hawaii. There they would finish their training and join the rest of the Fifth Marine Division and then depart on a forty four day sea voyage to Iwo Jima.

* * * * *

After a day at sea the troops began to relax. Card games and craps broke out and the scuttle butt began. Military gossip.

"Hey, Gunny?"

"Year."

"Where we going?"

"Hawaii for a nice vacation."

"Really?"

"No. We're going to Japan. This regiment is going to invade the home island. The rest of the Corps is going to Hawaii for a vacation."

"Gunny, you're bull shitting us."

"Why would I do that."

"Cause you always do that. We never get the straight dope."

"Sorry, Private. The General forgot to confer with me before we sailed. I'll have to kick his ass for that."

"See what I mean, Gunny. Bull shit."

"Relax, Mouth. You will get the word when we all do. Now shut up. I'm meditating. I'm searching for my inner self, my sphere of contentment."

"Gunny, you're going Asiatic."

"Sgt. Russo."

"I'm not here. Private."

"How long have you known the Gunny?"

"Since the Canal."

"Since the Canal."

"How is he in combat?"

"The best."

"How many kills?"

"Too many."

"How many you got, Sarge?"

"Don't remember."

"Why not?"

"They bug me at night when I'm sleepin.' How they're dead. You will see. They come alive in your head and bug you."

"So dead Japs ain't really dead. They live in your head."

"Right, Junior. You're learning. Now drop it. Rawlins is lookin' over here. He can hear us."

"How? He's in another compartment."

"He hears everything."

"How?"

"Cause he ain't human."

"Whata you mean, Sarge."

"When we was Raiders he shoulda got killed. Never did. Guys dropping all around him. Not Rawlins. Just keeps fightin,' even wounded. I'm telling you he ain't human. He's not meant to die in this war."

"No shit."

"No shit. Now leave me alone. I'm sleepin.'

* * * * *

When the troop ships pulled into Pearl Harbor the raw Marines got their first look at the war.

"Son of a bitch. Look at those ships. Dirty rotten Jap bastards. Those swabs didn't have a chance, bottled up in here like that."

"Yeah. The bastards. My brother is in that battle wagon

over there. Never knew what hit him. They're gonna pay for that. I promised my old man that much."

"Gunny. You been here before?"

"Yeah. Couple times. My brother-in-law is in the same ship as you brother, Henshaw. Just a kid. Just out of Annapolis. Dirty bastards."

* * * * *

When the ships docked, the Marines boarded trucks and headed for Camp Tarawa to begin training for the invasion of Iwo Jima.

"All right, ladies, play time is over. Stow your gear and grab a rack. Then get your ugly asses out here with rifle and pack. We're going for a little walk. Dismissed."

* * * * *

"Gunny, The Lieut. wants to see you."

"OK, Corporal."

Rawlins made his way to the C.P.

"You wanted to see me, Lieut.?"

"Sit down, Rawlins. Care for a drink?"

"Yes, Sir."

Lieut. Pruitt handed his Gunnery Sgt. three fingers of Johnny Walker.

"Just got briefed on the upcoming op."

"What are we in for, Sir?"

"Looks rough. Volcanic rock and sand, no water, sparse vegetation. Hot as hell and as many as twenty thousand Japs. Well dug in, lots of arty and heavy mortars."

"Sounds like Peleliu, Sir."

"Same shit only more of it. Lots of caves, too, and you

know how the Nips like that."

"Yes, Sir. Sounds like a lot of kids ain't comin' back from this one. It's gonna be a tough fight. They tell you where, Sir?"

"No, not yet. They will let us know aboard ship. Now get back to your people, Rawlins, and get them ready."

"Aye, Sir."

Rawlins left the hut, already feeling apprehensive about the new operation. He wondered if it was a Jap home island, not knowing that his guess was right on the money.

* * * * *

"All right, people. Get squared away. Line up in a column of twos. Let's go. I don't want to hear no whining about sore feet and sore asses. You have been loafing ever since Camp Pendleton. It's time to move your asses and learn how to kill the Jap. Right shoulder arms. Left face. Forward, march."

And out of the bivouac they marched. The crazy lifer and his children. And they marched and marched for fifteen miles in the hills of the big island of Honolulu, finally stopping at a small range. Here they stacked arms and had chow. Cold C Rations.

"Damn, I hate this shit. I wouldn't feed this to a dog."

"Quit bitching. At least you got something. Where we're headed we might have to eat dead Japs."

"I ain't eatin' no Jap."

"You never been hungry."

"Hey, Sarge, we gotta eat dead Japs?"

"It's easier that way. They squirm around too much when they're alive."

"Shit, Sarge, I ain't eatin' no Jap."

"Why not. They eat each other. They eat us. So why

can't we eat them?"

"Cause it ain't civilized."

"Neither are they. I hear the Krauts are eating the dead in Russia."

"That's different."

"No, it ain't. They're starving. Nothing there but snow and more snow."

"I still ain't eatin' no Jap."

"Relax, Smitty. The Japs will probably kill you and eat you first anyway, so you got nothing to worry about."

"Gee, thanks, Sarge. I feel so much better."

* * * * *

"Lunch is over, children. First and Second Squads, grab your rifles. Now listen up. When we close with the enemy and things get close you gotta change tactics. Since you're all expert riflemen now you gotta learn how to point shoot. You won't have time to use your sights or shoulder your rifle. You will shoot from the hip, beat the Jap at the draw. Sgts. Russo and Ramirez take First and Second Squads to the range and set up ten yard targets. Then instruct these Jap killers in the fine art of shooting close targets. Third Squad follow me to the grenade range. You will rotate with First Squad."

The two Squad Leaders instructed the young Marines in the art of close shooting.

"Keep your stock tight against your body, muzzle level with the center of the target. Now squeeze the trigger and walk the rounds in. Tommy gunners, tuck the stock under your armpit. Hold the front sling swivel strap to reduce muzzle climb. Now fire in three round bursts; no more or the weapon will climb over the target. Same goes for you B.A.R. gunners. Short controlled bursts."

The men were amazed at how proficient they became in a short period of time. The two Sgts. knew their stuff. Just like the Gunny.

That night was fire and maneuver practice on a gun emplacement range. The rifle squad leap frogged; one squad laying down fire on the target, the other making a flanking maneuver. Finally the flankers hit the pill box with grenades or flame throwers, then a thirty pound satchel charge. Very difficult at night.

Rawlins could see that a big island with well prepared positions would be the target. And for the first time ever he was nervous. Too much war for the old vet. It was taking its toll on him. Watching the young Marines burn and blow up the fortifications made the old vet sick to his stomach. It reminded him of seeing this in combat with live men inside the bunkers. One of his worst memories. Even though they were led to believe the enemies were inhuman monsters, they still screamed and died like people.

* * * * *

The next day the platoon was picked up by truck and taken to the wharf. Here they loaded onto L.S.T. transports and joined the rest of Baker Company. Out to sea for five miles and adjacent to the black volcanic and coral beach. Here they loaded into amphibious tractors, better known as alligators. A large rear loading ramp dropped and the Marines entered and sat along the sides of the craft. A bow mounted fifty cal. machine gun was the only protection.

"Man, I don't like this shit. I feel like a rat in a trap. There's no way outta this thing. If we get hit we're done for."

"Don't worry about it, Smitty. We get hit with something big enough to penetrate this armor you won't know it anyway.

You will become a telegram home in a hurry."

"Gee, Sarge, you always know how to make us all feel so much better. Sometimes I think you're working for the Japs."

"Sayonara, shit bird."

"I love you too, Sarge."

The alligators crawled down the L.S.T. ramp into the sea. After assembling in assault formation, they headed for the beach.

"Sarge. The diesel fumes and heat are making me sick."

"Quit whining, dummy, at least they ain't making you dead like the Japs will."

"Sarge. This tin can is leaking. The floor is covered with water."

"Don't worry about it. You can only drown once. What did you dummies think this was? A pleasure cruise on Lake Placid? Wait till we're gettin' shot at. This is nothin.' Now pipe down and act like real Marines. You're startin' to annoy me."

Gunny Rawlins was in the next am track with Second Squad. Just like in submarines when he was a Raider. Steel boxes in water was a bad idea in his opinion. He was getting nervous again and needed a drink.

"Hey, Gunny."

"Yeah Ramirez."

"You OK?"

"Yeah. Just a little sea sick is all. Like in the subs."

"Yeah, Gunny. Me too. Here, have a drink."

"Naw, don't like water."

"Go on, Gunny. It will help."

Rawlins took the hint. Taking a pull from the canteen was a surprise. Johnny Walker. He winked at his Squad Leader and friend and drank some more.

"Thanks, Carlos. You're right. It helps."

The steel craft hit the beach with a bounce and headed

inland. It finally stopping in a coconut grove and discharged its passengers.

"Shit. Am I glad to be out of that thing."

"Yeah, Smitty. You and me both," countered his friend Private Henshaw.

"Better than a rubber boat, children. That's what we had in the Raiders."

"Yeah, Sarge. And you're all nuts too. Didn't you volunteer for that insane shit?"

"Why, yes, my good man. After leaving my job in Chicago the regular Corps proved to be a trifle boring."

"What was that, Sarge?"

"I was big Al Capone's hit man."

"No shit."

"No shit."

Rawlins overheard the First Squad Leader's dialogue.

"Russo. Knock off the bull shit. These kids are scared enough. We don't want them afraid of us."

"OK, Gunny."

After a recon by fire exercise - then some hand to hand drills, the Marines dug in and went to sleep.

The next morning they were picked up by truck and returned to their bivouac. The day was spent packing gear and equipment. Then in the evening loading transports and L.S.T.s. Late that night the Fifth Marine Division left Hawaii for the Japanese home island of Iwo Jima. It would be the bloodiest and most costly battle in Marine Corps history.

Chapter Five

BLOODY IWO

Gunny Rawlins leaned against a bulkhead with a canteen of Johnny Walker and a Chesterfield. He was drinking all the time now. The only way he could cope with the stress. He had a feeling that this op would be his last. His apprehension was growing by the day. The farther out to sea they went the worse it became.

Oh, well, f**k it. Nobody lives forever. What's the difference.

His wife was gone. The war went on and on. His life was shit. Even the little nurse had turned on him. This war was killing everybody, one way or another. No way out. Only the white cross and purple heart. The guys that got it early in the war were lucky. They didn't suffer that much.

Rawlins thought of his father. Poor son of a bitch. His life had ended that day in France when a German artillery shell landed near him. He is so full of steel he lives in misery. Constant pain and suffering forever. Better to get it all at once. No suffering. Just gone. And all those kids in the hospital he had seen with missing members. Missing for the rest of their lives. Just kids. What a bunch of shit. And for what. It's all bull shit. Back in forty two when he had joined the Raiders he had believed in the war. Fight the good fight for God and country. For what? To make the rich richer and the politicians happy. This war is about the extermination of the young men of the world while the old men get rich and fat. It's the same all over the world. No matter what side you're on.

* * * * *

"Hey, Gunny."
"Yeah, kid."
"What's it like in combat?"
"Hot, noisy, smelly, exhausting, confusing."

"Not scary?"

"Naw, not really. You don't have time, you're too busy. You get scared after it's over."

"How many fights you been in?"

"Too many and it's always the same. Just do what you're told and you will be OK. Stick close to the vets, do what they tell you. They got the knowhow. The Jap ain't nothin' special. Just a man. They bleed and die like anybody else. And don't pick up souvenirs. They could be booby traps. I've seen men killed doing that. And make sure when you kill a Jap that he's dead. They like to play possum and throw grenades at people. If they're really dead they don't do much; just stink. And watch your mate's back. They like to let you walk past then shoot you in the back. Sneaky bastards, they are."

The youngster left to confer the combat wisdom with his buddies. Rawlin's depression returned.

Too bad they broke up the Raiders. That was a good outfit. They fought the war the right way. In the enemies bedroom, eyeball to eyeball. We showed the bastards a thing or two about soft Americans. This shit coming up is not civilized. Just annihilation. Huge Naval guns, bombs, napalm, flame throwers, tanks. No more man to man contest. Just mass destruction. Whoever has a man left standing wins the day. Bull shit.

Rawlins romantic side was showing.

No more cavalry charges with sabers, no spirit of the bayonet, no chivalry. Just mass death and destruction. Shit. Maybe it's better if I do get it. Just a damn dinosaur in a modern world. Should have been born two hundred years ago. Just don't fit in anymore. Like Susan told me when they hoisted my ass up the yardarm.

"It was only sex, Ken. I don't understand why you're so upset. You left me to fight your war. I was lonely and bored. You shouldn't have left me."

Maybe she was right. Maybe it was my fault. And maybe I should have let the swabbies take the little nurse. After all, she was shaking her ass all over the dance hall. Maybe I shouldn't have defended her since she told me what an asshole I am. Maybe she wanted to go with them. Young and exciting, not an old s.o.b. like me.

That's probably it. That's why the "go fight your war and kiss my ass, Jarhead." Makes sense I guess. She's probably there right now with some 4F joby shitbird. Shit. Why the hell did God make women so damn confusing. Why can't they be normal and think like men. Shit. Pain in the ass. I would rather put up with the Japs. At least they make sense when they're trying to kill you.

Rawlins began his pre-invasion ritual. His two forty fives and new Tommy gun were broken down and cleaned. Then the three thirty round Thompson magazines he had picked up at Camp Tarawa for a bottle of Johnny Walker and a Jap dagger. Finally he put an edge on his Ka-Bar fighting knife and his Sykes-Fairbairn stiletto, given to him by the British Commando. He didn't carry a bayonet. No place to mount one on a Thompson and besides he relied on his two pistols in a close fight. Far more effective.

* * * * *

"Hey, Gunny."

"What."

"Why do you carry two forty fives?"

"Banzai charge."

"What do you mean?"

"A Jap suicide bayonet charge. They all come at you at once. Hundreds of 'um. If my Tommy runs dry or jams I got back up."

"Ever happen?"

"Yeah. Twice."

"No shit."

"No shit."

"I gotta find me a pistol. Shit. They didn't tell us about Jap suicide shit in boot."

"They didn't tell you a lot of shit in boot."

* * * * *

Next Rawlins wrote a letter home thanking everybody for doing so much for him. Then one to Evelyn Trumbolt, apologizing for

being crude and ignorant and not understanding her feelings. He
didn't know if she would respond but he thought it was worth a letter.
There was something about her he didn't understand. Something
strange and unfamiliar. He had feelings for her that had never existed
before. He barely knew her but she haunted him at night like Russo
and his dead Japs. Always there in the background, calling to him,
reaching for him, then gone. Like mist in the rain. Weird. Almost like
she was part of him in some strange way from long ago, a time that
had existed in the past. But always just out of reach like a ghost in the
night, a fleeting specter in an unreal dimension.

Shit, thought the Marine, *thinking about her might get me
killed. Gotta put her away for now.*

* * * * *

The next day rubber relief maps of the target were laid out on
deck. Each platoon was briefed on their objective.

* * * * *

"Your target, gentlemen, is Iwo Jima. The first Jap home
island. There are around twenty thousand defenders waiting for us."

This hushed the men huddled around the map.

"There is no water, very little vegetation. It's a volcanic
island. Black volcanic sand beaches, lots of caves and rock ridges.
The Jap is not on the island, he is in it. There are miles of tunnels due
to sulfur mining. Just what the enemy likes. The Navy has been
pounding the hell out of the place for a month, so many of the gun
emplacements have been destroyed. You men of the Twenty Seventh
will land on Red Beach One and Two. Your mission is to secure
Motoyama Airfield No. 1.

Along with Fourth Division Marines on your right flank, on
your left will be the Twenty Eighth Marines. They will take and
secure Mt. Suribachi. You men will drive across the island at the foot
of the mountain after securing the airfield. When you reach the sea
you will wheel right and drive north. Elements of the Third Division
will be on your flank with flame thrower tanks. You will have Naval
guns, Naval Air, tanks and artillery when they are available.

Once Suribachi is isolated the Third, Fourth and Fifth Divisions will drive north in unison.

We expect this island to be secure in less than a week. Study this map. Your jump off positions are marked.

Carry on, gentlemen and good luck. The invasion is in two days. Feb. 19th. Two, you ex-Raiders. Gung ho."

* * * * *

Rawlins looked at the map.

Son of a bitch. This is bad. It's like a fortress and the Nips are in it. It's gonna be a slaughter on both sides.

Rawlins thought to himself:

Secured in a week. More like six months. That lousy Major is an idiot. This is going to be the toughest operation of the war so far. No wonder I'm gettin' bad feelings. The whole platoon might get it. There's no cover and they probably got every gun registered by now. They know we're coming. Shit. Sayonara asshole.

* * * * *

Later Russo and Ramirez found Rawlins on the fantail.

"Have a drink, Gunny. We got this jungle juice from that Bosun over there for a Jap flag."

"Gimme that shit."

The dubious liquid burned Rawlins throat but it was better than nothing.

"Half Aqua Velva, half boot polish. My favorite."

"Well, Gunny, what do you think?"

"It's gonna be a slaughter. You guys better tag your boots and get your paper work in. A lot of us ain't leavin' that shit hole I got a feelin.' "

This was bad. The two Sergeants knew Rawlins feelings were always right. Now they were nervous.

"They're sending in three divisions. We're used to fighting with three platoons or less. Shit. We ain't used to this major beach assault shit. It's a damn shame they broke up the Raiders. We were better off. At least we all knew each other and could rely on one another. Now I don't know. You might end up in a hole with a Joe you don't know and that ain't good, especially at night when the bastards are sneaking around."

"Maybe some of 'um are dead already. They been really poundin' hell out of the place."

"Shit, Russo. They're underground. We're gonna have to burn 'um out. It's the only way. I feel bad about all these kids. They ain't got a clue of what we're in for, poor bastards."

Rawlins, drunk again, started reciting Shakespeare. The young Marines around him began to worry.

"To be or not to be. That is the question I ask of Thee. Cry havoc. Release the dogs of war. We shall smite Thy enemy with tempered blade and righteous lance. Bugles sound and signal the charge. Our day of destiny is upon us."

"Hey, Sarge. The Gunny has cracked up ."

"He's all right. He's carrying a load. Got some jungle juice from the Bosun Mate. He's always like this before an operation. Always thinks he's gonna get killed."

"He acts like this on that island we're all gonna get it. The Japs will hear him a mile away."

"Don't worry about it. He will be OK."

"I'm sorry, Turnbolt. I didn't know you had feelings. Ha, ha, ha, ha."

"Man. He's really hammered."

"Don't worry about it. At least he ain't messing with us. Let him rave. Sooner or later he will pass out."

* * * * *

The next day was spent getting ready. While the Navy shelled the island the Marines cleaned weapons, loaded magazines, set fuses on grenades and mortar rounds, sharpened knives and bayonets. No one said much. They wrote final letters home and signed Next of Kin papers, stating who got the ten thousand dollars insurance if they were killed. They studies maps, re-checked equipment, put one dog tag in a boot in case the one around their neck was lost or destroyed. It would be the only way to identify the body in case of decapitation. All personal items were collected and locked in the ship's safe. In case of capture the enemy could gather Intel from these items.

Finally, lights out. Time for bed. No one really slept. Just talked or thought about home. Would they ever see it again.

* * * * *

Rise and shine. 0400 hours. Breakfast. Steak and eggs. The traditional invasion breakfast for all hands.

0600 hours. Disembarkation.

On the ships P.A. System:

"Ahoy, landing party. Stand by the starboard rail. Mount cargo nets. Load boats."

Rawlins felt sick as he climbed over the rail and down the net. Reaching the boat deck he vomited over the side.

Son of a bitch. I hate this shit. Another steel coffin to get buried alive in. Lousy Nips. Pain in the ass.

The fumes from the diesel boat engine and the rough sea made his head swim.

Soon the landing barge was full. They shoved off and headed for the assembly area, then circled for an hour while other boats loaded their human cargo.

When the flag ship gave the signal the landing craft assumed assault formation and headed for the beach. Three hundred yards off-shore Rawlins bellowed:

"All right, people. This is it. Lock and load. Keep your heads down. When the ramp drops, get out fast. Don't stop for anything. Drop your packs on the beach and move out. Don't hang around the beach. Move inland."

The black sand beach was a hundred yards away. A pall of smoke from the bombardment obscured Mt. Suribachi to their left. Machine gun bullets and shrapnel bounced off the steel hull. The Gunner's Mate behind the fifty cal. machine gun slumped over, a large hole in his helmet and head. Rawlins was dizzy. The beach before him was moving back and forth. Then they were there.

The ramp dropped and men scrambled to the waist deep water and jumped in, some slumping over and disappearing under the incoming waves, dead before they had a chance to fight.

"Move, move, move. Get your asses on the beach. This ain't no parade. Those are real bullets lookin' for you."

Rawlins cleared the boat and hit the beach. It grew strangely quiet as the men dropped their packs and crawled up the terraced black sand beach. The landing barge backed into the surf and was gone. Back to the ships for another Gunner and more Marines.

Rawlins and the first squad were alone, waiting for something to happen. All along the beach groups of men waited as the boats headed for sea.

Then it began. Just as the second wave came in, heavy artillery, mortars and machine gun fire from Mt. Suribachi. The enemy defenders walked the 150mm shells up and down the beach. The effect was devastating. Machine gun fire kept the Marines pinned down. Landing craft and AM tracks were being hit and destroyed with their crews. The carnage on the beach was terrible. Like Dante's inferno, General Kuribayoshi planned well. He would destroy these soft Americans that he had once known and loved. But now they were the enemy of his country and would be exterminated.

* * * * *

"Move out. Get the hell off this beach or we're all dead.. Head for the airfield. Let's go."

Rawlins and company stormed ahead through the smoke and steel of the enemy. Many men fell that morning. But they took the airfield and forged ahead, blowing bunker after bunker, never seeing the enemy. Only an occasional dead body. The enemy was in the island, not on it. The Marines commanded the surface; the Japanese the underworld. They lived like moles and fought like tigers. Very strange to a Marine's way of thinking.

Finally, night fell and the terror that came with it reared its ugly head. Two men to a foxhole. Infiltrators would keep them awake all night. Sleep deprivation was part of the enemy's plan. Wear down the nerves; make the enemy jumpy. A grenade in the Marine lines on occasion or a mortar round did the job. No rest for the invaders. And of course the Japanese Sapper, armed with grenades and a dagger, were an ominous threat. They crawled into the lines and attacked targets of opportunity. First they would kill a Marine or two with their daggers, then occupy the hole. Once they fixed the position of neighboring holes they would attack them with grenades. Sometimes they would strip the dead and don their uniforms and helmets. Then they would walk up to the line and attack the Marines with bayonets.

* * * * *

Rawlins was making a check of the platoon forward positions when he noticed movement in the mist.

Shit. Japs. A squad of 'um lying down on a small rise in the black sand .

He watched as they approached. Their long bayonet fixed Arisaka type 96 rifles looked odd compared to their short bodies. Rawlins pulled back the bolt handle of his Thompson, locking it open, ready to fire. Reaching into his grenade bag he pulled out two M2 frags and straightened the safety pins. As he watched, the enemy drew closer and closer. Rawlins felt odd watching these little men he was about to destroy. Alive for the moment but very soon to be dead. The Marine picked up a frag, pulled the pin and let the safety spoon discharge. He threw it at the enemy, quickly followed by the other mini bomb. At the detonation half of the intruders went down. Rawlins got up on his knees and burned half a magazine into the remaining bad guys. The muzzle flash on this dark, overcast night blinding him. Hitting the deck and rolling, he jumped into a shell hole and rose to return incoming fire. One errant shot came his way from a wounded son of Nippon. A three round burst flattened him. The whole line exploded with fire. Grenades on both sides detonated. Screaming enemies charged the Marines with bayonets. Now the fight was hand to hand. The Marines were being overwhelmed. Rawlins cut down two attackers, then dropped his empty Tommy gun and pulled out his forty five. No time to re-load. Japs all around him.

A big Jap tried to bayonet him. Rawlins side stepped the long blade and shot its owner in the face. Another butt stroked the Marine, knocking off his helmet and putting him down. Rawlins rolled on the ground, knowing the bayonet would come next. The Jap made a thrust. Rawlins deflected it, still got stabbed in the side, the blade glancing off his ribs. In a rage of pain and anger the Gunnery Sgt. kicked the killer in the crotch hard. The would be killer grabbed his crotch and fell to his knees. Rawlins pulled his backup pistol from its shoulder rig and shot the crotch holder twice. The bad guy's eyes crossed and he slumped over, quite dead. Rawlins got up with his two forty fives and walked toward the C.P.

He could hear Lieut. Pruitt's Browning shotgun. Boom, boom, boom, over the din of battle. Smitty was engaged in a choking match with a big Jap. Rawlins hit the Jap in the back of the neck with a pistol butt, dropping him. Smitty picked up his M1 and drove the bayonet into the chest of the senseless enemy, making sure he stayed down.

Russo was on top of a Jap Captain, stabbing him with his Ka-Bar. The officer slashed him with a Samurai katana. Before he could strike the finishing blow Russo was on him. As his eyes faded Russo asked:

"You stupid bastard. Why did you bring a sword to a gun fight?"

Much to Russo's surprise the Captain answered in perfect English:

"It is the way of Bushido, my American friend. Now I may enter the hall of fallen heroes with the seven Ronin."

The Samurai died with a smile on his face.

Son of a bitch.. These Japs are all crazy. They all wanna die and enter some bullshit shrine. Nuts.

* * * * *

Junior, the big farmer from Idaho, was with third squad. Two Japs jumped in his hole. One stabbed him in the shoulder, the other clubbed him. This enraged the huge Marine. He grabbed the knife wielder by the stacking swivel and shook him like a rag doll, then smashed his head on a rock. The Jap's buddy charged with his rifle and bayonet. The farm boy ripped it out of Tojo's hands and clubbed him to death with his own weapon.

They shouldn't have made me mad. Dumb Japs, he thought,

Rawlins made it to the C.P.

"Lieutenant. You OK?"

"Yeah. OK."

Dead Japs lay all around him, killed with his Browning A5 shotgun or his forty five cal. pistol. The platoon radio man sat at his set with a sword protruding from his chest, eyes wide open, seeing nothing. The fight was over. It was getting light.

"Son of a bitch, Gunny. They almost overran us."

"Yeah, Lieutenant. I bet the kids will wake up now."

"Yeah, Gunny. Wake up or die. These Japs are tough bastards. They don't give a shit for nothin.' Shit. Gunny, you're bleeding."

"Yeah, Lieutenant. Nip hung me on a bayonet. Not bad though. Just looks it."

"Corpsman. Get your ass in here. Gunny's bleedin.'"

The Navy Corpsman applied sulfa and dressed the wound, then gave Rawlins a syrette of morphine.

"Gunny. You want to be evaced?"

"Naw. Ain't that bad."

"You sure? Gotta hurt like hell."

"I've had worse."

"OK, Marine. It's your ass. But if it gets infected you gotta go."

"OK, Doc. I'll watch it. Go find Junior. He got it in the shoulder."

"OK, Gunny."

* * * * *

The new Marines did well. Some of them died that first night. But a lot more Japanese were destroyed than Marines. A preview of what was to come. The young Americans were blooded now. They knew they could beat the Jap on his own turf. They were going to win this fight and take this island. No matter what.

With the dawn came rain and mist. Quiet now. Only occasional sniper fire. The platoon was getting ready to move out. Begin the drive north. Rawlins was in the C.P. Captain Rogers, Company Commander, was there also.

"How's that wound, Rawlins?"

"OK, Sir. Good to go."

"Go check on the men, Gunny. Make sure they know what's going to happen."

"Aye, Sir."

Rawlins left the Command Post, re-loaded his Thompson, and began checking the forward positions. As he went from hole to hole a wounded Japanese Lieutenant watched him from a spider hole. The Jap decided that it was obvious that Rawlins was some type of officer.

His death will bring me great honor if I take him in the way of Bushido.

Unsheathing his katana, the Junior Officer left his hole and approached the big Marine from the rear. Just as he was about to strike the side of his head blew out, spraying blood and brains all over his intended victim. Rawlins spun around to face his attacker. Then he noticed that the Jap killer had only half a head.

What the hell happened to him. No grenades or mortar fire close by. Then he realized. Sniper. There must be a sniper close by. Good thing. That dead son of a bitch got the drop on me. Another dead Jap that ain't dead. Little bastards. Don't know when to quit.

Rawlins hit the deck in case another attack was coming. In a few minutes he noticed a tall, thin form in the distance walking toward him. The shape of his helmet looked Marine but you could never be sure. Could be a Jap trick. They had lots of tricks. Rawlins flipped off the safety on his Tommy gun as he watched. The tall form carried an M1 carbine and a long rifle across his back. Could be an Arisaka type 96 or a U.S. 1903 Springfield sniper rifle. The form was beginning to look familiar. The way he walked, the way he carried the carbine in one hand like a pistol. A big man. Too big for a Jap. He grew closer, then waved.

Son of a bitch. That's Eyes. Well, I'll be.

George Fisher, alias Eyes, Marine scout sniper, closed the difference between himself and Rawlins.

"Hi ya, Gunny. What's new?"

"You son of a bitch. Where the hell you been, Eyes?"

"I was with the Twenty Eighth Marines, over on your left. They told me to get my ass over here and see Lieut. Pruitt. I guess he drew me in a poker game or something."

"I thought you had some stateside lash up teachin' kids what a rifle is."

"Camp Perry, Scout Sniper School."

"Pretty sweet. What happened?"

"Somebody pulled my 201 file and decided they needed me more over here."

"Well, imagine that. The best sniper in the Corps and they decided to put you back in the war. Pity."

"Ain't it a shame, Gunny?"

"By the way, Eyes, thanks for recycling no mind over there."

"No problem, Gunny. Just like on Bougainville. I'm forever shootin' bad guys off your back."

"Yeah. Thanks. So did you make it home, Eyes?"

"Yeah. For a while."

"What happened?"

"Ah, you know how it is, Gunny. Nothing's the same. Gone too long, I guess."

"I know. I got it too. Mabel wasn't able. Thinks she's Betty Grable."

"No shit."

"She says I'm different. I'm socially inept now. A killing machine. All I care about is the war. So what's wrong with that?"

"I dunno, Gunny. You know how dames are. Too sensitive."

"Yeah. I know."

"All I did was tell her family about that Nip officer I blew off the bridge of that sub during the long patrol on the Canal. That was my best kill ever."

"Yeah, I remember. Hell of a shot."

"Well, anyway, here pansy ass college boy brother pipes up and says I have homicidal sociopathic tendencies and should be committed."

"So what happened?"

"I agreed with him. Broke his jaw, grabbed my sea bag and left. The hell with 'um all."

"No shit."

"No shit, Gunny."

"Well, don't worry about it. You got a home with us. And when the war is over, we'll go home and become movie actors and novel writers. Then they will all kiss our asses."

"Right, Gunny. Hey, by the way, did you see the flag go up on Suribachi?"

"Yeah, we saw it. Heard the klaxon bells on the ships too, and so did every Nip on the island. That's why they're so pissed off. Two of the flag raisers were ex-Raiders."

"No shit."

"You remember Mike Strank and Ira Hayes?"

"Yeah, I remember them. Two mud Marines and a Corpsman. And some AP wire guy got a picture. Said it was going to the States and they would all be famous. That's great."

"But for now I got bad news."

"What, Gunny?"

"Junior caught a blade last night and got evacked."

"How bad?"

"He'll make it. In the shoulder. I thought the big son of a bitch was invincible."

"Yeah. So did he."

"He had third platoon. Now I got an opening and since you're a Sgt. now it's your baby."

"You're kidding. I work alone, Gunny. You know that."

"Not any more."

"Shit. Son of a bitch. I ain't no baby sitter."

"Welcome to the Marine Corps, Sergeant. Now get to the C.P. and tell Lieut. Pruitt you're the new third squad leader."

"Shit, Gunny. This ain't fair."

"What the hell is? Now git."

"OK, Gunny. Shit."

* * * * *

Time to move out.

"All right, people. Let's move out. Nap time is over. Let's go."

The young Marines got out of their holes and pushed forward and the fire started. Enemy riflemen in spider holes or no seeums, as the Marines called them. The Jap would be in a small hole in a rock outcropping and fire at the Marines, then disappear, then pop up somewhere else and fire again.

"These lousy Nips are like gophers. Never in one place long enough to shoot at."

As the men forged ahead, two machine guns opened up. Everyone flattened against the rocky ground.

"Gunny. We're pinned down tight. What are we gonna do?"

"Clark. Gimme that handy talky."

Rawlins keyed the mike and spoke.

"Second platoon calling weapons platoon. Over."

"Go ahead, second platoon."

"Fire mission. Over."

"What do you need? Over."

"Smoke. Coordinates vector north 340 degrees, grid location hill 362A. Over."

"Fire spotter round. Will adjust. Over."

"Roger, second platoon."

An 81mm smoke round detonated right on target.

"Right on the money. Fire for effect."

"Roger."

A salvo of smoke rounds hit the ground in front of the two bunkers.

"Cease fire."

The smoke, mixed with the rain and mist provided good coverage for the Marines.

"Palmer. Get up here with that Zippo. You three guys get him up to that block house and roast 'um."

The four Marines charged into the man-made fog. Rawlins couldn't see them but he heard the firing. Then grenade detonations. Finally the whoosh of the flame thrower as jellied gasoline burned out the bunker. Screaming, burning men poured out of the bunker. The Marines mowed them down like they were rabid dogs, finally confronting the unseen enemy in the daylight on the Marine's terms.

"Burn, you bastards."

The other bunker went up in flames, escaping enemies shot down.

The Marines advanced uphill 362A in the thinning smoke, hidden snipers taking their toll. Sgt. Ramirez was shot in the arm and leg simultaneously by two different snipers. Rawlins noticed the Corpsmen working on him.

"Carlos. What happened?"

"Some son of a bitch shot me. Twice. Didn't even see him. Bastards.

"You lucky dog. Got a million dollar wound. Your war is over. Back to El Paso in one piece."

"That's OK with me, Ken. I've had enough of this shit."

"Yeah. Me too. It's fast becoming a pain in the ass. I liked it better when the Japs came out and fought like men. Not this hide and seek shit."

"Amen to that, brother."

"When you get home write me you lucky bastard."

"OK, Gunny. Semper phi."

As Rawlins walked back up the hill he passed three dead Marines. Killed by invisible hidden enemies.

Hell of a price for this pile of sand and rock. Damned expensive real estate.

The night replacements came up. The platoon was down to forty percent effective strength. So many new faces. Over half the kids Rawlins had trained were gone, dead or wounded. It made Rawlins sick. The price was way too high. He heard that the Regimental Commander had been killed, a mortar round landing next to his jeep. The place was like hell itself. Hot, smelly, dirty, and deadly. And no rest ever. Men slept standing up. It couldn't be helped. Days and weeks with no sleep. The only problem was if you fell asleep you could get a knife in the back.

The night was strangely quiet.

Must be some Jap holiday tonight, thought Rawlins. *Awful quiet.*

Ahead of the platoon lay an elevated ridge with caves and bunkers. Nishi Ridge on the map. The mist swirled up from the hot ground. As the air cooled, men waited for infiltrators that did not come. Rawlins wondered why. Maybe the Marines had killed so many Nips that their strength was down like ours. Maybe saving up for a banzai charge. Rawlins watched the dark ridge and thought, *tomorrow will be a slaughter. Those caves up there are full of Japs and heavy weapons. That's their favorite terrain. They love caves.*

As he watched he noticed a form in the mist, watching him. Bringing up his Tommy gun he realized it was no Jap. Too big and wearing camouflage like the Raiders had worn. And a Marine soft cover. No helmet. No weapon either or 782 gear.

He must be nuts or something.

As Rawlins watched the figure drew closer. Soon it was leaning on a rock close enough for a star shell to illuminate his features plainly. The Raider uniform, dirty and bloodstained with Corporal stripes, was all too familiar. Curly black hair under his cap and brown eyes, stocky build.

Son of a bitch. It can't be. He died in my arms on Bougainville. What the hell is this? Am I cracking up? That's the Joker. Corp. Heys from Pittsburgh.

The specter smiled and waved at Rawlins, then turned and walked toward the ridge.

I must be nuts. Too much jungle juice. He's dead. Long dead.

The figure stopped, turned toward Rawlins and waved for him to follow.

What the hell. Might as well follow him. Nothin' to lose

now.

The Marine picked up his Thompson, cocked the bolt and pushed off the safety lever.

Better be ready. Could be a Jap trick.

As Rawlins followed the ghost he felt tingly all over, like an electric impulse was hitting him. And cold. Very cold. He had heard about ghost stories where people felt the same thing.

Weird shit, he thought.

His dead friend looked back, smiled and waved.

Shit. It's him, all right. No mistake. How the hell can this be? Am I dead and don't know it? Is this hell? Is he here to take me there?

Rawlins felt his wounded side. The pain shot through him, almost buckling his knees.

Shit. I ain't dead. Not the way that felt. This has to be some supernatural shit. He came here to show me something.

The dead Raider stood on a large rock and pointed to a large cave, obscured by an outcropping until you were right on top of it. Two type 99 Nambu Woodpecker machine guns sat in the entrance, their snouts protruding out of the entrance. Rawlins could see a dim light and hear faint voices inside. It was the perfect ambush. Half the platoon would be wiped out before they knew what hit them.

The Joker continued to point at the entrance with a dead hand.

"Yeah, Joker, I see it. I'll take 'um out."

With this thought the Joker smiled, waved at Rawlins and jumped behind the big rock, never to be seen again.

I'll be a son of a bitch. He read my mind. Now he's gone.

"See you later, mate. I owe you one."

Rawlins pulled two frags off his web gear, crawled up to the cave and threw them in. At the detonations there were screams, then nothing. One more grenade was tossed to make sure.

It was getting light. Rawlins entered the cave. All down, some still alive. Then he saw a gruesome sight. A young Marine, maybe eighteen, tied to a stake naked, disemboweled with his genitals cut off.

"You dirty, filthy bastards."

Feeling sick and disgusted, Rawlins pulled up his Tommy gun and fired the whole magazine into the enemy murderers. None would survive this night. He took the boy's dog tags and left the cave. Later the contents of the cave were incinerated with a flame thrower.

* * * * *

Rawlins waited by the big rock while the platoon moved up. Russo spotted him first.

"What gives, Gunny? Why you out here alone?"

"I wasn't alone. Joker was with me."

"Gunny. Don't talk like that. People will think you're nuts."

"I took out that machine gun nest."

"Yeah. I see it."

"He showed me where it was. It would have wiped out half the platoon. You can't see it until you're on top of it. He showed me."

Now Eyes walks up.

"Gunny. You all right?"

"Yeah, OK."

"Why you out here alone?"

"Tell him, Vito."

"Ken says the Joker appeared and showed him that nest up there so he took it out."

"No shit."

"No shit."

"Where's Joker now, Gunny?"

"Disappeared. Back to where he came from I guess. But it was him. I got a good look at him."

"Did he talk to you?"

"No. Just waved at me and smiled and pointed to that nest up there. When I decided to take it he disappeared."

"Gunny. The Lieut. wants to see you."

"OK, Perkins. Go tell him I'll be right there."

The runner left the three ex-Raiders.

"Well, boys, I better check the kids. Make sure they're all ready to move out."

"OK, Gunny."

And he was gone; seeing to his children.

* * * * *

"Well, Vito, what do you think?"

"I think Rawlins is bucking for a Section Eight."

"How about you, Eyes?"

"I ain't so sure. Lots of weird shit happens in war. Remember in school when they told us about that Joan of Arc broad?"

"Yeah. What about her?"

"You know she led the Frenchies at the battle of the Somme in the last war. Stood in front of 'um, fifty foot tall with a big ass sword and ran off the Heinies."

"Yeah, I remember. But I thought it was bullshit."

"Not according to the Frenchies that were there."

"Ya know, Eyes. I heard a story about a Second Lieut. that got it at El' Gatar. This dogface claims that this dead guy showed up at Anzio and led his platoon against a Kraut bunker complex. He said they could see tracers go right through the guy but they had no effect. The platoon took out three bunkers behind this dead guy; then he looked at them, smiled and disappeared. So I dunno. Who the hell knows. Maybe Joker did appear to Rawlins. I know this though. That nest would have chopped us up bad. You couldn't even see it."

* * * * *

"Rawlins. Where the hell have you been?"
"Out front, Sir."
"Why?"
"Had to destroy an ambush site."
"All alone?"
"I wasn't alone, Sir."
"Who was with you?"
"Corp. Heys, Sir."
"What? You mean Joker?"
"Yes, Sir."
"Rawlins, he's dead."
"Yes, Sir."
"So who was with you?"
"Joker was, Sir."
"Are you bucking for a Section Eight, Gunnery Sgt.?"
"No, Sir. You asked me a question and I answered you, Sir."
"I don't have time for this nonsense. Get back to your men."
"Aye, Sir."
Rawlins returned to the platoon's jump-off position and waited for the word to come down to move out.

Soon they were advancing. This time with flame thrower tanks from Third Division. They hosed down the line of advance with burning gasoline to clean out snipers and machine gun fire. Then the infantry would move in and clean up any remaining enemy troops. It was gruesome work but it had to be done. There was no other way. The enemy would not surrender. They preferred to die at their post like good Samurai.

Days and nights became weeks. It all became a blur. The heat, then rain and cold, and the imminent stress of ever present death took its toll. Exhausted men, like zombies, pushed on. Many hoped to be wounded to escape this hell on earth. Some shot themselves out of sheer desperation. They had reached their limit of endurance and could endure no more.

One Sunday morning a Chaplain came up to give services. The enemy used the opportunity to bombard the church goers with the most intense barrage of the northern advance. The latest Japanese terror weapon was employed. The 320mm spigot mortar.

While Lieut. Pruitt and his radio operator transmitted counter battery coordinates, a flying garbage can, as the Marines called the new mortar projectile, found its mark. A direct hit on the C.P. Total destruction. The Lieut. and radio man were obliterated. All that was found was Lieut. Pruitt's hand with his Annapolis ring still on it and one foot, with an anonymous owner. Pruitt's Browning shotgun was driven into the ground by the concussion. Only the butt stock remained visible. This devastated the platoon. The Lieut. had been well liked by his men, especially the ex-Raiders like himself.

* * * * *

Major Wallace came up from battalion to confer with Rawlins.

"Gunnery Sgt. Rawlins."

"Yes, Sir."

"Your Captain is wounded and your Lieut. is dead. Can you take over the company?"

"Yes, Sir."

"Good man. We're really in a bind up here. There are very few senior N.C.O.s or officers left."

"Yes, Sir."

"I'll try to get you replacements, Rawlins, but they're getting hit as fast as they come in. Some companies are down to platoon strength. By the way, Gunny, your Lieut. put you in for the Navy Cross for taking out the machine gun nest alone at night. Congratulations. You deserve it.

"Thank you, Sir. I only wish Lieut. Pruitt was here to thank."

"Amen to that, Gunny. Good luck and carry on."

"Aye, Sir."

* * * * *

The Gunnery Sgt. formed up the forty odd men left in Able Company and moved out. They attacked the left flank of Motoyama Airfield Number Three. Third Division attacked the center. When they got close Rawlins ordered an all out charge.

"Up and at 'um, Marines. Give 'um hell."

The combat weary Marines charged, overrunning the enemy trenches near the airfield, throwing grenades and firing in relay as they went. The fighting, too close to call in support, was strictly an infantry fight. Up close and personal.

Eyes held back with his spotter and two man security team. Perched on a rock outcropping, the sniper readied Baby, his sniper rifle. As the Marines advanced the Jap would come out of the ground behind them. Eyes would eliminate them with precision out to four hundred yards. Sometimes the intended victim was saved with the enemy only three feet from him.

When this happened the Marines would comment:

"Boy, Sarge, your buddy Eyes is one deadly son of a bitch. Saved my ass twice today. Never seen a shot like him."

"Shit. This is nothin' kid. I saw him take out a submarine officer offshore on Guadalcanal."

"No shit. How far?"

"Twelve, maybe fifteen hundred yards."

"Damn. What a weapon. Why does he carry that carbine?"

"Baby's too slow on close targets. The way the Nips are popping out of the ground all over Eyes says it's better for 'um up close. The light weight and twenty round magazine is perfect. Those kid's guns are hard to get a hold of."

"Where did he get it?"

"Said he picked it up on the beach. The guy that had it didn't need it any more."

* * * * *

Rawlins jumped into the trench, Thompson at the ready. Rounding a corner he ran right into four Japanese. They looked dumbfounded at each other. One fired a Nambu type 96/8mm pistol at him, barely missing his head. The Marine opened up from the hip. The heavy weapon bucked in his hands as he cut down the enemy soldiers with the big forty five cal. bullets. Just as the Tommy gun ran dry a bayonet wielding Jap attacked from his rear. Rawlins deflected the thrust, then butt stroked the killer, now on his back on the ground. The Jap kicked the Tommy out of the Marine's hands, then kicked Rawlins in the crotch, dropping him. The Jap was on him with a dagger, choking him with one hand, trying to stab him with the other. Rawlins was losing ground fast, ready to pass out from lack of air.

Son of a bitch. This is it. This Nip is gonna kill me.

Then a bayonet appeared, protruding from the enemy's chest, on top of Rawlins. Blood poured out of the Jap's mouth and all over the Marine. The Jap had a shocked look on his face as he collapsed and died still on top of the Gunnery Sgt.

"Smitty. Am I glad to see you. I was done for. That bastard had me. I must be gettin' old."

Alowishis Josaphat Smith replied:

"You ain't supposed to die in this war, Gunny."

"How do you know, Smitty?"

"'Cause I know stuff like that."

"No shit?"

"No shit., Gunny."

The young Marine gave Rawlins a Camel.

"I gotta go, Gunny. Since I'm a Pfc. I got first squad. There's nobody else left."

"OK, kid. Go find your boys. And thanks."

Alowishis smiled at Rawlins and ran down the trench looking for his squad.

* * * * *

Russo and second squad were busy blowing spider holes and shooting the occupants. They would toss a grenade in one hole and the Japs would come out of another hole near by. Collins would mow them down with a B.A.R. he had picked up. It became a cat and mouse game. The Marines were almost enjoying it after weeks of hide and seek with the enemy. One hundred fifty Japanese died that day defending the airfield and probably many more underground killed by grenades, satchel charges and flame throwers.

The next day the regiment was ordered to stand down for the day for a much needed rest. The odd mortar and sniper fire came in like every day but no attacks. Most men stayed in their holes and slept. They needed it.

The field kitchens brought up hot chow and hot water, the first in weeks. And mail. The first mail since D-day. Rawlins got a letter from his ex-wife, Susan.

> Dear Ken:
>
> Hope you're feeling better since being wounded. Sorry I didn't see you when you were home. Didn't think it was appropriate.
>
> I'm writing to tell you I'm getting married. Didn't want you to hear it from someone else. I met an executive from General Motors. He is older but treats me well and is stable. Doesn't intend to get involved in your war.
>
> I've decided not to be a sea widow like my mother was. And after losing my brother and my father to your war I have had enough.
>
> Good luck and goodbye.
>
> Susan

* * * * *

Well, I'll be a sad Sailor in a cheap whore house. She went for the money. I shoulda expected it. That's how she was raised. Big money all around. What a dumb bastard I am, thinking she would come back to this mud Marine. Never happen. Oh well. F**k it. I'll probably get killed anyway. Just as well.

Then he opened his other letter.

> Dear Ken:
>
> I'm sorry I insulted you like I did. I didn't

mean what I said. Daddy told me if you went
AWOL for me I would eventually hate you and
think you're a coward. And he is right. He said
you did the right thing. One hell of a Marine, he
said. Damn good man. I should be honored to
know you. And he is right. You frightened me
the way you fought with those Sailors. I didn't
expect you to be such an expert. Daddy got mad
at me. He asked me what the hell I expected and
that you're a Marine, pure warrior. He said I was
lucky you were there or the outcome might have
been far worse. Not too many men would
defend a woman against two knife wielding
attackers. He said to give you a break. He's
not one of the kids you grew up with. He's
a real man and you better hope he shows up
here when he comes home. Good men are
hard to find.

I'm sorry, Ken. Everything Daddy
said is true. I hope you can forgive me. I'll
be praying for you.

Love, Evelyn

* * * * *

*Well, imagine that. The old man likes me and Turnbolt is
sorry. Reminds me of another father I once knew. Too bad he's
gone. Hell of a Sailor he was.*

* * * * *

Rawlins fired up a Camel and stripped his Tommy gun.
It hadn't been cleaned since the landing. Then his pistols. The

whole time he was contemplating the vagaries of the opposite sex.

Well. Imagine that.

* * * * *

The next morning all three divisions began the final drive to the end of the island. A massive Naval and artillery bombardment was followed by air strikes from Navy Corsairs and TBF Avenger dive bombers.

Then the Marines jumped off. It was strangely quiet. Not much firing from the enemy.

Were they all dead? Not likely. They were up to something. The sneaky bastards, thought Rawlins. *They should be firing like hell at us. They're up to something.*

"All right, people. Watch your asses. The Nips are up to some new shit."

Sure enough as Able Company advanced a platoon of bad guys poured out of a cave and attacked their right flank. Third Division tanks and infantry opened up on the flankers. Then Rawlins directed artillery against them.

"105mm batteries fire mission. Over."

"Go ahead, Able Leader. Over."

"Coordinates baker niner two six, northern sector of grid, map reference four able six. Massed infantry. Fire H.E. proximity fuse ten foot airburst. Over."

"Fire spotter round will adjust. Over."

The shell came in and landed fifty yards behind the advancing enemy.

"Raise fifty."

Another round fired, landing in the middle of the enemy unit.

"Right on the money. Fire for effect. Give 'um hell."

The barrage lasted for a minute and a half, the tanks joining in with their 76mm guns. The effect was total devastation. Three or four Japanese survived to disappear into spider holes. The rest of the platoon was destroyed. Bodies and parts of bodies littered the volcanic landscape. The battle was over.

The three divisions converged on Taichi Point, on the northern end of the island. Here they took a few prisoners but the majority of troops still alive, killed themselves. This included General Kuribayashi, the cavalry officer that had once loved America.

The Twenty Seventh Regiment of the Fifth Division dug in on the northern end of Motoyama Airfield No. 3 and waited for orders. Work on the airfield had already begun by the Seabees. Two B29 super fortress bombers, shot up over Japan, landed there. The first of many. Their bases on Guam, Tinian, and Saipan were too far to return to with this amount of damage.

*   *   *   *   *

Two days later a squadron of Army Air Corps P51 fighters landed on the field to escort the bombers to Japan.

Iwo Jima was declared secure thirty four days after the invasion. Three days later a finale banzai charge was attempted. Three hundred Japanese formed up for the final assault on the airfield. The last survivors out of over twenty thousand defenders. They charged the Army bivouac where pilots and ground crew lived, throwing grenades, stabbing and slashing sleeping men with swords and bayonets. They even killed wounded aircrew men in the field hospital. They showed no mercy.

Finally, the Army ground crews and Navy Seabees

organized a defense and stopped them. Then the Marines showed up and wiped them out to a man. The last Japanese on the island were dead. In the way of Bushido they had made a final bid for glory and honor.

Rawlins and Able Company received orders to re-deploy to the landing beach for pick up. They were leaving the island alive. On the way they stopped at the Fifth Division cemetery to say goodbye to their fallen comrades. So many. Hard to believe. Able Company alone had been replaced twice from eighty percent casualties.

Rawlins turned command of the Company over to a new Captain just in from the States. He also received his Navy Cross and Purple Heart.

General Howlin' Mad Smith himself decorated Rawlins. The medals were sent home to his parents with a letter saying he was OK. The battle was over.

Next the Marine was flown to Tinian Island by Navy P.B.Y. flying boat. From there he would begin the journey to Tehran, Iran. There he would begin a joint O.S.S./M16 mission in Bavaria. The inventors of the German V1, V2 buzz bombs and Messerschmitt 262 Rocket fighter had to be brought out of Germany.

Scientists like Dr. Erik von Braun and associates were of great interest to the Russians, Brits and Americans. It was feared that if the Russians got their hands on these men the balance of power would change dramatically. The Russian Army was ready to enter Bavaria at any time. This was the supposed hiding place of the aforementioned Nazi scientists.

Rawlins and his British counterpart would find and remove or eliminate these people. Allowing them to fall into Russian hands was unacceptable.

Chapter Six

O.S.S AND M.I.6

The Fifth Division, minus Rawlins, sailed for Camp Tarawa to re-arm and re-train for the invasion of Japan. Because of the atomic bomb and Japan's surrender in early September the planned invasion never occurred. Instead the Fifth Marine Division stood occupation duty in Japan from September tc late December. As a result of the end of the war the Fifth Division was disbanded at Camp Pendleton in January 1946.

* * * * *

Rawlins flew on a C47 Dakota transport from Tinian Island to Walaboom Allied Airfield in central Burma. Here he hitched a ride on an American lend lease British operated B24 Liberator bomber. Next stop - the almost secret British Commonwealth air base at Cocos Keeling Island in the Indian Ocean. This was the base that Bomber Command used to target Java, Sumatra and Borneo and the Japanese strongholds there.

Next hop on a British Lancaster bomber to Dhubulia Airbase in northern India. Here there was a two day layover. That was fine with Rawlins. He liked aircraft about as much as he liked submarines. Coffins with wings, he called the aircraft.

India was a strange place. Totally foreign to what he was used to. Dressed up elephants in the streets, throngs of people everywhere, tigers on the outskirts of town eating the inhabitants on occasion. And the Ghurkas guarding the base were surprising to say the least. Indian Commonwealth troops, they were very proud, very serious. Rawlins remembered the stories of how they terrorized the Germans in North Africa. They would go out at night with their famous bolo knives and decapitate sentries, then put their heads on a rope and stake them out in front of their lines. They did the same thing to the Japanese in Burma. Their enemies were terrified of them. The Brits loved them. "Bloody good show," they would say.

Even the food in this exotic place was strange. Everything hot. They put curry and pepper on everything, even eggs. He was beginning to miss C Rations. At least they didn't burn your mouth. The Brits would laugh at him in the mess hall. "Bloomin' Yank. Can't handle wog food."

Finally departure day. Another C47, equipped with an extra fuel bladder for the long flight. They would fly over the Kandahar Mountains bordering India and Pakistan, then down the Swat Valley into Afghanistan, then south west into Iran. There should be no enemy fighters on this route. It was British controlled in the sky and on the ground.

When they reached Tehran, Iran's capital city, Rawlins was grateful to land. He was taken to a meeting place in Tehran from a secret airfield in the desert. A British Major escorted him to the meeting room. Here he met his British counterpart, one Royal Marine Commando Sergeant Major Benjamin Rothchild. Rawlins knew him from 1942 in the days when Rothschild had been his instructor in the Commando. Back when the Marine Raiders were being formed and trained.

"Rawlins. You bloody Yank prima donna."

"Well, I'll be a son of a bitch. Rothschild, you old walrus, I knew you were too miserable to get killed."

"Yes, Rawlins, you were right. I had a feeling we would meet again. Bloody Jerry has some new toys. And we're going to grab the playmates before the ruddy Commies do. The war in Europe is almost over."

"Yeah, I hear. Too bad the Japs won't give up. They're gonna fight to the bitter end."

"We heard that bloody Iwo Jima was a bloody great slaughter on both sides."

"You heard right. I just left there. Worst combat I ever say. My company was wiped out twice. Almost six thousand killed and nobody knows how many Japs got it. Over twenty thousand is the estimate."

"Bloody shame. What a waste. Sounds like our Holland debacle. We jumped on top of General Models SS Panzer Division and got creamed. Bad Intel. Never knew they were there. Ruddy slaughter. So bad Jerry let us bury our dead and gave us medical help. Almost human, they were."

"This war is nuts. I'm glad it's almost over."

"Amen to that, Yank."

* * * * *

The next day the two agents flew to Gibraltar in the modified Dakota. Then, after re-fueling at the British base there, on to England and Southbury Airfield near Southampton, this time with a British Spitfire escort. German Messerschmitt and Focke-Wulf fighters and JU88 Junker bombers were harassing shipping and planes in the area. There was a hidden base nearby in Portugal, not yet found by the Allies.

* * * * *

Finally, they arrived at MI6 headquarters in London.

"Gentlemen. Your mission is to parachute into Bavaria disguised as German officers. You will make contact with an Abvere agent. This agent is actually a double agent. He works for us and the Germans. He will lead you to your targets. He will also assist in any way possible. You will jump at night in two days. Study these files. They contain instructions and other important information. Do not leave the complex. This is a high security matter. That is all."

Next the two agents were led to wardrobe. Here they were fitted with German officer uniforms. One a Major and the other a Captain. The 354th Alpine Mountain Regiment would be their unit. It was one of many Alpine Regiments in the Wehrmacht stationed in this area.

"Rawlins. You look like a proper Nazi with your blond hair and blue eyes. The uniform becomes you."

"Good. Maybe after the War I'll become a movie star and do war films. You look good too only the mustache better go. Not too

many walrus look-alikes in the German Officer Corps."
"Bloody hell, Yank."

* * * * *

Next day - final briefing.
"Gentlemen. You will jump into Bavaria south of Munich
near Berchtesgaden. Your contact's name is Carl Steiner. He will find
you in Bergdorf. There is a small inn located nearby named the
Slouse Gasthouse. It's on the banks of a small river. Steiner will
watch for you at the bar, then light your cigarette, then you will leave
together after an appropriate time. Your contact will be dressed as a
Wehrmacht Infantry Lieutenant, home on leave. Steiner will take you
to the hiding place of the scientists. From there you will make your
way southwest to the Swiss border. Once across you will find the
British Consulate in Zurich. There you will hand over the defectors to
British authority, then remain there until the war in Europe is over.
When normal flights from Switzerland resume you will return here.
You leave tonight 2300 hours. Good luck, gentlemen."

* * * * *

Next the new Nazis went to the armory and were issued
German P38 Walther 9mm Parabellum pistols, the standard German
officer sidearm in 1945. They were also given Walther PPKS pistols
in 9mm Kurz, a small pocket pistol popular with German pilots and
staff officers. This would serve as a back-up gun along with a Sykes-
Fairbairn stiletto. If things got personal this should suffice for
weaponry for the mission at hand.
     Next a ride to the airfield. The German uniforms were packed
in kit bags with the weapons, except the PPKS pistols and knives
which were kept hidden. The two warriors packed their chutes, not
trusting anyone else to do it. Now they had a little time to kill. They
were permitted to enter the closed and guarded hanger where the
captured Dornier Flugzeugwerke transport was hidden. Its white and
black Alpine camouflage paint was a stark contrast to the O.D. green
Spitfires next to it. The plane was like new, captured on the ground

on a small airfield hidden in the Ardennes Forest in Belgium.

Finally, with nothing left to do, the pair of infiltrators studied maps and drank coffee. They began to talk.

"Well, Rawlins, are you ready for this?"

"No."

"Bloody hell, Mate, no time to get squeamish. The show is on."

"Yeah, I know. Just tired. Tired of this war, tired of seeing people die."

"Yes, Rawlins. Quite. I've lost a lot of mates in the bloody fracas."

"Me too. Too many."

"Now I understand why my old dad acted so strange half the time. Bloody shell shocked I wouldn't wonder. Served in the Black Watch. Saw too much of the Hun in the Great War."

"My old man too. He's the same way. All shot up. Full of Kraut steel. Battle of Belleau Wood."

"Bloody shame. Hope we don't end up the same way. How did you make out with your wife, Rawlins?"

"No good. Said she had enough of war types. Got a letter on Iwo saying she's marrying some old guy who's stable."

"Bloody she wolf. You're better off."

"Yeah, I know. But it's still a rough deal."

"Yes. Quite."

"How about you? You see your wife lately?"

"After Holland. We spent two weeks together."

"How did it go?"

"Bloody marvelous. I think she actually missed me. It was like a second honeymoon."

"Good for you. At least someone is waiting for you."

"Yes. I got lucky with her."

* * * * *

2300 Hours:

Time to go. The two spies boarded the Luftwaffe Dornier and it was pulled out to the tarmac in the darkness.

Both men were silent on the flight to Bavaria; each with their own thoughts.

Rawlins was contemplating the nurse back in Niagara Falls. Should he get involved and take another chance or should he forget her. Could he handle another break up if it didn't work out? Or should he play it safe and avoid the whole situation? He just couldn't decide.

Oh well, I'll probably get killed before I get home anyway.

"Rawlins. Have a drink."

"Thanks."

The Marine took a long pull on the German silver flask, full of brandy.

"Nice. Where did you get it?"

"Took it off a Jerry prisoner. A Colonel. Nice old fellow. Said he hated the war as much as he hated Hitler."

"Well, imagine that. A Nazi that hates war."

The brandy helped relax the warriors and so did the Chesterfield cigarettes they smoked.

Finally, after what seemed like an eternity, they were at the target. The Jumpmaster gave the commands.

"Stand up and hook up."

The jumpers attached their ripcords to the cable above their heads.

"Stand in the door."

Rawlins moved to the door, wind blasting his face and jumpsuit.

"Go, go, go."

The OSS man stepped into space, then felt the jerk of his chute opening. Now suspended in the cool, black mountain air, like another dimension, he just hung there in empty space. Then the black ground came rushing up at him and wham, he was down, legs folding and rolling like he had been trained. His partner landed thirty yards away.

They buried their chutes and donned their German uniforms. Then they took a compass bearing and headed for Bergdorf on a mountain trail before the local Gestapo showed up to investigate an unauthorized airplane fly over.

The two agents followed the trail into the small hamlet,

traffic coming and going on the main road. All military. The Russians were closing in from the east, the Americans and Brits from the west and south. All available units were being deployed for the defense of the Fatherland. The end was in sight.

Finding the inn on the river, the two spies ordered a room overlooking the river, then headed for the bar to wait for their contact.

Rawlins ordered for the pair.

"Schnapps und beer bitta."

The fraulein tending bar got their drinks.

"Vegates, Herr Major?"

Rawlins answered:

"Sere gut, fraulein. Danke."

Right on schedule a young Lieutenant approached Rawlins. The Major pulled out a cigarette, then searched for a match.

"May I be of assistance, Herr Major?"

"Why yes. Thank you, Herr Oberleutnant."

As the contact lit the cigarette Rawlins spoke:

"Are you stationed here, Oberleutnant?"

"No, Herr Major. I am home on furlough."

"I see."

"And you, Sir?"

"The Hauptman and I are couriers for Field Marshall Kesselring. We come from the Po River Valley, en route to Berlin."

This was the identification exchange required. This was the contact.

* * * * *

An SS officer sat at a table in the corner watching the three travelers. After a few minutes he stepped up to the bar.

"May I inquire as to your reason for being here, Herr Major?"

"We are couriers en route to Berlin, Herr Hauptsturmfuhrer."

"I see. Und papier bitta?"

"Ya, ya. Must the SS always bother soldiers? Don't you have better things to do?"

"May I remind you, Herr Major, the SS are the overseers of the Wehrmacht?"

"May I remind you, Hauptsturmfuhrer, that you are a Captain and I am a Major. In any army I outrank you. Is that understood? And one call to Field Marshall Kesselring's headquarters and you will be shining boots for the duration."

The SS man shrank away from the bar and went back to his corner to pout. He would see about this. No lowly Army Major was going to show disrespect to an SS officer. This would not be tolerated. As the miffed Socialist planned dire straits for the Army at the bar the Army went upstairs.

"Rawlins. That SS bloke isn't done with us. You insulted him and they're all ego."

"Yeah, I know. I screwed up. Couldn't help it. Didn't know what to do but pull rank."

Soon there was a knock on the door.

"Shit. It must be him."

Rawlins pulled the stiletto from under his tunic and motioned for Rothschild to open the door. The Sergeant Major pulled the door open and there stood the SS Captain. As he stepped into the room Rothschild addressed him:

"Good of you to come, old man. Would have been a bloody bother to find you to shut you up."

The SS man looked horrified.

"Britisher. Mein Gott! You are a Britisher."

"Why yes. Frightfully so, old boy."

The Nazi killer tried to pull his pistol but too late. Rawlins grabbed him from behind, shutting off his air, then sank the stiletto into his neck, up to the hilt. The SS monster kicked and bucked, then went still forever.

"Bloody good show, Yank. One less goon to deal with. And their German friend. SS pig. Kill them all, I say."

Rawlins searched the body, taking papers, ID tag and Walther P38 pistol with spare magazine. Then he hoisted the body through the open window and into the river below. The body slowly sank out of sight.

0400 Hours:

"We better get the hell outta here before someone misses Captain asshole."

The trio left the inn and took the SS officer's car, a black Mercedes. Their German contact drove down the main road south, then took an unimproved road going up in the mountains to a small cabin in the woods. Behind the cabin, a hundred yards into the woods, was an underground bunker. In the bunker were three German scientists, ready to defect to the Allies.

*****

Carl Steiner, the German contact, drove the car back to the river. With the help of Major Rawlins they pushed the Mercedes over the bank and into the water. They hoped that if the SS Captain's body was found and the car found it would be considered an accident.

Next they walked to a small inn they had passed earlier and stole another car, a pre-war Saab, then back to the cabin. The three men and Rothschild were in the cabin. One of them was cooking potatoes over a small smokeless fire. They all ate and drank some Schnapps found in the pantry.

After dark the German spy and Rawlins decided to recon the area. Leaving the cabin they headed into the woods parallel to the road, keeping in the woods for fifty yards or so. No surprises this way. Reaching the bottom of the mountain they headed south, checking the main road. A kilometer from their starting point they discovered what they had feared they would find. SS road block with a platoon of Waffen-SS troopers for backup.

"Shit, Steiner. We can't get out this way. We can't take on a whole platoon."

"Nein, Herr Major. And any other direction is the wrong way out of Germany."

"Do we have any options?"

"The river. We steal a boat and float southwest and away from here."

"Sounds good, Steiner. Let's get back to the cabin and discuss this with our people."

* * * * *

"All right. This is the situation. Down the road heading to Switzerland there is an SS roadblock with a platoon of Waffen-SS. Too many for us to handle. So we're going to take the river out of here. We will steal a boat and float to the southwest toward the border. So let's get in the car and head to the river and find a boat."

"Major. There are patrols on the river."

"Yes, I figured on that. We'll deal with that problem when the time comes."

Rawlins already had a plan. Steal a patrol boat and masquerade as German sailors. The international boat crew loaded into the Saab and headed into the dark night in the opposite direction of the SS sight-seers.

"Herr Major. What if there is trouble? We are not soldiers."

"Don't worry. We are. Just stay out of the way."

Reaching the other side of the mountain, the river lay in front of the travelers. They turned onto the river road and headed north. Many small row boats were seen. All too small.

Suddenly, as they rounded a curve in the road, there it was. A German Kreigsmarine patrol boat, tied to a dock, being fueled.

"Bloody hell, Rawlins, look at that. Bloody perfect and only two guards plus four sailors that I can see. There may be more. That's perfect, Rawlins. We can pose as ruddy Jerry swabbies, no one the wiser. Jolly good show, old man."

Rawlins was thinking the same as he drove by the boat and crew. Hide in plain sight. It was even being fueled for them.

The Waffen-SS Grenadiers saluted the imitation Major as he slowly drove past.

"Bloody grand, Yank. They already think you're Hitler's long lost son."

Rawlins drove a half kilometer down the road, then took a side road into the woods. Her he drove the Saab into a grove of pines as far as it would go, in the soft earth. Well hidden from prying eyes.

Then the spies made ready for the attack. The placed silencers on the PPKS pistols, then loaded them with subsonic ammo. The only noise would be that of the slide racking at the shot. These

These weapons were placed inside their tunics. Their P38 pistols remained in their uniform holsters. Their Commando stilettos were in easy reach also.

The three men were instructed to wait in the woods by the intersection of roads near the river. They would only come out when they saw the boat.

Rawlins, Lieut. Steiner and Rothschild walked down the dark road back to the boat. Thirty foot in length and fueled, ready to go, her engines were even idling, warming up.

As soon as the officers came into view the SS troopers came to rigid attention.

"Heil Hitler, Herr Major."

"Kiss my ass, dummy."

With a shocked look the trooper tried to unsling his Mouser rifle. Too slow. Rawlins pumped two 90 grain, 9mm Kurz bullets into his chest.

Another misguided fool dies for the Fatherland.

Rothschild gave the same treatment to the Schmeisser machine pistol carrying Socialist lackey. He never got the change to become the mass murderer his Fuhrer had hoped for. His beloved SS would reign with him for a thousand years. In hell.

The sailors, oblivious to the carnage that had taken place on shore, came to attention when the officers boarded their boat. Only one was armed with a Schmeisser MP40 burp gun. The others were busy wrestling fuel drums. The petty officer with the machine pistol got two rounds in the head. No more whorehouses on the Danube for him. The two boatswains mates doing the fueling tried to come to their comrades aid but were both gunned down in short order.

Rawlins pulled out his stiletto and descended the bridge ladder below deck. He knew there was one more crewman somewhere. Not wanting to damage any equipment from bullet over penetration he would use his knife to dispatch the Kreigsmariner. Listening intently he heard the rattling of dishes, pots and pans. Stepping quietly to the middle compartment he found his target. A German sailor washing dishes. Sneaking up behind the busy cook he grabbed the Nazi by the hair and back of the head and drove his head into the sink full of water. Placing his knee in the Nazi's crotch he held him motionless with his head under water. As the enemy tried to fight back Rawlins gently slit his throat. Gouts of blood spilled into the water as the cook bled out and died. Then Rawlins removed his uniform and went topside with it.

"Here, Ben, put this on. No blood on it."

Then he took the head shot petty officers uniform for himself. The bodies were thrown into the river and drifted away.

After donning the Kreigsmarine uniform Rawlins started the engine and slipped away from the mooring. Increasing the twin diesel engines to fifteen hundred revolutions per minute the patrol craft headed downstream in the direction of Switzerland.

The new petty officer picked up the Schmeisser MP40 submachine gun left on the deck by the dead petty officer. The weapon was laid on the wheel house combing. Out of sight.

Rothschild readied the twin Spandau MG42 7.92mm machine guns in the anti-aircraft mount. He also removed the limit pins so the guns could be depressed to fire on level targets. Another Schmeisser was found below deck and given to Lieut. Steiner.

It was getting light as the escaping Germans passed the SS roadblock on shore. Everyone waved, never guessing there was a new crew on board and their Nazi comrades were fish food.

Rawlins felt odd dressed as a German sailor on the bridge of this German gunboat. Another story for the old man.

With the sunrise came a Luftwaffe Messerschmitt. It flew low over the boat looking things over. Then left. After a half hour it was back. Looking harder. Then left again.

"Bloody hell, Yank. They know we're up to something. That bloody Messerschmitt pilot was too curious. We must be in the wrong place."

Just then the radio crackled to life. A German voice was demanding a password and explanation. Of their location.

"We're in for it now, Rawlins. They're on to us."

"Yeah. And here comes the reception committee."

Another patrol boat was heading upstream in their direction.

"Rothschild. Get on those guns. We're gonna have to take them. No way out of this."

The enemy craft drew closer. Then, over a bull horn:

"Heave to. Prepare to be boarded."

"Rawlins. They mean to board us."

"Yeah. I heard um. When they pull alongside let 'um have it."

"Right, old man."

Rawlins pulled back the throttle levers and the boat settled down to a stop, now dead in the water.

The German sailors, all on deck, prepared to jump aboard and were perfect targets.

"Let 'um have it."

Rawlins fired the full thirty two round magazine into the shocked enemy boarders. So did Carl Steiner. Dead Nazis littered the deck, which was now awash with blood. A German Sub Lieutenant, who was in command fired a pistol from the wheel house. Rothschild hosed the helm with the twin MG42s, destroying the officer and the wheelhouse. Then the Englishman sprayed the length of the boat below deck. A fire broke out and the little ship began to list to port.

"Rawlins. Get the hell out of here before it blows!"

As the dead men's ship sank and burned Rawlins powered its sister ship downstream.

Wham!!! The fuel tanks went up. And the Nazi patrol craft slipped beneath the surface, burying her dead crew.

"Shit. That was close. Too close. We gotta get off this tub. If they send a couple of planes after us we're dead."

Rawlins found a small tributary and headed the German craft into its channel. A mile or so inland they put their charges ashore and scuttled the Nazi gunboat. Paddling a rubber raft to shore the two agents watched as their former transportation rolled over and sank. They made sure they sank the life boat, leaving no trace of their passing.

Entering the woods on shore they found the scientists and Carl Steiner. Here the intrepid agents donned their German Army uniforms and buried the Kriegsmarine jumpsuits they had borrowed. The two MP40 machine pistols were retained along with their Walther pistols. Also German rations and a map which they had found on the boat were kept. The small group moved deeper into the forest. Prying eyes could give away their position. There was no doubt the German Army and SS were looking for them by now.

As it grew dark the escapees from Socialist murder ate German Army field rations. Smoked sausage and biscuits. And cheese.

"Bloody hell, Rawlins, their rations are better than ours. Bloody Jerry has the best of everything."

"Yeah, Rothschild. Too bad they're losing the war. Break out that map. Let's see where we are. Here's where we left the main river. We should be about here. In the forest. There's two main roads. We'd better check them out. Steiner, stay here with your people. Keep one of the Schmeissers in case of company. Let's go, Ben."

Rawlins felt better now. Back in his element. This espionage stuff was getting to him. Hide and seek with the SS ultimate bad guys. He preferred regular warfare with regular soldiers. Not stick a knife in somebody and then run and hide. This just wasn't right. Borderline murder. Even if they were the enemy.

The dark woods reminded the Marine of Guadalcanal and the long patrol. Red Mike Edson's First Raider battalion, including Sgt. Rawlins, had slipped into the jungle and stayed for a month, harassing the Japanese defenders. That was Rawlins kind of war. Soldier to soldier. Man to man. No politics. No mass civilian murder. Kill or be killed. The ultimate contest. The Japanese Samurai loved it. And so did the Marines, secretly. The thrill of intense close combat. With light weapons. No bombs, no artillery. Just rifle, pistol, bayonet, bare hands. The ultimate test of the warrior.

* * * * *

The two men were quiet as they slipped through the forest heading for the road. No talking. They knew the enemy was looking for them and could be anywhere.

With the moon rise they could see reasonably well. As they passed a grove of blue spruce trees the road lay before them. And on the road, heavy traffic. All military.

"Shit. A convoy. Must be a regiment moving up. From what I can see it looks like Wehrmacht Alpine troops. No SS. Must be something big going on."

Little did the two agents know that Germany was being

invaded. Russian General Zukov had broken through on the eastern
front and was heading for Berlin. American General Patton's Third
Army was in the Ruhr Valley. British General Montgomery's Eighth
Army had come through Holland and Belgium and was in northern
Germany. In the south on the Po River line in northern Italy German
Field Marshall Kesselring's southern Army group had its back against
the wall. American Thirty Sixth Division and Tenth Mountain
Division troops were putting overwhelming pressure on this front.
The end was in sight. All reserve and People's Guard troops were
activated. Hitler's Plan Valkyrie was in effect. All men from fourteen
to eighty years of age would defend the Fatherland. Period.

* * * * *

     "Bloody Jerry is everywhere. How in blue blazes are we
going to escort our Nazi boy scouts out of here now? I say we shoot
them and hide out till our troops get here."
     "We can't. Our governments need them to jump ahead of the
Russians. Remember?'
     "Bloody hell. Flaming Jerry."
     "Well, one thing is clear. We can't use the roads. The Army
and the SS are everywhere on the move."
     "Well, Yank, you're in charge. What will it be?"
     "We fly out."
     "Fly out!! You're bloody daft, man."
     "I saw an airfield on the Kraut map. They're sure to be flying
troops to the front. We'll steal a plane and its pilot."
     "Bloody brilliant, Yank. Just go commandeer a plane full of
ruddy Jerry and fly away to a better place. You're bloomin' mad."
     "All we gotta do is find a place to hide near a transport, wait
until they start the engines for warm up, and then rush the plane
before the troops board. And take off. No problem."
     "No problem. Just like that. You bloody Yanks are all
crackers. Round the bloody bend. But I guess it's worth a try. No
other options at this point. Bloody hell."

* * * * *

As the two agents made their way back to the forest hide site a conversation was started by the ex-Nazi scientists.

"Herr Steiner. Why have you turned on the Fatherland?"

"I haven't."

"But you have killed our people."

"I have killed Nazis. Not people. The Socialists are destroying Germany. Just like you destroyed London. Where many of our friends once lived, now they hate us all. Because of you scientists and your death machines at Pina Munda. In my opinion you should be shot as traitors along with Hitler and his SS."

"That's dangerous talk, Steiner."

"If you don't like it, Nazi, go surrender to the Russians and see what happens. Because Admiral Canaris, head of Intelligence, went to Spain and made a deal with the Allies on your behalf, you may survive the war. If your friends don't find us first. And if you try to contact the SS in any fashion I will kill all three of you before they kill me."

So much for conversation. The three old men decided to remain quiet and not provoke this madman. He might kill them out of spite.

Just then the Yank and Brit showed up.

"All right. This is the deal. We're hemmed in on all sides. Troops are using the roads. There must be a big push happening. They're moving by battalion and regiment in convoy. Lots of SS roadblocks. And patrols. They're still looking for us. The only way out is by air. We will steal a plane from the airfield on the map and fly to Switzerland."

"Rawlins, you must be mad," countered Steiner.

"They will kill us all. There is no chance. The Waffen SS guard that field. We'll never make it."

"We have to. There's no other way. All we need is a diversion. We'll blow a couple of plane's fuel tanks, then take a running plane."

The plan garnered looks of disbelief and consternation but the Yank was in charge. And they knew he was right. No other way out.

"Rawlins. How do we blow a plane with no explosives?"

"Simple. We steal some."

"How?"

"That Alpine regiment we saw pulling out is sure to have left something useful lying around their barracks.

* * * * *

0300 Hours:

"Well, Yank, there it is."

"Steiner. Stay here and watch the three stooges. We don't want 'um wandering off here in SS land."

"See that big tent, Ben? Let's try that."

The two Commando trained agents crawled through the underbrush and entered the tent from the rear.

"Bingo. Supply tent. There's gotta be something here we can use."

First they found ammo crates. From them they took ten loaded MP40 magazines. Next, rations. Ten field rations. Then ten potato masher grenades and two Teller mines. Then German voices from someone entering the tent, talking about the big move north. Rawlins took the corporal with his silenced Walther PPKS as the unfortunate Service NCO rounded a corner of stacked crates. The soldier thought he had walked into a German Major. He came to attention and the Major shot him twice in the chest. The Corporal died without a sound.

The other German was nearly beheaded by Rothschild's commando knife. Dead before he saw his enemy.

"C'mon, Ben. Let's get outta here."

"Right behind you, Yank."

As they left Rothschild grabbed a new STG44 Sturm Gevere assault rifle in 7.92mm Kurz. Germany's new battle rifle. He also grabbed the four loaded magazines left next to it.

After the thieves made their escape and were safely away from the dump, Rawlins looked over the new weapon.

"Watcha got there, Ben?"

"STG44. Jerry's new toy. It's a cross between a rifle and a machine pistol. Like a crossbred Sten gun and Bren gun. Bloody different. Saw some in Holland."

With their new found arsenal the intrepid warriors and company made their way to the airfield.

"There it is, Rawlins. And guarded by SS Grenadiers."

"Yes, Ben. And there's our transport. That Dornier they're fueling near the woods. That's our ride outta here. And on the end of field it looks like two Messerschmitt ME109s and two Focke-Wulf FW190s. Both painted with Alpine white and black camo."

"Meaning, Rawlins?"

"They're stationed here; not visitors. They have to go or we won't get ten miles. They will shoot us down for sure. Blowing them will also give us the diversion we need. Get your Limey ass down there and wire them up with those Teller mines and grenades. I'll stay here with Steiner and get the plane. Watch out for guards. There has to be at least two. And don't blow the planes until you hear this one start. We'll taxi down the runway and pick you up."

"Bloody hell."

* * * * *

As Rothschild made his way through the woods toward his objective he noticed two guards with slung rifles walking around the fighter aircraft.

Luftwaffe troops, not Waffen SS. Bloody good show.

The Commando crept up to the first half dozing guard and grabbed him from behind. As the German began to struggle, his killer pushed the thin blade of the Commando knife into his neck to the hilt, then dragged the enemy guard into the woods

One down.

Slinging the STG44 over his back, he picked up the dead man's Mauser rifle and attached the bayonet from his belt frog.

Bloody good club, thought the Englishman. Creeping back to the planes he watched as the Luftwaffe soldaten rounded a corner. Slipping behind him, Rothschild butt stroked him in the back of the head, knocking off his duck-billed helmet and shoving him to the ground. The confused and bewildered German sat up and held up his hands in the dark. No matter. The Commando sank the bayonet into his throat, killing him. Dropping the rifle, he proceeded to place

Teller mines in the cockpits of the inside planes in the lineup.
Grenades were wedged between the mines and fuel cells under the
seats. A piece of cord was tied to the grenade's pull strings. At the
right time he would pull the cord from the woods and detonate the
mines with grenade blasts.

* * * * *

Rawlins and Steiner watched from the woods as the ground
crew and pilots did the pre-flight check. Then the pilots boarded the
airship and fired up the engines. The ground crew returned to the
main hanger.

The Marine noticed a formation of Luftwaffe Fallschirmjager
(paratroopers) standing fifty yards away, waiting to board the plane.

"Well, Steiner, it's now or never. Let's do it."
The two imitation German officers and their Gestapo looking charges
walked to the plane, across the tarmac. The German troopers watched
curiously. The trespassers boarded the Dornier transport. Rawlins
walked up to the forward cabin, pulling out the silenced Walther
pistol. The co-pilot watched as he cleared the rear hatchway. Then the
German flight officer noticed the pistol in the American assassin's
hand. Pulling his own Walther, the Nazi tried to engage the Yank bad
guy but to no avail. Rawlins was faster, shooting the co-pilot in the
head from six feet. Stepping over the body, Rawlins shoved the pistol
in the pilot's face, then explained that he was next if he didn't
cooperate. The German flight officer began to taxi down the runway
as instructed.

The troopers in formation watched their ride to the front leave
them behind. With total discipline they never moved. Good Nazis
followed orders to the letter.

Wham!! Boom!! The fighters went up in a huge fiery
explosion. Flame shot a hundred feet in the air from high octane fuel
fires.

Jolly good show, thought Rothschild.

Ground crew and troops ran to and fro to their battle
positions. Rothschild ran out on the tarmac and began firing on
people heading his way. The STG44 proved deadly for close range

work like this.

Rawlins commanded the pilot to stop. Through the open outer hatchway he yelled.

"C'mon you Limey walrus. Get your ass in here."

As Rothschild clambered aboard, Steiner told the pilot to take off and fly south. The pilot gunned the engines and spun the plane into the wind. Slowly advancing down the runway the plane began to lift off. An anti-aircraft flak Panzer 20mm automatic cannon crew found the range. As the lumbering transport lifted off the AAA crew sprayed the hull. Doctor Stephen Kranz from Munich University, Applied Physics Dept. was decapitated from a 20mm round. Carl Steiner would never leave Germany alive. He was cut in two when a burst of 20mm shrapnel blew through the hull, killing him instantly.

"Shit. Steiner and one of the old Krauts got it. Tell the pilot to fly to Switzerland and find an airfield. Tell him if he lands this crate and we survive he goes free."

When Rothschild delivered the message the German officer looked relieved and headed for the border.

"Well Yank, it looks like we pulled it off. No fighters following. We're in the clear. Bloody good show, I say."

* * * * *

Rawlins was tired. So tired. Tired of war. It felt like his whole life had been war, starting with his father's war stories, then his father-in-laws, then his own. All he knew was war and killing. Could there be another way for him. Could the little nurse show him how to live again. Live without fear. Live without carrying a gun to survive. Find love and understanding where there had been only hate and misconception. Rawlins wondered. *Imagine that,* he thought.

* * * * *

"There's the border, Yank. We made it."

The German pilot had found a small field ten miles from the border. He secretly had plans of his own to defect to this neutral country when the Russians came. Russians were not kind to German prisoners. And they all knew it. He had memorized the location of this field for his planned escape. In perfect English he said to Rawlins:

"I wish to defect if you will allow it, American."

"You got us down safe; you got a deal, Fritz."

* * * * *

When the plane landed the occupants were immediately greeted by Swiss defense forces Military Police. They were instructed to leave any weapons on the plane and come out. The German officers, real or otherwise, were taken to an internment camp and placed in the guarded compound. Many men from different countries were there. Deserters and defectors from Italy, Russia, Austria, Czech Republic, Germany, America and Great Britain. They all got along reasonably well. Their war was over and they were alive.

Finally the scientists convinced the camp Commandant to take them to the British Consulate in Zurich. Their contact people were there waiting for them.

The German pilot remained in the camp with his German comrades. The others were transported to the Consulate.

A British Colonel greeted them.

"Welcome, comrades. Jolly good show, Rothschild. We knew you could pull it off. The PM sends his thanks."

"I had some help, Sir."

"Yes, yes, we know. The Yank and a German double agent. And where is he, Sergeant Major?"

"Dead. Killed in that bloody Jerry excuse for an airplane."

"Pity. Oh, well, he served his purpose. Just another Jerry. Make yourselves comfortable. You will remain here until further notice. Anything you need, let us know. Cheerio."

Rawlins and Rothschild shared a stateroom. So did the Germans. A bottle of Johnny Walker and a bottle of Beefeaters gin were delivered to the room. The two allied warriors got very drunk. Happy to be alive.

The next day: full debriefing and After Action Report.

Two Days Later:

The war in Europe ended. Admiral Doenitz, in place of the dead Adolph Hitler, surrendered. All German military forces were unconditionally capitulated to the Allied Supreme Command.

* * * * *

After a week of celebrating and boozing the two warriors returned to England, their charges with them. After more celebrating in Piccadilly they said their goodbyes. RSM Rothschild returned to his wife and the Commando to await his next assignment.

Rawlins boarded ship out of Southampton. The relaxed atmosphere among the officers and crew made him nervous. Particularly at night. No zig zag. And full lighting. He waited for the torpedo that never came. The last time he had made this trip, back in forty two, the North Atlantic had been alive with German U-boats. He recalled the horrible sound of torpedoes blowing up ships in his convoy. And screaming, dying sailors in the dark Atlantic night. Now all the U-boats lay on the bottom of the sea for all eternity, their dead crews on a patrol in hell. Everything they had fought and died for gone. All for nothing. It was hard to believe. The North Atlantic was a cemetery. But the war in this part of the world was over. Never to be repeated.

In a week the ship docked at Philadelphia Naval Yard. Three days later he was on a train bound for Buffalo, NY. Home at last. And alive.

Chapter Seven

BACK TO THE CORPS

When Rawlins' train pulled into the Buffalo Station he was greeted by his family and the little nurse. She threw her small body against the big Marine and hugged his neck, suspended in mid-air. Then hugged him around the middle and almost made him collapse.

"Ken! What's wrong? You're hurt."

"No big deal. Caught a bayonet on Iwo. Just a little sore" Rawlins lied. It was killing him.

"You better have that looked at, Son. I know what can happen with a wound like that. I'll take you to the VA Hospital tomorrow."

"OK, Dad."

They all piled into the old man's Chevy and drove to the family home, the nurse holding the Marine's hand all the way.

At home Rawlins relaxed for the first time in months. His father gave him a glass of Johnny Walker and a beer, then a Camel.

"So how was Iwo Jima? We heard it was a real slaughter."

"It was, Dad. On both sides. We lost almost six thousand killed. We killed over twenty thousand of the bastards. That island is a cemetery now and a lot of my mates are still there. Did you see the flag raising?"

"Yeah, I saw it."

"Two of the raisers were ex-Raiders. Now one of them is dead along with two mud Marines that raised it. My company was wiped out twice. I was in command of the company at the end. All of our officers were gone."

"We got your Navy Cross in the mail. What happened?"

"I can't tell you."

"Why? It's over."

"You will all think I'm nuts."

"Why?"

"'Cause its crazy. Or I'm crazy."

"C'mon, Kenny, tell us. We won't tell anyone. We love your

stories. We want to know what happened."

"Evelyn already thinks I'm a little off."

"Oh, c'mon Kenny. I want to hear too. I won't run out the door. I know strange things happen in war. I heard a lot of strange stories from the boys on the hospital ship."

"All right, but I warned you. You may all think I'm buckin' for a Section Eight. But here goes.

We were at the base of Hill 362a. Rainy, foggy. Jap infiltrators all around us. All of a sudden I see this guy walk out of the mist. No weapon, no gear, no helmet. And he's comin' right at me. I figure it's a Jap trick. So I push the safety off my Tommy gun, ready to fire. He gets closer. I see in a star shell burst that he's dressed in Raider camo. Bloody and dirty. Not dungarees like regular Marines wear. He gets closer. Another star shell. I look at his face. And son of a bitch, it's Joker."

"Your friend from Pittsburg?"

"Yes. And he's dead. Died in my arms on Bougainville. Now he's smiling and waving for me to follow. I'm thinking I must be dead and don't know it. He's here to take me wherever I have to go. Then I touched my side and almost passed out from the pain. *Well, I thought, I ain't dead yet. Probably will be before long. I might as well follow him.* I got up and walked behind Joker's ghost for a way in our front. He jumped up on a big rock and pointed at a hidden gun emplacement. You couldn't see it from the ground. It was in a cave up the hill a ways. In the morning it would have chopped us up good when we advanced. He was trying to save us. Just stood on that rock. Smiling and pointing. Finally, I thought without saying, *I see it, Joker. I'll take it out. Thanks, Mate. I owe you one.* He must have read my mind. He smiled, waved and jumped behind the big rock and was gone, never to be seen again."

"Kenny. Did you feel anything while this was going on?"

"Yeah. Kinda cold and electric all over. Like the air was charged with electricity."

"My God. You won't believe this, Ken. In school my Paranormal Psych class. The professor told us that exactly what you describe happens during a paranormal visit. Wow. Wait until I tell him this."

"He'll probably have me committed, Sis."

"He might want to talk to you for his case files. He told us lots of stories similar to yours. There are many of them from Gettysburg. Lots of paranormal activity. So many men were killed there."

"So what happened with the gun, Ken"

"Well, Dad, I could see a faint light up there and hear Nip voices. So I snuck up the hill to the cave entrance. I heard 'um talking and laughing. So I tossed in a couple of frags. Then I entered the cave. Nips lying all over. Then I saw it."

"What, Kenny?"

"A young kid, maybe eighteen, tied to a stake, bayoneted, disemboweled, with his privates cut off. And they were laughing at him, the filthy bastards."

"Oh, my God, Kenny. What did you do?"

"I killed every last one of them with my Tommy gun. Murdering bastards. Then I took the kid's dog tags. Spiked the guns and met my unit coming up the hill. Later, I had the Zippo man burn out the cave. It was the best I could do for the kid. Graves Registration was way behind us."

"Did they ask you why you were out front alone?"

"Yeah, Dad, they did. And the Lieutenant didn't believe me. He was killed soon after that so it didn't go any further."

Silence. No one knew what to say. Everyone was shocked. So the subject was changed.

"Where were you after Iwo, Ken?"

"Bavaria."

"Why?"

"Me and a Brit and a Kraut posed as German officers and smuggled three German scientists out of Germany before the Russians got them."

"No shit?"

"No shit."

"So how did you pull it off?"

"We jumped in near Berchtesgaden. Met our contact man in a hotel nearby, then borrowed an SS officer's car. He didn't need it any more. The roads were crawling with troops on the move. SS roadblocks blocking our way."

"So what did you do, Kenny?"

"We stole a Kraut river patrol boat, then posed as Nazi sailors."

"You're kidding."

"No kidding. It was the only way to move out of there."

"A Luftwaffe patrol spotted us. We were in the wrong place and they were on to us. So here comes another gun boat. When they came alongside us and tried to board we let 'um have it. Their boat burned and sank in the process. So we found a tributary and sank our boat and headed into the woods. The Brit and I did a recon and found the whole area hemmed in. The SS were looking for us and the Army was on the move. Convoys everywhere."

"So how did you get out?"

"We stole a plane and flew to Switzerland."

"Are you serious?"

"Yes. There was no other way. And the SS were closing in so we headed for an airfield we found on a map. Stopped at a Kraut Regiment bivouac and stole some explosives and better weapons. Then to the airfield."

"How did you take the plane?"

"We waited in the woods until they fueled and started a Fallschirmjager Dornier transport. As they warmed up the engines we just walked up to it and boarded it. There were several fighters on the end of the field and the Brit sabotaged them with the explosives. This served as a diversion."

"Didn't anyone try to stop you?"

"We were dressed as Nazi officers and the scientists looked like Gestapo. No one bothered us. Not even the Fallschirmjager platoon standing nearby waiting to board the same plane. But we did get some strange looks."

"Kenny, you're nuts."

"That's what the Krauts who were with us said."

"Must be true. You have more courage than brains."

"I guess I'm like my old man. You should hear his stories if you think I'm crazy."

Everyone laughed at that.

"What about the pilots?"

"I had to shoot one of them. He gave me no choice. Came at me with his sidearm. The other one cooperated after I placed my pistol at the end of his nose and asked him to fly us to Switzerland. We found out later that he had been planning to defect when the Russians showed up. We just helped him."

"What about the Brit?"

"We taxied down the runway and picked him up, then took off."

"Did everyone make it?"

"No. A flak Panzer found the range and killed one Kraut defector and the German agent. Everybody else made it. The Kraut pilot even thanked me in the Internment Camp with all his Kraut buddies who had defected before him nodding and blinking. A month ago they would have killed us, being good Nazis. Now they want to hold hands and sing songs with us. Weird. And that's pretty well it. The war in Europe ended a few days later."

"Wow, Kenny, what a story. You should be a writer. If you wrote a book about your war experiences and made a movie picture you would be rich."

"Yeah. Me and a million other guys. No big deal, kid. All in a day's work."

"You've even been around the world. Amazing."

* * * * *

That evening Rawlins and Evelyn went out for dinner. They had a long talk, something he wasn't much good at. As he tried to eat a rare steak the blood on the plate made him sick. It reminded him of Iwo Jima. He gave up on that and had a Scotch and a Camel. The little woman talked non-stop about nothing, then began to cry.

"What's wrong?"

"You're here."

"So that makes you cry?"

"Yes."

"Why? I thought you liked me."

"I love you but you scare me."

"Why?"

"You take too many chances. You're crazy. You're not bullet proof, you know."

"Yeah. I found that out."

"You're going back, aren't you?"

"Yes."

"Why?"

"I have to. The war is not over. I have to rejoin my regiment. The special mission is over. I have to go to Hawaii to Camp Tarawa. That's the Fifth Division bivouac. My regiment is there."

"You don't love me."

Rawlins was getting mad.

"How the hell do you know that?"

"I can tell. You don't talk."

"Wadda you mean? I'm talking."

"You're not saying anything. You treat me like a stranger. You don't want me. I'm not pretty like your ex-wife."

"How the hell do you know that?"

"Your sister showed me her picture. She looks like a movie star. I'm just a plain nurse. Nothing special. Not what you want, Ken. I know. You have never even tried to make love to me."

Rawlins didn't know what to say. He was mystified. What the hell was with this woman. Fine one minute, crying the next. Shit. They're all nuts."

"I was trying to treat you with respect."

"No you weren't. Don't give me that line. You just don't want me. You're still in love with your wife."

Now the Marine was mad. *The hell with this squirrely broad. I don't need this shit.*

"I guess you're right. This is a waste of time. Let's go."

Rawlins drove the nurse home in the old man's Chevy. No one said a word. There was no point. Rawlins realized she was probably right. The whole time he was seeing Evelyn he felt like he was cheating on Susan. Now he could see why prostitutes were so popular. No bull shit. No whining. No lies. Yes, I love you. No, I don't love you. I have loved you. I will love you forever.

Kiss my ass. All bull shit. Better to pay for play and the hell with the rest. This shit is worse than combat.

When they arrived at her house she said:

"I'm sorry I don't measure up. I don't want to waste any more of your time. When the war is over go back to your movie star wife. That's where you belong. Goodbye."

And she was gone.

Well, f—k this. The hell with this dame. She tells me I'm crazy. Gets jealous of an old picture. She's the nut case, not me. I can't handle this shit. Civilian life ain't for me. I gotta get back to the war. Where everything is normal. All I gotta do is kill bad guys. I don't have to talk to them. Or cuddle their asses. Or listen to college bullshit. These broads around here are all crazy. I'll find some island fuzzy wuzzy dame and stay out there. The hell with Buffalo. No more freezing weather and no more frozen women.

That night at O'Malley's Bar the Marine got very drunk and disorderly. He was in a very bad mood, made worse by booze. Two sailors walked in, home on leave. As they sat at a table nearby, they stared at Rawlins. After getting their drinks, they began to talk.

"Look at Sgt. York over there. Must have won the war all by himself. Look at those decorations. Damn Jarheads are all alike. They love it. Crazy bastards."

"What are you deck apes lookin' at? Never seen a Marine before? Or are you queer and want to play with me?"

That did it. The sailors jumped up and attacked the drunk Marine. Bad mistake. Rawlins hit one in the face with a beer bottle, dropping him. The other one Rawlins grabbed by the hair and polished the bar with his face.

When the police showed up they beat the Marine to the floor with clubs, then cuffed him and hauled him to the drunk tank. Rawlins began his usual "singing when drunk" ritual, much to the displeasure of surrounding occupants.

"In the brig again. Bread and water till I'm dead. I'm an old sea dog with half my head. When I had a woman she always said to me. Kiss my ass, Marine if you wanna stay. There was a man from Nantucket and I can't remember the rest. You can beat me, shoot me, run me to death, just don't bore me. Susan was her name. Her ass was

Just the same, until a swabbie used her for a pottie. Now her name is
Jane. Ha, ha, ha, ha.

"Shut up in there, Jarhead."

"Kiss my mothers green ass, flatfoot. You and your faggot
buddies. Are you in love or is it just sex. Ha,ha, ha."

About that time Bill Donovan from the O.S.S. walked in.
Addressing the desk Sgt. he asked, "Are you holding a Gunnery Sgt.
Rawlins?"

"Yeah. He's in the tank. Drunk as a lord. Who are you?"

"Bill Donovan, Office of Strategic Service, from D.C."

"Well, if you want him it's fifty dollars bail."

"Donovan was led back to the cell area.

"Well, I'll be a sad sailor in a cheap whore house. Wild Bill.
How the hell are you?"

"Better than you, Marine. I came to get you out. Your father
called me."

"Please, Mister. Take him. He won't stop singing. And it's
pretty bad."

"C'mon, Gunny. You're going home."

* * * * *

The next morning the senior Rawlins took the Marine to the
VA Hospital on Genesee Street. A Navy surgeon looked at the
bayonet wound.

"I have never seen a man with so many scars. I'm amazed
you can still function. Your wound is healed. The pain you're
experiencing is from two fractured ribs. That will take a while to
heal."

The doctor taped up the ribs and the two Marines headed for
home with a slight detour to O'Malleys.

"Wait a minute, Rawlins. I don't want that mad man in here.
He almost killed two sailors in here last night."

"They started it, Bill."

"Yeah, and you finished it and my business. All my regulars
that were here are afraid to come in now. So get the hell going before
I call the cops again."

Father and son left the bar. They found another one down the street. After getting their drinks they sat down at a table.

"What happened last night, Ken?"

"I got dumped again.."

"She saw Susan's picture. Decided she didn't measure up. Told me I'm still in love with my ex-wife."

"No shit. Sounds like a woman. They're funny about other dames."

"Yeah. I'm finding that out. What the hell has my ex got to do with her anyway."

"Competition."

"That doesn't make any sense. Susan is long gone."

"Doesn't matter. She knows there might be a return."

"C'mon. You gotta be kiddin.'"

"I'm telling you, they're like that. They worry about what could happen. Even your mother. One time we were in the A&P Market and we ran into this woman I went to school with. This dame lays one on me and gets all buddy, buddy. Well, shit, after that your mother had cast iron pants for six months. Swore up and down I was having an affair with this broad. And I hadn't seen her since school."

"No shit."

"No shit."

"So what do I do?"

"Nothing."

"Nothing?"

"Nothing."

"Just like that?"

"Just like that. For now. Let her think for a while. She's convinced herself she can't compete with a memory. Give her time to calm down."

"How long?"

"Six months. A year maybe. Go finish the Japs and look her up when you come home."

"The hell with it. Just another dame."

"You sure about that? She looked pretty happy when you got off that train. Good broads are hard to find. Think about it while you're gone. You owe yourself that much."

"OK, Dad. Father knows best."

"You're right, son. Now drink up. Mom is waiting with dinner.

* * * * *

After dinner Rawlins and his sister had a discussion.

"What happened, Kenny"

"I got dumped because of Susan's picture. And I don't get it."

"Sorry about that. My fault this time. I showed her your wedding picture. She looked a little sick at the time."

"I don't understand this shit. Susan's gone. Why the bullshit."

"You don't understand women. Susan is very intimidating to other women. I was even jealous of her."

"What the hell for?"

"You were too nice to her. It was disgusting. 'Yes, dear, no, dear, right away, dear, let me kiss your bum, dear. She turned you into a chump."

"Really?"

"Yes, really."

"Well, son of a bitch. Why didn't you tell me this before?"

"You wouldn't listen. You have a head like a mallet."

"Gee, thanks."

"This girl is just the opposite. Not a prima donna. Very sensitive. And she really loves you."

"How do you know?"

"When we got the letter from your C.O. about your Navy Cross and Purple Heart she cried and cried."

"Why?"

"She was afraid you would be killed like some other guy she knew who was killed early in the war."

"Yeah. I remember her talking about it."

"And another thing, you big dummy."

"What did I do now?"

"You don't even know her name. Her name is Eleanor, not Evelyn."

"Oh, shit, I forgot. That's right. I asked her when I met her if she was the President's wife. Shit. Memory is shot. Shell shock too many times."

"Do you know how insulting that is? To be called another woman's name? You big dummy. That's how I know she loves you. I would have left a man right away for that. And another thing. Don't call her Turnbolt. No woman wants to be named after a gun you dumb Jarhead. What are you going to name your kids? Pistol or bayonet?"

"What kids?"

"You know what kids."

"I do?"

"Yes, you do."

"I don't understand."

"When you get married."

"I'm not getting married again."

"Yes, you are."

"No, I'm not. Marriage is for married people like Mom and Dad. Not me."

"Well, I heard different."

"Waddaya mean, different?"

"Eleanor told me."

"Told you what?"

"You're getting married."

"What?"

"She asked me to be a bridesmaid."

"Bullshit."

"She did, Kenny. It's already done."

"Like hell it is. She's long gone. Don't' wanna know me no more."

"We'll see."

* * * * *

O.S.S. Commander Donovan called and made a lunch date with Rawlins for the next day at the Statler Hilton. After arriving early, Rawlins waited at the bar for his Commander.

"Barkeep. Gimme a Johnny Walker."

Lighting a Camel, he nursed his drink. He wondered what

mayhem the O.S.S. had planned for him this time. The war was winding down. Maybe the Commander just wanted to hear about Bavaria.

"You always drink alone, Marine?"

"Oh. Sorry, Bill. Didn't see you there. Barkeep. Another Scotch."

"Let's go to a table."

They both ordered steak, Rawlins' favorite.

"I got a cable from M16. They claim the snatch and scoot was a great success. Congratulations, Ken. The P.M., Winston himself, sends his thanks."

"Well. Imagine that."

"What I am about to reveal to you is ultra top secret. You can't tell anyone. Period."

"Aye, Sir."

"The invasion of mainland Japan is scheduled for September. Your division will land on Honshu in the south of the main island. There is a problem that must be dealt with. Chichi Jima. It's 150 miles north of Iwo Jima. And in a direct line with Japan. It is the Communication Center for the Western Pacific area. In direct contact with Tokyo and the Japanese Imperial General Staff. There is a small mountain on the island. Mt. Asahi. It holds a communication array that must be destroyed."

"Can't the flyboys do it, Sir?"

"They have been pounding it for a month. The Army from Iwo Jima and Saipan, the Navy from carriers. But signals are still emanating from there. It must be underground. Like on Iwo. The Japs are like moles. They live underground so our aircraft can't get to them. You will find this array and destroy it. When you get to Camp Tarawa, pick your team. Ex-Raiders or other combat vets only. No boots on this trip."

"Aye, Sir."

"You will travel to the Bonin Islands by submarine. It's the fastest, safest way."

Like hell, thought Rawlins.

"Secondary target. One Lieutenant General Tachibana. The cannibal."

"What, Sir?"

"You heard me right, Rawlins. According to reports from Islanders who have been feeding us Intel, he is a cannibal. He has been seen killing and eating American pilots shot down over the Island. Kill this bastard if you get the opportunity."

"Aye, Sir. With pleasure."

"As far as enemy troops go, most were transferred to Iwo Jima before the invasion. But be careful. The ones that are left are crack troops."

"OK, Sir."

"Move only at night. And set your charges so you have plenty of time to get the hell out of there."

"Aye, Sir."

"So far, Rawlins, you have done an outstanding job for O.S.S. This will probably be your last mission. The President is disbanding us at the end of the war. He feels we won't be needed. So be careful and good luck. I'll see you after the war."

And out the door he went. Rawlins had another drink and contemplated the mission.

Sounds like a tough nut to crack. Better get what's left of my Raider platoon for this job. No place for amateurs.

⊁ ✳ ✳ ✳ ✳

Rawlins left home before dawn. He hated saying goodbye. Back to the train station. As he boarded the train full of service men heading for the west coast he wondered how many were going for their last ride. How many would never see home again. Petty Officer Nickerson, the head cook, made him breakfast. He was a Sailor from Niagara Falls. Always had a joke and a cigarette. Didn't like officers or M.P.s. Just like every other guy on the train. This had been the cook's last time home until after the war. He had been home just long enough to tell his little brother Leslie what not to do.

"If you join up I'll kill you myself. The Japs won't have to."

So much for that idea.

The Sailor and Marine became friends on the long ride to San Francisco. They even got drunk together on an overnight stop in Kansas City. Nickerson knew the local hot spots. He had been making this run since forty two. Every time he volunteered for combat duty they told him he was needed here. The Sailor always managed to get the hard ass Marine to laugh. Always performing. Imitating an officer or some other object of dislike. The life of the party. When they pulled into Frisco they said their goodbyes. Maybe they would meet again if they both made it home some day.

Rawlins boarded ship in San Diego Harbor. An APD Destroyer taking Fifth Division Marines to Hawaii. Next stop, Pearl Harbor. Then Camp Tarawa. Back to the Twenty Seventh Marines and the beginning of a new mission.

* * * * *

"Well, look who's coming this way. Gunny Rawlins. The son of a bitch is back. Where you been, Gunny?" asked Sgt. Russo.

"While you tourists were here lounging by the pool I was in Europe ending the war for the Army."

"No shit, Gunny."

"No shit, Sgt. So what's the scuttlebutt, Vito?"

"We're gonna hit Japan. That's the word. Top secret, of course."

"Where?"

"We heard Honshu but who knows. All I know is this is the big one. Lotta guys ain't coming back. The Nips are saying they will fight to the death. Even the kids."

"Yeah. It figures. Crazy bastards. We got another job first. I got a top secret mission. Gotta pick my team. You just volunteered."

* * * * *

Rawlins stowed his gear. Then he went to Supply and picked up another Thompson and five magazines, new 782 gear and dungarees. Also a bottle of Johnny Walker from the Supply Sgt.'s hidden stash. Then back to the NCO tent. While getting drunk he cleaned the new Tommy gun, removing the Cosmoline from action and barrel. Then he loaded the magazines with 45 cal. 230 grain full metal patch ammo. He also cleaned his forty five pistols and sharpened his two combat knives.

0800 Hours:
Next morning there was a mission briefing. An Army S2 Major from Intelligence briefed the team.

"Your target, gentlemen, is Chichi Jima in the Bonin Islands. This small island is the Communication Center for Western Pacific radio traffic for the enemy. It has to be knocked out before the invasion of Japan. Mt. Asahi, the Island's highest point, contains the longest range transmitter in the West Pacific area. The Navy and Air Corps have been pounding hell out of it for weeks. But it is still transmitting. We believe the main transmitter is underground. Out of reach of air attack. Your mission, gentlemen, is to penetrate this underground complex and destroy the transmitter. And kill as many enemy offices and NCOs as possible. If this mission fails, the enemy will have advance notice of the invasion of the home island. And this could be disastrous for the invading troops. This may be a one way mission men. So it's volunteer only. We need experienced men only. Ex-Raiders and Para Marines. Gunnery Sgt. Rawlins will lead the mission."

Next a Navy Lieut. Commander spoke to the group.

"You men will board the submarine U.S.S. Tigerfish. When you reach the Island you will deploy in rubber boats and land on the opposite side of the Island from Susaki Airfield, between 0300 and 0400 hours, then hide the boats and proceed to your target. After reaching target wait until the following night to attack. Make your attack at 0300 hours. Then get the hell out of there. The sub will be at the pickup area watching for you. You will have until 0500 hours for pickup. After that it will be too light for the sub to surface. If you miss the pickup head for Haha- Jima just south of Chichi Jima. There's better cover there and fewer troops. Most of them were transferred to Iwo Jima just before the battle there. Three days later Tigerfish will surface off the western coast of the Island at 0400 hours. Paddle out to sea and she will find you. Any questions?"

"What about wounded, Sir?"

"This s a top priority mission. You will be given cyanide capsules. If anyone is wounded severely enough to leave for the enemy, he must be dispatched. The same goes for capture. The enemy will torture you without mercy and keep you alive as long as possible to do so, then kill you and eat you?"

"Eat us, Sir?"

"That's right, Corporal. We have received reports from local natives that these Japanese kill and eat their American prisoners. These people are cannibals. So you see, men, the cyanide is a much better option. If any man wishes to leave do so now. It won't be held against you."

No one moved.

"Very good, men. There are relief maps here for you to study. Then take the rest of the day to prepare your gear. We shove off at 0500 hours tomorrow. That is all, gentlemen. Good luck."

* * * * *

"Well, boys, it sounds like we got a tough one this time."

"Yeah, Gunny. Sounds like the Toulabong raid back in forty two."

"Same shit only bigger."

"I don't like this submarine shit, Gunny. I would rather jump in like we did on Ruwawa. Remember?"

"Yeah, Collins. I remember. But you ain't Paras and we ain't Raiders anymore. Now we're just mud eaten' Marines. I don't like those sunken tin cans either but it's the only way to get in undetected. Junior. How is the shoulder?

"OK, Gunny."

"You ready for this?"

"Yeah, I'm ready. Getting bored sittin' around this rock with all these square heads."

"Russo. You got the Tommy guns?"

"Yeah, Ken. Five including yours with five mags a piece. Three frags a piece. Four forty fives with three mags a piece. You got your own. I still have the Colt Woodsman twenty two with suppressor and two clips for it."

"Good. We'll need it. How about Composition B?"

"Enough to blow up half the world. With fuses and

detonators."

"All right. Let's go to the range and fire these weapons."

After cleaning and assembling the weapons the Range Master, an old grisly Master Sgt. who had seen better days, took over.

"All right, people. Let's get this right. I ain't tellin' you again. Ready on the left? Ready on the right? Fire."

The explosion of fire sounded like a war in itself. Thompsons on full auto ripping through thirty round magazines. Then the forty five pistols with their loud report due to the short barrel. Rawlins' ears rang for the next four hours; but the weapons checked out. All OK.

Next the team went to chow, then packed their gear. Finally, time to play cards and get drunk. There was nothing else to do.

0100 Reveille:

Then back to Pearl Harbor. The Shore Patrol led the Marines to the sub pens where they boarded the Tigerfish. This would be their home for the next week.

Leaving the harbor at 0400 for security reasons, they were on their way. The aft torpedo room would serve as the Marine barracks for the trip to the Bonin Islands. And the closest raid to the Imperial Home Island thus far was underway.

"Hey, Rawlins."

"Yeah."

"I thought this sneak and peek stuff was over."

"It is. You're imagining all this. You're really with some skirt telling her how you won the war. And she's thinking what a bull shitter this Jarhead is."

"C'mon, Gunny. I always tell the ladies the truth."

"Oh, yeah. Like the time in Frisco you told that dame you were a government assassin and were on your way to eliminate Tojo."

"I didn't lie, Gunny. I just didn't tell her when. She even believed me."

"You silly bastard. She thought you were nuts and humored you."

"Gunny, you're no fun any more. What's the matter? You

having sub paranoia again?"

"Naw, I'm all right. Like that Chief Boats told me, if we get hit we won't know it. It will be over that fast. So don't worry about it."

"Gee, Gunny, I feel so much better knowing that."

"Yeah. So did I."

"Collins. You OK ? You look green."

"I'm sick, Gunny. I don't like water. That's why I joined the Para Marines. Airplanes don't bother me. I never expected this under water shit. You guys, being Raiders, are used to this. And besides, you're all nuts anyway. So it don't matter."

Still on the surface, the hum of the diesel engines and generators charging batteries lulled Rawlins into passive reflection.

Will this be the last operation of the war or will they put us ashore on the Japanese home island with some crazy pre-invasion mission like Ruwawa.

He wondered about Susan and her older husband.

What a joke. He'll never keep her home. Maybe he doesn't care. Maybe she's just a status symbol.

Devious thoughts entered the jilted Marine's mind.

I think I'll look her up when I get back. What the hell. Why not. Might as well have a little fun. She was always good for that. Shit. Everybody else is. Maybe I can shake up the rich old bastard that has her in tow right now. He deserves it. It's about time I raised a little hell.

He didn't think much about the nurse. What was the point. She had dropped him for no good reason. Just because she doesn't have the looks his ex-wife does.

They're all crazy. Too much to deal with. Combat was much simpler. When this war was over he would have to find another one. Become a mercenary. That's all he knew how to do anyway.

* * * * *

Day after day the same monotonous routine. Surface at night and charge batteries. Run submerged during the day to avoid detection. Sleep was almost impossible. Sailors standing watch or swabbing decks and bulkheads constantly. And the drills. Three a day. The Skipper was a fanatic about trimming the boat during a dive. And the time it takes to do so. Drill, drill, and more drill.

Finally, their target was reached. Final briefing. The Captain gave them the word in the Ward Room.

"All right, men. 0300 tonight we will surface, three hundred yards off shore. You will deploy in two rubber boats. You know the rest. Tomorrow night we will surface at the same time. If for any reason we're not there remember to proceed to Haha-Jima. In three days we will surface on the western side of the island. 0300 hours, maintain a position three to five hundred yards off shore. We will find you. That is all and good luck. One more thing. There will be no radio issue because the enemy has tracking equipment. A transmission could endanger the whole mission and this boat. Carry on, men."

The Team donned their new Marine Corps special duty camouflage dungarees with soft cover. No helmets. Final weapons and gear inspection next. Then boot black on faces and hands. They were ready.

The Skipper surfaced, the Tigerfish decks awash. Battle surface. Keeping a low profile so as not to be seen from the island. The Marines looked like prehistoric lizards as they slid their little boats from the sub deck into the sea, then silently boarded them and paddled for the island. The Sailors on deck watch wondered if they would ever see the crazy Marines again. As the dark swallowed them it gave the Navy men the impression that they were entering hell. They couldn't have been more right.

* * * * *

Reaching the shore, the Team jumped into the breaking surf and dragged the black rubber boats into the tree line. Hiding them in the underbrush was the first order of business. Just as they finished, Japanese voices could be heard as a beach patrol approached. The Team hit the deck. Russo pulled out the suppressed twenty two. The others had their combat knives. Now almost on top of the Americans, the enemy troops turned and walked away. Rawlins gave the signal to stand fast. Let them go.

After a time they talked in low whispers.

"Gunny. We could have taken them with no problem. You getting soft or something?"

"Collins, you're a dummy. Now I know why you like to jump out of perfectly good airplanes. Don't you think the Nips might begin to wonder what happened to their missing brethren and send out more patrols to find them, then a company or battalion when the patrols don't return? You dummy."

"Sorry, Gunny. I didn't think."

"Yeah, Collins. And not thinking will get you dead. You should know that from Iwo. Don't worry. You'll get plenty of killing before this op is over. This island is probably crawling with the little yellow brothers. Just like Iwo was. Remember?"

"Yeah, Gunny. I'll never forget."

Soon it was light. The Team spent the day hiding in the thick woods between the beach and Mt. Asahi, their target. They could see the antenna network on the summit and the concrete building below it. Barely visible in the side of an outcropping, half way up the mountain, was a steel door with a trail leading up to it. Tunnel entrance. Just like Iwo Jima. No wonder the pilots couldn't see it from the air.

Smart little bastards, thought Rawlins.

"You guys see that tunnel entrance? That's our way in."

"How, Gunny? We don't dare blow it. The Nips will be all over us."

"Tonight when someone shows up and opens it, we're in."

Soon after night fall a Japanese officer and two guards pulled up to the entrance in a staff car. The Team was in position, waiting for this opportunity. They had to be quiet or blow the whole operation. As the Japanese Captain unlocked the steel, blast proof door, Rawlins jumped him, driving the divine warrior's head into the door from behind, then pushing his knife under the Captain's jaw bone to the hilt. Rawlins dropped the dead Jap and opened the door. Collins butt stroked a guard and caved in his head with the butt of his Tommy gun, then threw the body over the bank of the small parking area. Russo shot the remaining guard with his Colt .22 cal. suppressed Woodsman pistol, placing two 40 grain solids behind his right ear.

Sayonara, bad guy. Eyes stayed hidden in the brush, to offer cover fire if necessary. Junior stuffed the dead Japs in the car and pushed it over the embankment. It came to rest in the woods below. Hopefully, it would look like an accident of any searchers for the Captain showed up.

The Team entered the tunnel leading to the Communications Matrix. Dim yellow lights lit the concrete cavern. Like Mt. Suribachi on Iwo Jima, the mountain has been hollowed out by the Japanese. Only this time instead of a fortress it was turned into the most comprehensive communication facility in the western Pacific area. Linked to Tokyo, it was the ultimate warning system. It was even equipped with stolen British radar taken by a German raiding party on the east coast of England. German scientists had studied and duplicated the radar system and then had given it to the Japanese. It had to go. It would jeopardize the whole upcoming invasion.

* * * * *

Lights ahead. The Team entered a large room full of radio transmitters and receivers. The two operators were eliminated. Junior picked one out of his chair from behind and snapped his neck. As the dead man's partner looked on in horror, trying to pull a pistol from his belt, Russo shot him. The 22 served again.

"All right. Wire this place up. Use thirty minute acid fuses."

Junior crushed the copper fuse sleeves with pliers, allowing the acid to eat through to the primary detonator in thirty minutes. Then he stuck the primed fuses in the Composition B blocks. These bombs were placed against all of the equipment that looked important. Then the entrance door was locked closed. Next they re-entered the tunnel from the other side of the room. Another low lit cavern. As they rounded a corner they came upon a network of cables and electrical conduit. This was the main induction center for the antenna network above them. As they worked on setting charges on the junction boxes three Japs came around the corner from the other direction. One opened fire with a Nambu pistol, barely missing Russo and Collins. Eyes opened up with his Tommy gun, cutting down all three with the heavy forty five slugs.

Rawlins gave the order.

"Let's get the hell out of here. Someone had to hear that. Back the way we came in."

When the Team entered the Communication Room they booby trapped both doors. Grenades were taped to two blocks of high explosive, making two mines. String was tied to the safety pins which were straightened and almost removed. The other end was tied to the door pull on both doors as they re-entered the tunnel. When the doors were opened there would be a very nasty surprise for the visitors to this room.

A Japanese Lieutenant with a squad of men was right behind the Team. They were Security responding to the firing they had heard. The son of Nippon opened the heavy door and looked in horror at the two dead radio wizards lying in a grotesque pile of bloody death. As he drew his Nambu with pearl grips, a present from his mother, the booby trap exploded. The Nippon officer disappeared along with half of his squad in the horrendous blast. The rest were down from the mass concussion in the tight confines of the room.

"Hear that? They're right behind us. Move out."

Rawlins and company ran down the tunnel to the exit. As they emerged a Mitsubishi truck full of soldiers was coming down the road, Soldiers standing up and firing as they came. The ex-Raiders melted into the trees and brush below the road.

"Grenades. Prepare to throw."

The truck stopped above their position and began disgorging troops.

"Throw."

Five M2 frags landed around the enemy troops and wreaked havoc upon them.

"Let 'um have it," bellowed Rawlins.

Five Thompson sub machine guns on full auto fire raked the enemy as they tried to deploy. Fifteen enemy Soldiers dead in a matter of seconds and a burning truck to add to the confusion.

"Let's go."

Down the mountain they went, stumbling and falling in the darkness. When they reached their hide position they all formed a circle, weapons ready, expecting the enemy to find them and attack.

Wham! Boom! The charges detonated. No more Communications Center in this mountain. Mission accomplished. Now they had to stay alive long enough to catch their pickup from Tigerfish.

"Eyes. Break out Baby and get ready."

"Right, Gunny."

The sniper loaded his rifle with five rounds of 30 cal. M2 ball ammo.

"They're comin.' Get ready."

Another truck load full of Soldiers came down the road. Only this time stopping two hundred yards away from the scene of death and destruction.

"Find a good position, Eyes, and thin 'um out. Junior, watch his back."

"OK, Gunny."

The two seasoned vets moved to the left, staying in the trees. Eyes found an open spot with a clear field of fire, then engaged the targets, placing Baby's crosshairs on the officer in charge as he waved his sword in the air. As the Major ordered the attack, bam; 150 grains of Supersonic death entered his chest. The superior hero of Nippon looked down in surprise at the hole in his chest, then fell forward, very dead. Still clutching his family's class signature. The troops in his charge hit the dirt and tried to hide. No heroes of Nippon here. Just conscripts trying to survive the war. The heroes died long ago. A Sergeant with slow wits propped himself up for a better look and tried to urge his squad to advance on the enemy. As he talked his brain became part of the terrain as Eyes blew his head apart. No motivation here to charge into the enemies ranks. As the spectacle progressed into lunacy, Rawlins, Collins and Russo flanked the pursuers. At Rawlins' signal they threw grenades, then rushed the inexperienced enemy squad. It was quickly over. Three Tommy guns firing point blank had a devastating effect. Two Soldiers ran off into the forest. The rest were dead without firing a shot. Rawlins almost felt sorry for them.

"The dumb bastards didn't have a clue of what to do. They weren't even trained. Not like the Nips back in forty three."

"That's 'cause their good troops are all dead, Gunny. The hell with 'um. Let's go, Gunny. We gotta find that sub."

"Yeah, it's time. Let's go."

They picked up Eyes and Junior on the way down the mountain. Then back to the hidden boats.

* * * * * *

As they headed out to sea, Rawlins was uneasy. This was too easy. It went too well. He couldn't help but feel that they weren't out of danger yet.

As they made deep water off shore they spotted the sub.

"There she is, Gunny."

"Yeah. I see her."

As they paddled toward their pickup there was a tremendous light. The Tigerfish, now fifty yards away, lifted out of the water and broke in two. Wham!! A huge explosion. The Team was blown out of their boats from the concussion.

In the water now, boats and submarine gone, every man swam to Haha-Jima, including two Sailors from Tigerfish. The only survivors. To return to Chichi-Jima now would be suicide and their orders in case of foul up were to go to the other island and wait for pickup.

Reaching the sister island, the survivors stumbled ashore. They emerged on a small beach with trees near the water's edge.

"Get in the trees," commanded Rawlins.

"They may be looking for us. And stay down. All right. Who's missing?"

"Collins, Gunny. He didn't make it."

"What happened to him?"

" He just disappeared. Got blown out of the boat. Never came up. Gear must have dragged him down. Or he was knocked out by the concussion. He's gone, Gunny."

"Son of a bitch. He was a good man. Shit. What the hell happened anyway?"

"Torpedo, Gunny," answered a Sailor.

"We had intermittent sonar contact. Slow screws. No engine noise. Shadowed us for two days, then disappeared. Must have been an I-boat. (Japanese submarine) They must have figured we were picking up downed flyers like usual and decided to wait us out. Must have heard us surface when we blew main ballast, then surfaced and threw the spotlight on us to blind our gunners. Then they hit us with a fish. That's the only thing that would break the boat in half like that."

"What's your name, Sailor"

"Wilson, Gunner Mate Second Class."

"And you?"

"Andrews, Motormac. First Class. We were standing deck watch up on the tower when we got hit and blown over board. Lucky for us. I'm surprised the Nips didn't machine gun us. They didn't see us or they would have Standard procedure with those bastards."

"All right. Let's see what we got left. Weapons?"

"Four forty fives with eight clips. One .22 with one clip. Four K-bars. Two frags. That's it, Gunny."

"Rations?"

"None."

"Water?"

"Two full canteens."

"OK. We live off the Japs until we're picked up or the war ends. We gotta avoid contact. If the Japs find us we're finished. If you gotta take one, hide the body. Don't leave 'um laying around for the Japs to find. There's lots of stuff to eat in these islands. And there's Jap rations. It's getting light so stay in the trees. Don't move around. They may be looking for us. Whatever we do will be at night unless it's something in easy reach like those coconuts over there."

"Hey, Gunny, look at that."

"I figured as much. Those Japs are looking for us in that flotsam from the wreck. Good thing it happened at night. Don't move around. Those Nips are lookin' all around. If they see movement they'll be over here. And we can't afford a fight."

Chapter Eight

SURVIVAL

Through the day the Team relaxed and ate coconuts and mangoes. Patrols traveled the road near their position but never stopped. Finally darkness fell and the stranded Americans went on a scavenger hunt. They prepared by filling their canteens with water from a small stream and adding iodine tablets to the water in case of malaria bacteria.

In a remote spot in some rock outcroppings on the sea coast they made and set fish traps. Kunai grass and small tree branches were used for this. The traps were anchored to the bottom with rocks in ten feet of water. No floats were used in fear of discovery by the enemy. The traps were baited with land crabs found on the beach and killed for this purpose. The enemy would have to swim to get to these outcroppings. Not much chance of that happening.

A Jap patrol could be seen in the distance on the long thin beach, moonlight reflecting off their helmets and fixed bayonets.

"Hit the water," Rawlins ordered.

Everyone slid off the rocks and into the sea, nothing exposed above water but their heads. Hiding behind rocks, they watched as the patrol walked by.

"OK, Gunny. They're gone."

"Let's get to shore and in the woods."

In the dark the marooned warriors followed the Jap patrol at a comfortable distance.

"Where we going, Gunny?"

"Same place they are. We gotta find their stores and supplies and figure out how to raid them. In a couple days things will calm down. They'll assume we're all dead. Then we hit them and take what we can."

After traversing a major trail in the woods the patrol arrived in a clearing. Tents, tables, chairs. Radio shack, officers mess and head.

"Must be a company bivouac."

" They gotta have lotsa stuff, Gunny."

"Yeah. Alright. Eyes and Junior. Check those tents over there. Russo, you're on me. We'll recon the north end. Can you Swabbies handle a forty five?"

"Yeah, Gunny. We trained with 'um."

"Here. Take mine. Eyes. You got your hideout .380?"

"Yeah, Ken, right here."

"Give your .45 to the Gunner Mate. If we come back with Japs on our tail you guys take them when they're close. OK?"

"Got it, Gunny. We'll watch your back."

"OK, Navy. Let's move out."

As an afterthought Rawlins flipped a grenade to the Gunner Mate.

"Here, Guns, these are always fun. You might as well keep it."

"Thanks, Gunny."

The men low crawled through the camp, avoiding enemy troops as they went. The ex-Raiders checked every tent they could. Finally, Eyes lifted the edge of a large tent. Much to his delight, it was the Stores tent; or, as Junior would describe it, "lots a stuff."

"OK, big fella. This is it. Let's get back to the woods."

Ten minutes later all hands were at their infiltration point. In whispers they conferred.

"We found it, Ken."

"Where?"

"See the big tent with the Nip writing on the side?"

"Yeah."

"That's it."

" Stores?"

"Lotsa stuff, Gunny."

"OK, guys. Good work. We found something interesting too. On the north end of the complex there's a movie screen with lotsa chairs in front of it."

"We goin' to the movies, Gunny?"

"No, dummy, but the Nips will be. And that's our diversion.

Each night we'll move close to this position. When we see light in the trees from the movie we hit the place. Sound OK?"

"Sounds good, Ken."

"The most we'll have to deal with will be two to four perimeter guards. But if we time it right we may be able to get by them. Better we don't take 'um unless they see us. Now let's mosey outta here."

After reaching the rock outcropping they headed inland a safe distance.

"OK, everybody. Clean your weapons. They're full of sea water from our little dip in the pool. By morning they'll rust up. Better clean 'um now."

Soon the sun came up and the survivors went to sleep. All but Rawlins. He took first watch. As he fought the need for sleep, the Marine began to think about their situation.

Well, this is a fine mess we're in. Just like the island I was stranded on back in the Solomons when we were Raiders. Just the same as when the PT boat I was on then blew up. Same shit, different day. At least we're not in jungle like that time. These islands are a lot farther north. Just a few coconut trees someone planted. Lucky for us. I wonder how many Nips are here. Didn't see many in that camp. Maybe the majority went to Iwo like the other island. And maybe they're not looking for a fight since the war is almost over.

* * * * *

I'll love you forever. I can't live without you.

Son of a bitch. She's back. Every time I finally forget Susan she shows up to torment me. She's re-married and still she torments me. She doesn't love that old bastard. He can't even do his own screwing. He's just the support group. She's still in love with me. That's why the letters and talking to my parents. She just won't admit it. Too much pride. When I get back I think I'll wreck her marriage like her Swabbie playmate ruined mine. I'll show the rich old bastard what a Marine can do. He ain't got a chance. Geriatric son of a bitch.

"Gunny I'm hungry!!"

"Shit, Junior. You scared the hell out of me."

"I'm starving, Gunny."

"We all are. Eat one of those coconuts."

"I can't. They make me go all the time."

"Well, then, chew on your boots. What the hell you want from me?"

"I'm goin' to that camp and get some food."

"You can't, Junior. The Japs will see you for sure and we're all dead. Let's go get some fish. How's that?"

"OK."

"Russo."

"Take over. Me and the kid are goin' for fish."

"OK, Ken."

The two jungle experts slipped through the forest to the beach. Seeing nothing in the area, they sprinted for the water one at a time. Swimming to the rocks, they hovered above the traps. Rawlins dove down and retrieved a trap. Then another. Small amberjacks. The traps were full of them. The two fishermen emptied the traps, then took a quick look around. Nothing. They swam for the beach and returned to the hideout.

"Ken. You got fish."

"But of course, my good man. Did you expect anything less? You guys know how to clean fish?"

"Yeah, Gunny. Give 'um to me. My old man was big with this shit. He taught me."

"OK. I'll start a smokeless fire. You other guys find some small, dry wood."

The survival expert dug a hole in the soft earth with his Ka-Bar, then lined the bottom with small beach rock. Next, dry leaves were placed on the rock; then small dry sticks. Then his ever present flint and striker were used to ignite the leaves. Then the sticks caught and bigger sticks were placed on these. As they burned down and made hot coals, Rawlins made a rack using green tree limbs and vines. Then he suspended this over the fire, propped on rocks. The gutted fish were placed on the rack and allowed to cook. Ten minutes a side.

"Gunny. That smells good. Now I'm really hungry."

"I just hope the local Nippon population doesn't smell them."

When the fish were cooked everyone ate ravenously.

"Damn, Gunny, that was good. You should open a restaurant."

"Yeah, Eyes. The new hot spot on Jap Island. We better move outta here in case some Jap smelled this. It's getting dark. Let's go. Russo. Take the rear. I'll take point."

Heading west, they found another road and followed it. They were amazed to find a plantation house, now serving as a Geisha house. It was full of semi-naked Japanese women and Japanese Imperial officers.

"Gunny. Look at that. They got naked broads in there. We gotta go get some."

"Cover your eyes, dummy. You wanna lose your head over a piece of tail. Wise up. We're in bad ass land. Remember? And these Japs eat people."

"Yeah, Gunny. I forgot for a minute."

"Forget again and some Nip may eat your sorry ass. You guys see those cellar windows? We gotta get a closer look. There may be Stores down there. You guys stay here. I'll check it out."

Rawlins inched through the dark trees flanking the lawn of the huge house. When clouds covered the moon, he dashed to the cellar window and lay on the ground. Looking in the semi-lit room, boxes with Japanese writing were evident. Also shelves with canned goods and bottles of beer and sake. The Marine pulled his Ka-Bar and jimmied open the window. Just as he was about to enter a Jap Soldier, bottle of sake in hand, rounded the corner of the house and tripped over Rawlins, falling next to him. Without hesitation the Marine grabbed the enemies face and covered his mouth and nose, then drove his Ka-Bar under the Jap's sternum and twisted it. Blood covered his hand as it erupted from the Jap's mouth. The son of Nippon's eyes went wide and he grunted in shock. Then nothing. Eyes open wide, seeing nothing.

Shit, thought Rawlins. *This ain't good. Sooner or later this deadbeats gonna turn up AWOL. Then the shit will hit the fan.*

He dragged the body into the woods and returned to the cellar. Entering through the window he grabbed all the canned goods he could, stuffing everything into a laundry bag he found. Then exited, closing the window. Back to his comrades who marveled at his find.

"Listen, you guys. I had to kill a Nip. He fell on me. No choice. Let's grab his body and beat it."

Junior picked up the small body like a rag doll and they were gone back in the forest. Finding a swamp, they sank the body in the muddy water, weighing it down with rocks, then moved around the stinking abyss and found some high ground. Here they would spend the day, thankful to have food.

"Damn, Gunny. This is good shit. These Nips eat better than we do. Lobster, crab, salmon. Rice cakes with fish and veggies. What a feast."

"Go easy, guys. It may have to last a long time. Who knows how long we'll be here."

* * * * *

From their perch the Marines could see enemy patrols. They were searching the beach areas.

"Must be they're on to us, Gunny. The missing Jap must have done it."

"Yeah. They know something is up. Probably figure survivors from the sub are lurking around down there."

The Team lay in the trees, watching the enemy in the distance, all day. That night they formed a perimeter defense and stayed where they were until the heat was off. They couldn't afford a fight with a platoon or more of Japs.

"Hey, Gunny."

"Yeah, Vito."

"What ever happened with that little nurse that was polishing your ass at Bougainville? Ever meet up with her?"

"Yeah. I looked her up when I was home."

"How did it go?"

"Not so good."

"Why not?"

"She saw a picture of my ex."

"Yeah. That would do it."

"Whata ya mean by that?"

"Your ex old lady is one of the best lookin' dames in captivity. Regular broads hate women like that."

"Why?"

"They think you're goin' back with her."

"I told her I wasn't."

"Don't matter. They don't believe guys. They only believe what other broads say. How did she see the picture?"

"My sister showed it to her."

"That's bad."

"Why?"

"Family broads are the worst traitors."

"Why?"

"They're always jealous of new dames on deck."

"Why the hell is that?"

"They don't know. And neither do guys. Brothers, fathers, cousins. They all get shit revealed about themselves between broads."

"But I'm divorced and Susan is re-married."

"Don't matter."

"Why not?"

"Still a return threat. Especially good looking ones. Boy, Gunny, you don't know shit about broads. You better stay in the Corps and become a flat top lifer. Women are too complicated for you."

"So what do I do about the nurse?"

"Let your sister handle it."

"You just said she's a traitor."

"Not any more. Now she's an asset."

"How?"

"'Cause now she'll play matchmaker."

"Why?"

"She feels guilty about the picture."

"What if I'm not interested?"

"Don't matter. They have decided you're getting married."

"But she don't like me any more."

"How do you know?"

"She told me to beat it."

"Means nothing. She was just punishing you for having a good looking ex."

"Why?"

"'Cause she's a woman, dummy."

"Russo. You're as nuts as they are."

"Maybe, but I know women."

"Hey, Gunny, look at that glow in the sky."

"Yeah, Junior, I see it."

"What is it?"

"Gotta be the movie theater in the camp. Boy, they don't worry about security, do they?"

"Maybe the war is over."

"Naw, couldn't be. The invasion ain't for a while yet."

"Maybe they just gave up."

"Not these boys. They don't believe in giving up."

"What if they're ordered to?"

"Then maybe it's possible."

The movie lit up the sky at the camp for two hours.

"That's the perfect diversion for us to raid the camp Stores."

"Right, Gunny. Look at the stars, Ken. I never have seen so many. There's millions of 'um."

"This is the first time on a Jap island that I'm not worried about getting knifed in the middle of the night. These Japs don't seem to give a shit about the war."

"They know they're gonna lose, that's why. As far as they're concerned, it's already over. The movie proves it. Normally they would never do that. They know there's no ships or aircraft in the area."

The night passed slowly. Staying awake while on watch was difficult. So peaceful. No mortars or artillery. No infiltrators. Just the buzzing of insects and the chirping of frogs.

All the men were thinking of the homes they had left so long ago. A thousand years. They were just kids. Now they were tired old men. They had seen too much war. Lost too many friends. Too many battles fought. Nothing would ever be the same. If they made it home some day how would they cope with civilian life after this.

"Hey, Ken. What's it like being home?"

"I don't know."

"Whaddaya mean you don't know? You were just there."

"Ain't the same. Everybody's different. Or maybe I'm different. It was hard to talk to them."

"Why?"

"'Cause of the questions. They wanna know everything. Details. Like seeing men killed in combat. What's it like to kill a man with a bayonet. Or did it make you sick when your best friend died in your arms with his guts blown out. They're all so damned curious. I just wanted to stay drunk. Not talk at all. Just leave me the hell alone. I don't belong there any more. I guess my ex was right. I belong in a jungle. I'm no longer civilized. Just a killer. I guess she was right. How about you, Eyes?"

"Same shit. They asked me about my kills. So I told them. Then they looked at me like I was crazy. Then they got real quiet. Wouldn't even look at me no more. So I left and never looked back. F**k it. I think we should become mercenaries when this shit is over. Killing is all we're good at. And we don't fit in society any more."

"Gunny. I hear leaves shuffling. Somebody's walking this way."

"Yeah, I hear 'um. Sounds like three or four. We gotta take 'um quiet. Can't give our position away."

As the footfalls grew louder and closer the Team prepared for close combat, drawing their knives and getting into position next to the trail. Junior was closest to the noise. He would be the first to engage the enemy.

Dark, indistinct forms came into view. They seemed to be grunting or talking some strange code words. The big Marine thought, *I'll take the last one to crawl by. The others can have the lead Nips.* As the low crawling forms passed by Junior jumped on the last infiltrator and sank his Ka-Bar fighting knife in its back to the hilt. A great squeal escaped its furry lips. Its snout, with twin tusks, spun around, searching for its killer. The huge Marine grabbed the menacing snout with a great bear paw of a hand and stabbed the boar in the neck. The beast finally succumbed to its wounds. Its fellow infiltrators were long gone.

"Junior. What the hell is that" Some new Jap secret weapon?

The Order of the Wild Hog? Ha, ha, ha, ha, ha."

"It ain't funny, Gunny. It tried to bite me."

"Gee, imagine that. You sink a Ka-Bar in his back and he gets pissed off. Ha, ha, ha."

Everybody laughed at the embarrassed Junior.

"Well, kid, you did good. Now we got something to eat."

The next morning Rawlins gutted and skinned the wild boar, then made a fire pit. Just like before only bigger. Rocks were laid in the bottom. Then a fire was started on them. A rack was constructed and the pig suspended above the coals. A mixture of Japanese beer and coconut milk was used for basting. A forty five round was taken apart and the powder sprinkled on the meat for seasoning. Just like the mountain men did one hundred years before. Some canned rice was opened when the meat was ready to consume along with some canned veggies. All the empty cans were filled with equal parts of the mixture and some convincing rations were created. Everyone ate their fill and drank some Japanese beer to go with it.

"Wow, Gunny. You can really cook. That was good."

"Glad you liked it."

Even the Sailors spoke up.

"We thought all Marines could do was kill people and march. That was good, Rawlins."

The remaining meat was wrapped in palm leaves and placed under the bank, suspended just above the water, in a stream they found. It would stay cool and hidden there. The remainder of the canned food was buried nearby. Hidden from the enemy.

"Gunny. What do we eat now?"

"Fish. And pretty soon we raid the camp."

The Team stayed near the beach through the day, watching the coast road. More patrols. They were still looking for them.

"Gunny. Look what I got."

"Where the hell did you find that, Junior?"

"Me and Eyes were watching the beach and this thing crawled out of the water. So I grabbed it."

"Shit. It must weigh fifty pounds. Looks like dinner tonight."

Rawlins killed the great sea tortoise and Junior carried it to their hide in the wooded hills. Their fire pit was revived. The turtle

was placed on the hot coals and buried with dirt. They left the area
but would return after dark and eat the great find.

Traveling deeper into the woods, the Team found a spot
where a shot down F4U Navy Corsair had crashed. They buried the
dead pilot, taking his ID tags. Then they looked over the wreckage to
see if anything had survived that was usable.

"Gunny. The radio looks OK but the batteries are smashed."

"Grab it. We can steal a battery."

Everything else was destroyed. The pilot's 38 cal. Revolver
and survival knife were also taken. It was growing dark as they
returned to their camp, disregarding their own rule of no traveling in
daylight. The Team was becoming lax, apathetic, tired. Rawlins saw
the signs. The men were reaching a dangerous place. Letting their
guard down could be fatal.

* * * * *

The turtle was ready. It was dug up and devoured. Enough for
everybody.

"Gee, I never ate turtle before. It's kinda like the dark meat
on a turkey. I never saw a turkey like this on Thanksgiving."

After the meal Rawlins cleaned out the shell and would use it
to cook in. If it wasn't for the men in his charge he could stay here for
the rest of his life. War or not. It was his element. This is where he
belonged and he knew it. A wild, untamed place. No rules. No right
or wrong. Just survival of the fittest.

* * * * *

"Gunny. You hear that? Sounds like heavy bombers. Lots of
them. B29 strike from Tinian or Saipan."

Chichi Jima was the target. Tons of bombs rained down.
Sheets of flame erupted from the airfield and radio towers. The
surrounding sea boiled from the heat of detonations in the water.

"Well, boys, that's it. We're on our own. They think we're
dead. We're here for the duration for sure now. Unless we can
convince someone on the radio otherwise. It also means the invasion

is on.

* * * * *

The telegram arrived at the Rawlins' home in Buffalo on August 30, 1945.
We regret to inform you that Gunnery Sgt. Rawlins, U.S.M.C,. is missing in action and presumed dead. The submarine, Tigerfish, which transported his Team on a special mission behind enemy lines is overdue, presumed lost with all hands.

* * * * *

His father read the news in stunned silence. His mother and sister wept uncontrollably. As she sobbed, his mother kept repeating:
"I knew he would die in this war. I just knew it would happen."
The next day Wild Bill Donovan, O.S.S. Commander, stopped by the house. He was home on leave from Washington. The house was quiet as a tomb when he entered. He tried to console the shattered family.
"Nothing has been confirmed. Even if the sub went down he may not have been on it. He has had advanced survival training through the O.S.S. And he was marooned once before and made it out. The war is almost over. I think he will turn up on an island in the Bonins when they are occupied. That's where the mission was. And he's tough. Hard to kill. As resilient as he is deadly. That's why the O.S.S. recruited him. I think he's alive and well. I can't say the same for the sub crew. They probably were discovered during drop off or pickup and sunk. It's happened before. That's how the Argonaut went down. He probably made it to shore and is hiding until the war ends."
The family didn't believe a word he said but thanked him anyway for coming. Rawlins sister called Eleanor, the little nurse. They had decided to keep in touch The effect was immediate. Hysteria. Eleanor said the same thing as the Marine's mother.
"I knew he would die if he went back. And I was right. How am I supposed to live with his memory and nothing else. He didn't

even leave me with a baby like I had hoped he would. He said he was trying to treat me with respect. Now I have nothing but a dead man's respect. I might as well be dead too. He made me love him and now he is gone forever."

* * * * *

"Hey, Junior."

"Yeah, Russo."

"You ever see that dame from New Zealand again?"

"Yeah. After I got wounded on Iwo. The hospital ship went to Australia and I got a three day pass after a month. An Aussie Captain who got hit on New Guinea took a liking to me. He knew a Dakota pilot who gave me a lift to Wellington."

"So what happened?"

"Remember her dead old man?"

"The Anzac that got it in Italy?"

"Yeah. Well, it turned out he ain't so dead."

"No shit."

"No shit."

"So what happened?"

"I walk in the crumpet joint where she worked and here she is sitting with the dead guy. But he ain't dead no more."

"OK."

"She sees me and almost passes out, then asks me why I'm there. So I tell her I got wounded on Iwo and they gave me a pass to get married. Then the Limey look alike pipes up like this:"

"Is this the bloody Yank you told me about?"

"Yes, dear, that's him. Just wouldn't leave a girl alone. And he's back again."

"Well, I'll see about this. You bloody great cur, step outside. I'm going to give you the thrashing you deserve. Try to take a man's wife from him."

"So what happened? Tell us."

"We get outside and he slaps me in the face."

"No shit. Is he still alive?"

"Yeah. I didn't break him or nothing. The Shore Patrol was down the street and besides my shoulder wasn't healed yet."

"So what did you do, Junior?"

"I picked him up by his blouse with my good hand and shook him 'cause he made me mad. He shouldn't a made me mad."

"Then what?"

"Then I smashed his head on a tree real easy like."

Now the Navy men were looking at the big Marine like he was crazy.

"Then what?"

"I threw him through the front window and left."

His fellow Marines were not surprised. Junior had a temper. You shouldn't make him mad.

The Sailors were thinking, *this guy is more dangerous than the Japs. Nuts too. Typical Marine.*

"Hey, Gunny. When we gonna raid the camp? I'm hungry again."

"Tomorrow night if they have a movie. Here, eat some of this meat I saved for you. And a can of rice. I don't want you getting pissed off at us 'cause you're hungry."

The next day was quiet. No activity at all. No patrols, no fly overs. The Team rested up for the raid that night.

* * * * *

As darkness fell the Team moved down the road, closing on the camp. As they drew near they dispersed in the woods and formed a defensive perimeter. After about an hour the movie began.

"It must be Saturday night. There it is. Let's move."

As the Team reached the edge of the Japanese bivouac they checked the outdoor theater. A Japanese cowboy movie. Their favorite. Only this time the Indians were American or British and carried sticks and rocks. The cowboys were Samurai warriors with ten gallon hats, on horseback and armed with swords, lances, and bows. The ridiculous spectacle made the American castaways laugh. But the movie had the desired effect. The theater was packed. Every seat and ground space was occupied by a loyal son of Nippon.

"Alright. This is it. Le:'s go."

The six men, weapons ready, converged on the supply tent. Two guards were in front of the entrance. Two more walked the perimeter of the camp. When the roving guards walked by Rawlins and his Marines cut their way into the rear of the tent. The Sailors stayed behind and covered the rear so the thieves wouldn't be cut off from escape.

Rawlins and Russo each grabbed a guard from behind and knifed them, then dragged the bodies into the tent.

Eyes and Junior filled canvas ammo bags with rations. When they had all they could carry they left the tent taking the dead guards with them.

Russo noticed a Mitsubishi truck parked nearby.

"Ken. Look at that truck. There's our battery."

The others headed for the stream stash site. Russo and Rawlins stayed behind to get the battery.

The roving guards walked by, not even noticing or caring that the tent guards were missing.

"OK, let's go."

The two Marines had the battery and were on their way in less than two minutes. On the movie screen the Samurai slaughtered all the bad American Indians. The onlookers cheered and clapped.

Silly bastards, thought Rawlins. *They actually believe that bull shit.*

Reaching the hide by the creek, the survivors buried most of their find. The rest they took with them to their high ground hide. They also buried the guards they had killed.

"OK, boys. What do we have?"

"Lots of canned stuff, Gunny. Like from the house. Some beer and sake. Grenades and two Nambu pistols. And a battery."

The next day the Team watched from their mountain hide as patrols combed the woods around the camp. Also the beaches and road.

"Gee. Pretty active today. We must have pissed them off. No more movies this month. You guys get that radio working?"

"Yeah, Gunny. But we can't transmit. Only receive."

"Shit. It figures, the way our luck has been. Keep listening.

Maybe we'll hear something useful."

"So far all we can get is Tokyo Rose telling us how the Tigerfish was sunk with all hands by the Imperial submarine, Ichigowa, and fifty B29 bombers were shot down over Hiroshima."

"What a bunch of shit. Lyin' bitch. I hope General LaMay's boys burn their cities down like they did in Germany. They deserve it."

"Why, Gunny. Do I detect a hint of hostility and resentment in your tone of remorseful admonition?"

"Eyes, kiss my green ass before I set you on fire."

"Now, now, Gunny, we musn't get testy with our fellow castaways."

The two Sailors looked at each other and agreed. *They're all nuts.*

"Gunny. My bum hurts."

"What?"

"My bum, it's sore."

"What the hell do you want me to do about it. We're all out of baby oil, Junior."

"It really hurts, Gunny."

"Alright, dammit. Let's go to the stream. You can take a bath and use some of that Jap soap on it. Maybe that will help. Then put coconut milk on it. As a matter of fact we're all stinking. Time for a bath."

At the stream two men stripped and washed at a time. The rest stood watch. Sure enough, when Rawlins and Eyes were in the water, disaster struck. A Jap patrol walked up to the stream. Both men instinctively dove under water and swam downstream, bullets landing all around them. Then muffled explosions on shore. When the two Marines surfaced, dead Japanese lay on the opposite shore, killed with the Gunner Mate's grenade and the stolen Japanese mini bombs. Russo used a captured Nambu pistol to finish off the wounded.

"Boy, Gunny, it's a good thing we had those Nip grenades. They would have had us for sure otherwise."

"Let's get the hell out a here."

They scampered back to the hills, before the whole bivouac turned out to find them.

The Team ate pig meat taken from the stream hide as they watched the Japanese from their elevated position. Patrols were all over the island. Finally, a platoon began the ascent up the mountain where the Team was hidden.

"Shit, Gunny, we better get out a here. We can't handle a platoon of these heroes."

"Yeah. Let's head for the rocks in the water."

Slipping through the trees, the antagonists evaded enemy patrols and made it to the water's edge.

"You guys hide the radio?"

"Yeah, Gunny. It's under some tree roots along with the Jap rations."

"OK. They don't look too interested in finding us anyway. Alright. Two men at a time, head for the rocks, you swabs first."

The Sailors ran across the narrow beach and into the sea, then swam the short distance to the rocks. Then Eyes and Junior, followed by Rawlins and Russo. As they hid in the rocks, darkness fell. They could see enemy Soldiers marching by in the moonlight. By midnight all was quiet. No more patrols. The Japanese had given up for the night.

"OK, guys, two at a time, head for the mountain. Navy first. When you clear the beach wait in the trees for us. Now go."

The stranded Submariners swam for shore and crossed the beach. Then the Marines did the same.

"Alright. Ten yard intervals. Russo, you got point. Move out and stay quiet."

After half a mile, Russo returned to the main body in a hurry.

"Ambush fifty yards ahead, Ken. Looks like four Nips and a Nambu Woodpecker light machine gun."

"Let's have a look. You guys stay here."

The two seasoned ex-Raiders flanked the ambush and approached from the rear, Russo with his silenced .22 and Rawlins with his Ka-Bar. As they low crawled up to the position the Marines could hear the ambushers talking.

Hard to believe, he thought. *These people must not have been trained. Just put here as a last resort. All their good troops are gone, used up in battles long ago.*

Silently, deadly, the two combat experts crawled up to the Japanese, close enough to smell them. Fish and sake.

They all smell like that, thought Russo as he shot the gunner and the loader. The 22 rounds entered their heads from the rear. They never knew it.

Rawlins grabbed No. three by the mouth and nose from behind, then shoved his Ka-Bar in the enemies back to the hilt. The Soldier bucked and kicked, then expired, making no noise. No. 4 spun around, trying to draw a pistol when Russo grabbed him from behind. With his free hand, the Marine administered a wicked knife edge chop to the Jap's throat, then a double knuckle punch behind the son of Nippon's ear. Between the two deadly strikes the would be ambusher moved no more.

"Thanks, Vito. That Nip had the drop on me."

"No problem, Gunny. We gonna bury them?"

"No time. No point anyway. They know we're here."

Rawlins returned to the waiting men.

"All clear. Move out."

Russo joined them and they made it back up the mountain in the dark, spending an uneasy night in the large trees.

The next day they watched for patrols but there were none.

"Gunny. I don't get it. They ain't lookin' for us. Why?"

"I dunno. Something ain't right. After we took out their ambush they should be all over this rock. It doesn't make sense. Eyes. Fire up the radio."

"OK, Gunny. No Tokyo Rose today. Only static."

" Must be atmospherics, Gunny" offered the Motormac.

"Or the battery is getting low. Something ain't right. I'm telling you guys. No patrols, no Nip broad. What the hell gives?"

The rest of the day and that night there was no activity. Nothing. The next morning the Team watched as a Japanese officer lowered the flag in the Camp assembly area and a bugler sounded taps.

"Gunny. Something weird is happening. It's like they're leaving or something. They lowered their colors."

"What! You're shitting me."

"Look through these field glasses."

"I'll be a son of a bitch. It's like they're surrendering. Turn on the radio."

TO ALL ALLIED FORCES IN THE PACIFIC AREA. THE EMPIRE OF JAPAN HAS UNCONDITIONALLY SURRENDERED. THE WAR IS OVER. CEASE ALL HOSTILITIES. THE WAR IS OVER.

The message repeated all day.

"What do you think, Ken? Could be a Jap trick to lure us in and then kill us. I don't believe it. Not until I see Americans land here."

And three days later, they did. A contingent of Marines landed and took the surrender from General Tachibana, Commander of the Bonin Islands garrison, and Major Matoba, Commander of Haha-Jima.

The Team walked down to the Camp and presented itself to the Marine Captain in charge of the landing party.

"Gunnery Sgt. Rawlins reporting, Sir, with survivors of the Chichi Jima mission and the submarine Tigerfish, Sir."

"My God, man, we thought you were all dead."

"No, Sir, most of us, Captain, but not all. We have been hiding out here since the sub was sunk."

"Well, men, the war is over. We dropped a new super bomb on Japan and they gave up."

"Thank God for that, Sir."

"Amen., Gunny."

Chapter Nine

HOME ALIVE IN FORTY FIVE

On the ship headed for Pearl Harbor the men contemplated peace and civilian life.

"So, Ken. What are you gonna do now?"

"I think I'll lock up my ex old lady just for the hell of it. Got plenty of time and money. Might as well waste some. We got thirty days survival leave coming. Might as well have a little fun."

"What about you, Vito?"

"Back to Chicago, the old haunts, see who made it back, check on some broads I knew, and maybe open a gin mill."

"Junior?"

"Back to the farm, I guess. It's all I know. Help out the old folks."

"Eyes?"

"Stay in and try to get my instructor position back. It was a good deal and it's all I know. Maybe get a pension out of it. I can't believe it's over. It's like a dream. Never thought I would make it. So many guys didn't."

"How the hell are we gonna fit in, Ken? We're killers. We been out here so long. We don't belong in society anymore."

"Yeah. Us and a million other guys. We'll adjust. Just like we got used to the war, now we gotta get used to the peace. Just remember, if somebody pisses you off you can't break his neck or cave in his head. They don't like that in society. Just look at the dummy and remember you could kill him so fast with your bare hands he wouldn't know he was dead. That should help some. But don't do it. A life in prison ain't worth it for some asshole. Let somebody else do it.

Back at Pearl the Team tied on a good one at Samson's Post, the watering hole of the Raiders back in the beginning of the war.

Now it was quiet. No brawls or inter-service rivalry. Just a few Sailors and Marines happy to be alive.

"Boy, Ken, remember this joint. All the fights."

"Yeah. Joker always starting something with the Navy, or anybody else. He was a pain in the ass, but a good Marine. He will be missed."

"Yeah, Ken. Him and a lot of good Marines. Hell of a price, this victory."

"I wonder how Ramirez is doing."

"I dunno. He got hit pretty bad on Iwo. Hope he's OK. He was a good Joe. I remember when he killed that Nip on Toulabong with a knife, then found out he had a wife and kid when he checked his pockets. Damn, he got sick."

"Boy, that sure changed. By Iwo he was a stone killer."

"Yeah, Eyes. Just like us. We all changed. In the beginning we all struggled with killin' the enemy. I remember on the Canal the first time time I killed a man with Baby. He was sitting behind a Woodpecker in an ambush position five hundred yards away. I was on a ridge I had crawled up on. I put the cross hairs on his forehead. At the shot I saw a little black hole appear between his eyes and the back of his head blew out. He just sat there dead like nothing happened, staring ahead with dead eyes. Gave me the creeps. I got cold all over, then I got sick. Hell of a thing. After a while, it all changed. They just became targets. Not even human. Just do your job and move on. Don't think. Hard to believe it's over. Can't get used to the idea. And what comes next. Factory worker, hit man, farmer, truck driver, who the hell knows. It ain't gonna be the same ever again. That's for sure."

* * * * * *

When the men reached San Francisco they said their goodbyes and promised to keep in touch. Rawlins boarded the train for New Orleans and his ex-wife, Susan. He would give it one last try. He owed himself that much.

The train was full of service men going home. They played cards and shot craps to kill the time. All were very happy and excited to be alive and going home.

Rawlins sat in detached silence, thinking: *Where was home? Buffalo? the Corps? He didn't know any more. The war had taken him around the world. He had seen and done some terrible things. How could he be a civilian now. The boredom alone would be too much. A life of memories, good and bad would be his future. As the train moved ponderously across the plains the Marine remembered the flaming death of Iwo Jima, the stinking jungle rot of Guadalcanal and Bougainville and the diseases of the tropics. Everyone had the jungle rot if they had been there. Sores that never really healed, oppressive heat and rain, like a blanket of depression. Now it was over. Four long years in the earth bound hell called the Pacific Theatre. All he knew was war. How would he function now. Would he go to college with the children? Would he take a factory job and work himself to death? He didn't know. All that was certain was that he had survived and Susan was on his mind.*

Pulling into the New Orleans station was strange for the returning Marine. It was home but wasn't. He had lived here with his wife Susan during the time he was assigned to the Higgins Boat Works as an advisor. Susan's Navy Captain father was in charge of designing a new landing barge for the Navy and Marine Corps. Rawlins was on his Team. They soon became friends and Rawlins met Susan at a party. Soon after that he began seeing the tall, blonde woman. Soon after that he married her and soon after that the war separated them. Then a young, debonair Navy fighter pilot took the Marine warrior's place. Said pilot relieved Rawlins of his wife and finally his rank, after the jilted Marine caved in the Lieutenant's face. A year later lover boy resides at the bottom of Truk Lagoon, rotting away with his Navy Corsair fighter. The Japanese Imperial Navy made short work of Mr. Playboy. Fine with Rawlins. He had decided to kill the bastard anyway if he survived the war. Better the Japs did it for him.

* * * * *

Next stop. The Waldorf Astoria and a room, then the bar. Rawlins ordered a sandwich and a Johnny Walker, then sat at his table, getting drunk, watching civilian life and thinking: *How strange it is. How could I ever adjust. People laughing and talking, the juke box blaring, no officers staring at you demanding respect. No boots to train and cajole, no regimentation, no revelry, no inspections, no reports. Just people enjoying life. He was used to people dying and killing around him, artillery and mortar rounds crashing down, not a juke box. Rifle and machine gun fire, not bourbon and scotch.*

He noticed a Navy Chief Petty Officer watching him. He had many battle ribbons on his blouse, like his own. Then he recognized the Sailor. Chief Sanderson. He was on the Higgins Boat Advisory Board also. Rawlins knew him well. Getting out of his chair, he staggered to the Sailor's table.

"You old sea dog. You made it."

"Rawlins. You son of a bitch. I thought you were dead."

"Not yet, Chief."

"Your wife told me you went down with the Tigerfish."

"Almost. Made it to an island and stayed there till the end of the war."

"I guess somebody told her otherwise."

"No shit."

"No shit."

"I didn't know I was missing."

"You are presumed dead."

"Maybe I should try to collect my insurance. Sure, what the hell. Better than some broad getting it. By the way, Chief, where did you see Susan?"

"The Jitter Bug Club on Bourbon Street. She hangs out there."

"I'm surprised her old man lets her."

"He's out of the picture. They're separated."

"No shit?"

"No shit."

"I think I'll check the place out."

"Don't do it, Ken. She's got some young joby with money in the van."

"Yeah. So?"

"So another trip to brig, bread and water you don't need. This time they will bust you to private and give you hard labor."

"I ain't gonna slap down some deadbeat punk she's takin' for a ride."

"Bull shit. One wrong word and he's history. I know your Gyrene ass. Just a word from the wise, Ken. It ain't worth it. Better to walk away. There's plenty of loose broads around. You won't have any trouble getting' in trouble. Now sit down and let me buy you a drink so you can tell me all about it."

The Sailor from New Orleans and the Marine from Buffalo got very drunk together, trading war stories back and forth, reminiscing about old mates that didn't return and far off places they had both seen. Susan's father, the Captain, was discussed. He was missed by all who knew him. A regular guy for an officer and a good father-in-law to Rawlins, even after the divorce. Some men connect no matter what.

They talked about the young Ensign that died on the Arizona with eleven hundred and fifty of his mates the day the Japanese started the war with America. The old Captain never fully recovered and neither did Susan. The two children were close in the years before the war.

* * * * *

The next day Rawlins had his uniforms cleaned and pressed. The house barber gave him a high and tight hair cut and a straight razor shave.

"Where you been, Marine?"

"You name it, Mac, I've been there."

"By the look of those ribbons you ain't lying. My son is in England waiting for transport home. He was with Patton from North Africa all the way to Germany."

"How did he make out?"

"Never got a scratch and he was up front the whole time. Every time a friend of his got it he would write home wondering when it would be his time. He didn't expect to survive when so many died. Now he feels guilty to be alive when so many men aren't. Strange, ah Gunny?"

"Not at all. I feel the same way. You wonder why you're alive after seeing so many die. So many lost friends. What a waste."

* * * * *

Rawlins shined his leather and brass and dressed in service dress greens, sub tropical. The red stripes and hash marks were a stark contrast to the dark green jacket. He brushed the fore and aft cap and polished the Marine Corps globe and anchor hat device. He was ready for action, only this time the action was of a different kind. He was going to seduce his wife for the first time in years. He owed it to himself, he figured. To hell with the old man who was hulling ship for her. His mistake.

The Jitter Bug Club was alive with people, mostly servicemen and young women looking for servicemen. A table with three young Marines sat near the stage and dance floor. Rawlins noticed them staring at him. Finally, one got up and approached him.

"You looking for a seat, Gunny? C'mon over here. We got room."

"Shove off, Junior. I'm on a mission."

"But, Gunny."

"Beat it. I ain't in the mood to tell you children about the war you missed."

"OK, Gunny, but if you change your mind."

"Yeah, I know. Now beat it, Private."

The young boot was not about to question this older combat Marine. He wasn't ready for that.

Rawlins found a table in a dark corner and ordered a drink, then lit a Camel. After watching the people on the dance floor and listening to the band play for a while he was getting bored. He began to wonder if the Sailor had been on the level. It was Saturday night. Susan's favorite night to play. Just as he was getting up to leave, Susan cleared the door. Black, low cut evening gown, white pearls, high heels, long legs and long blonde hair. She looked the same as Rawlins remembered. As she walked to the bar heads turned male and female alike. The queen had arrived.

Since she was sitting with her back to him, the Marine planned a rear attack. Walking up on her blind side he leaned on the bar next to her.

"Buy you a drink, lady?"

Recognizing her dead husband's voice, Susan turned to him with a shocked look on her face.

"Ken. My God, you're alive."

Throwing herself on him, she kissed him long and hard.

"They told me you were dead. They said you died in a submarine."

"Who told you that?"

"Your parents. I called them to find out when you would be home. I wanted to see you. I didn't know they had been notified. No one told me. What happened to you?"

"We got dropped on an island to destroy a radio complex."

"My God. No wonder you're so thin. I don't remember you being this thin."

"Between short rations and malaria most of us are like this. Cost of war, I guess. Where's Grandpa?"

"We're separated."

"What happened? He ask you to make dinner or do the dishes?"

"That's not fair, Ken."

"Sorry."

"I see you're still a smart ass."

"Isn't that why you love me?"

Susan got red in the face at this remark but didn't answer.

"He's an old fuddy duddy."

"Meaning?"

"He never wanted to do anything so I started going out and then he got mean and hit me."

"Why?"

"Because I became friends with one of the Junior Executives

in his office. He didn't like that either."

"Gee. I wonder why."

"So I left and moved back to the family house and he went back to Detroit, thank God. You know, Ken, the drinks are cheaper at my place."

As the two exes walked by the young Marine's table the boots yelled,

"Semper phi, Gunny. Way to go" and clapped and saluted.

"Friends of yours, Mister Hero?"

"Naw. Just baby boots raising hell. Lucky they're still able to. A lot of guys ain't."

"Yes, I know."

* * * * *

The Marine didn't waste any time. He pinned Susan against the living room wall and kissed her, then unzipped her dress and let it fall to the floor. She pulled his uniform off and he carried her to the bedroom, throwing her naked form on the bed and driving his manhood deep inside his wife's lower region. Susan swooned with passion. It had been so long. She met his pounding strokes with abandon, scratching his back with long painted fingernails, biting his neck and ear to spur him on. When it was over she whispered in his ear,

"I'll always love you."

Rawlins blood went cold. The last time he had heard that was just before he found out about her affair with the flyboy. As he got dressed he realized it was finally over. There was no feeling any more. It was gone. The sex was just mechanical release. He was finally free of her clutches, her ownership of his very soul. There would always be a hidden place where she would forever dwell in his mind and she would visit him in this place during long, lonely nights, but then disappear like his dead mates from the war. They also would visit him in his sleep for the rest of his life.

Rawlins looked at his ex-wife as he left. Almost with sympathy he said good-by. His object of pain and frustration for so many years sat in stunned silence and said nothing as her man walked out of the room and out of her life forever.

As the Marine reached the sidewalk he felt free. As he walked along it began to rain and with the rain came thoughts of Nurse Trumbolt. Maybe he would look her up when he got home.

* * * * *

Rawlins stopped at Camp Lejeune on his way north to Buffalo. He decided to end his time in the military, at least for now, and give civilian life a try. After nine years of service the Corps would take him back as a Drill Instructor if need be. Since he had survived the war it was time for a new life and maybe a new wife.

Entering the Personnel Administration building at Lejeune he spoke to the desk Sgt.

"I would like mustering out papers, Sgt."

"OK, Gunny. Have a seat."

The clerk returned with papers in triplicate for Rawlins to sign.

"Fill these out, Gunny. Your D.D214 and final pay will be sent to the address on the forms. They will be mailed as soon as approved. Welcome back, Gunny. Good luck."

Rawlins thanked the Sgt. and left, then took a cab to the home of Master Gunnery Sgt. Eugene Parker, a friend from the Raiders.

"Well, I'll be a son of a bitch. You're supposed to be dead."

"Not yet, Master Guns."

"We heard you went down with a sub right at the end on some special op."

"Almost. But I made it out."

"You always were a lucky bastard. Everybody said you weren't gonna die in that war. You're too ugly to die anyway. Scare hell out of the Japs with that mug."

"How are you, Gene?"

"I been better, but I been worse. Just bored. Wasn't meant to be a paper shuffler. I hear you got the Cross on Iwo."

"Yeah."

"How the hell did you manage that? Let me find a bottle and you can tell me all about it."

"You won't believe me if I tell you the truth."

"Waddya mean?"

"I'm tellin' you, Gene, you won't believe what happened."

"Try me."

"It was night, kinda rainy and misty. Japs all around. Lots of hide and seek shit. You know how they are."

"Ya, ya, go on."

"Well, I see this form in the mist, just standin' there, lookin' my way. I figure it's a Jap so I cock the Tommy and get ready to give him a burst. Then he moves closer, and he's wearing camo and a soft cover like we wore as Raiders. All bloody and dirty, so I figure it's a Marine that lost his mind and was wandering around. No weapon either, or 782 gear. A definite Section Eight. Then he gets even closer and it's him."

"Him who?"

"The Joker."

"You mean the dead Joker from Second Raiders?"

"The same. I saw him close. Black hair, brown eyes, and that stupid smile. It was him, Gene."

"So what happened?"

"He motioned for me to follow him so I did."

"Where?"

"Out front, up a rise in some rock outcropping on this hill we had to take in the morning. He gets up on a big rock and points to a cave. In the cave are two woodpeckers and a gun crew, hidden where they couldn't be seen. They would have taken out half my platoon. So I wasted them with grenades."

"What about Joker?"

"He jumped off the rock and disappeared, never to be seen again."

"Well, ain't that some shit."

"I told you you wouldn't believe me."

"I didn't say that. I been hearing lots of strange stories about dead guys gettin' back. Yours ain't the first. It's like they hang around and try to help their buddies. Weird shit. One guy told me about four Japs walkin' by his platoon at night. They were twenty yards to their front. Everybody opened up on them and they just kept walkin' by. Their rifles were even slung right shoulder. Tracers goin' right through them and they kept walkin.' All at once they just disappear. Gone. This guy still has the creeps over it. How did your Raider buddies make out?"

"Eyes and Russo got through it OK. Ramirez and Junior got wounded along with me but we made it."

"How about Lieut. Pruitt? He was a good kid."

"He didn't make it, Gene."

"No shit. What happened to him?"

"Spigot mortar landed on him and his radio man. It took out the CP. They were obliterated. Nothing left to bury."

"Damn. That's a shame. He was a good officer, good Marine. Too bad. You write the letter?"

"No. The Major took care of it."

"Not the Captain?"

"He got it too."

"Shit. I heard it was bad but not that bad."

"It was the worst we ever saw, Gene. On both sides."

"Glad I missed it. How about your old lady? Ever see her again?"

"Yeah. Two days ago."

"How did it go?"

"Nothing there. Just a body."

"No shit. Too bad."

"How about that little broad that was mothering your big ass at Bougainville?"

"I'm thinking on it. Last time I was home she saw a picture of my ex."

"Oh, shit. That's bad."

"Why, Gene?"

"Your ex is a movie star under glass compared to regular broads. She probably feels threatened. Did she dump you?"

"How did you know?"

"'Cause I know dames. Remember our talk before?"

"Yeah. I remember."

"Just look her up like nothin' happened. You didn't kick any ass near her, did you?"

"Well, kinda."

"Shit. That's bad too. When the hell you gonna learn women ain't Marines? They got feelings and brains and stuff. You gotta cuddle 'um and take shit when you're with 'um. Otherwise they think you're a brute or worse."

"But I am a brute."

"Shaddup and tell me what happened."

"Two deck apes tried to pick her up. I tried to dismiss them nice and gentle like. One pulled a shiv. So I put 'um down for a nap."

"You didn't kill 'um?"

"Naw. Just a little bit."

"Well, that ain't so bad. But you should have let her take care of it."

"Why?"

"Makes 'um feel important and you don't look like a killer."

"But I am a killer."

"That's beside the point. You don't want her to know that. Most broads don't like that killer shit. They prefer pansies."

"Really?"

"Yeah, really. So when you get home kiss her ass and see what happens. Call me if you need further instructions. I've instructed Colonels and Majors already. Even one general. So I can teach you. "

"OK, Master Guns."

*　*　*　*　*

On the train ride north Rawlins contemplated everything Parker had said. He knew his word was good. He had known him for a long time.

The weather was getting cooler as they reached Maryland. It was late September and Rawlins was used to the tropics. His dress green jacket did little to keep him warm but the Johnny Walker he nursed helped some. His first winter in many years was fast approaching and Buffalo had some of the worst in the world. Good old Lake Erie saw to that.

Oh, well, the Marine reasoned, *better than getting shot at but it would be hard to get used to. He kept thinking about how surprised*

*he was to be alive. He had never thought he's make it. He had
thought he would die in Japan for sure with a million other poor
slobs. That was the casualty estimate he had heard. No one at Camp
Tarawa expected to live through it. The Fifth Division was one of the
spearhead divisions for the final invasion. Men were mailing home
their pay and personal effects so the grave diggers didn't get them.
Writing last letters home, figuring it was their last chance. Tough
bastards they were. Most of them kids. They took it like men, stared it
in the eye and laughed it off. Typical Marines. Wattaya want? To live
forever? Quit whining. You would be bored as a civilian anyway after
all this fun. And you won't have to worry about getting' old. Even the
Chaplains joined in. Remember, boys, when we meet St. Peter, tell
him this: "One more Marine reporting, Sir. I've done my time in
hell." A lot of surprised boys going home, I bet.*

Then it occurred to Rawlins that in two weeks he would be a
civilian. How the hell would he handle that? He might have to look
up Eyes and take an Instructor position since he had pull in that
department. Maybe being a lifer like Parker wasn't so bad. He wasn't
complaining. But that would be the end for him and the nurse. If it
wasn't already over. That he had to find out. He just was not able to
let her go. Couldn't stop thinking about her. There was something
about her. She wasn't beautiful or a fashion plate but there was
something he just couldn't describe that held him in her grasp. Her
smile, her gentle touch. The warrior had not experienced that before
and it was over-ruling his judgment. It was confusing and exciting all
at once, like some school kids first romance. Like nothing he had
known before. The family even liked her and her parents liked him.

"Oh, well, shit. She's probably long gone with some pansy
college boy by now. What the hell. Can't expect dames to wait on a
lost cause, especially dead ones. I'm sure my parents told her I was
missing. I'm probably better off with bar broads anyway. They ain't
so confusing. Get in, get out fast. Semper phi. Any port in a storm."

* * * * *

Finally reaching Buffalo, Rawlins hailed a cab.
"Where to, Marine?"

"Hertel Avenue."

When the cab pulled up in front of the house the Senior Rawlins was mowing the lawn. The Marine grabbed his sea bag and exited the cab. His father stood motionless, hanging on to the mower, tears streaming down his face. The son dropped his sea bag and grabbed his father, picking him off the ground and holding him in his arms, weeping with him. His mother and sister ran out of the house to him, and held him for a long time. Neighbors came over, seeing the commotion, and they grabbed the big Marine and held him and wept with him.

"We thought you were gone, boy. We heard you weren't coming home."

"They were wrong. I made it. It was close but I made it."

That evening became an unscheduled home coming party for Rawlins. The whole neighborhood and all the relatives showed up to see their long lost Marine. It would be one of the happiest occasions of the Marine's life and the beginning of a new one. A life without death and killing but including a mysterious woman he didn't understand but could not forget. It would continue until 1950 when a new threat appeared on the horizon.

* * * * *

The next day Rawlins borrowed the family car and headed for Niagara Falls. Instead of going to Eleanor's house he rented a room at the Statler Hilton Hotel, right by the Falls. The place was full of service men going home, everybody happy or drunk or happily drunk.

Rawlins changed into a fresh uniform and headed for the dance hall where Eleanor and her friends wasted time in the evenings. Picking a table by the wall in a dark corner he ordered a drink and waited. Firing up a Lucky he smoked and nursed his scotch. The place was filling up. Zero hour at 9:00PM, thought the Marine. And there she was, in the company of a young Soldier, a Buck Sergeant.

Shit. I was afraid of this, thought Rawlins. *Oh, well, have to make a flanking move. When Junior goes to the bar or head, I'll move in. Hope I don't land in the brig for this. Junior might start something I'll have to finish.*

They got up and danced. The little nurse clung to the Soldier and Rawlins burned with jealousy.

Son of a bitch. I better get a grip. Haven't felt like this in a long time. Could get me in some real shit if Junior says the wrong thing.

He ordered another drink. The waitress tried to get friendly but he ignored her.

Just what I need. More woman trouble. Her old man is probably on the way home right now. I gotta be nuts coming here. Just asking for an ass kicking. She's done with me. Dog face is seeing to that.

Finally the Sergeant went to the bar and the Gunnery Sergeant moved in. As Eleanor watched the twirling bodies on the dance floor, Rawlins made his move. Walking up on her blind side, he said:

"Care to dance. lady?"

Eleanor spun around in her chair and stared in shock at the long lost Marine.

"Oh, my God. Ken. You're dead!!"

"No I'm not or did they forget to tell me."

The nurse from Bougainville jumped out of the chair and grabbed Rawlins around the neck.

"I love you, you big jerk. Don't get killed again or I'll hit you next time."

The people at the surrounding tables clapped and yelled. All Eleanor's friends; all aware that the Marine had been missing.

About this time the Soldier re-appeared.

"Welcome home, Marine. We know all about you. Have a drink with us."

"OK, Sergeant, I'll do that."

"Ken, this is Billy. We were friends before the war."

"Hi, Ken. Pleased to meet you."

"Likewise, Bill."

"Glad to see you made it."

"Amen to that, brother. Where you been?"

"Normandy, Bastogne, Aachen, the Rhine. Bad shit, Gunny. Lost a lot of friends."

"Yeah, me too."

"By the look of those ribbons you must have won the Pacific War single handed."

"Naw. They hand these things out to anybody that lived through it. Don't mean nothing."

"Well, kids, I'm gonna shove off."

"That little blonde in the corner is alone. Go get her, Soldier."

"OK, Marine. Good to be home, ain't it?"

"You know it, brother."

"Well, you two sure hit it off. I was afraid you would hit him."

"We both had enough of that for a while. It's understood."

"Aren't you jealous?"

"No, I'm dead, remember?"

"Stop it, Ken."

"You said it."

"I didn't mean it like that."

"Like what?"

"Like you're really dead."

"Then why did you say it?"

"You know."

"Know what?"

"Why I said it. Now stop or I'll cry again. I've been crying for a month, you big jerk."

"Sorry. I would have called but there's no phone in the jungle."

"So what are your plans now that the war is over?"

"I mustered out."

"You what?"

"I retired from service. I signed the papers on the way home. At the end of the month I'm a civilian."

"Really? Why?"

"I've had enough. I'd like to see what a normal life is like and get married."

"Get married?"

"Yes, married. Do you object?"

"No, I don't mind. Marry who?"

"You."

"Is this a proposal?"

"I'm trying."

"Then the answer is yes."

"Are you sure?"

"Yes."

"OK, then."

Rawlins shocked himself. He hadn't planned this but he was alive so he might as well be married too. What the hell.

That night in Rawlin's room, they finally made it official. Rawlings felt a thousand different feelings he had never felt with Susan. Strange, terrifying. Like the future was already planned by some unknown force. Like he had been re-united with this woman from some primal age and place. Things could only get better from here on. Tomorrow they would tell her parents.

* * * * *

The next day the couple shared the news with Eleanor's parents. They weren't surprised. They had seen it coming. They both liked Rawlins and knew he would make a good husband.

Rawlin's family was surprised. Except his sister. She's known all along this would happen.

They didn't know about his meeting with Susan and the finality it had brought between them. The jilted husband was ready to move on. Finally.

The next day Rawlins and his soon-to-be father-in-law went fishing on the Niagara River.

"What happened when you were missing, Ken?"

"Jap sub torpedoes our sub during the pickup. We were all in the water and swam for another island. We hid out there until the war ended. We lived on fish, wild pig and Jap rations we had liberated."

"Were you on Iwo Jima?"

"Yeah. I was there."

"Was it as bad as the press said?"

"Worse. My company was replaced twice. I was in command at the end. The officers were all gone. Lost a lot of good friends there."

"Did you see the flag go up?"

"Yeah. We saw it."

"I guess Okinawa was almost as bad."

"I missed that one."

"Sounds like you saw enough."

"Guadalcanal, Toulabong, Ruwawa, Ulithi, Bougainville, where I met Eleanor, and Iwo. And Chichi Jima at the end. Not to mention a couple of jobs in Europe with the O.S.S."

"You're with the O.S.S.?"

"I was. Truman is disbanding the Unit. Figures we're not needed any more."

"You think that's a mistake?"

"With the Commies on the rise I would say yes. Sooner or later we're gonna have to fight them. And the espionage has already started. Just before the end, me and a British MI6 agent got three German scientists out of Germany. The Allies were afraid the Russians would grab them."

"Why?"

"They invented the V1 and V2 rockets."

"Wow! You have really been around, Ken."

"Yeah. Me and a lot of other guys. No big deal. I'm one of the lucky ones. A lot of guys ain't coming back. Hell of a war."

"How did you get wounded?"

"On Bougainville. A Nip officer shot me with a pistol after we roasted his bunker buddies with a Zippo. Pissed him off, I guess. That's when Eleanor took care of me on the ship. Picked up some grenade fragments, too. Then on Iwo a Nip got me with a bayonet. Right here in the side. Little prick almost killed me."

"I take it he is no longer with us."

"No. Him and twenty thousand of his mates on that stink hole of an island."

The exhaust fumes from the boat engine were making Rawlins sick; reminding him of the smell of burning flesh and flame thrower gas. The fish flopping in their death throes in the back of the boat bothered him too. He had seen men do the same thing. It sickened him. Finally the torture ended. Back at the house the old man produced a bottle and they got drunk together. Rawlins' favorite sport as of late.

"So, Ken, where is the Corps sending you next?"

"Nowhere. I'm done. Signed my papers."

"Really?"

"Yeah. Had enough. Time to try a normal life with a new wife. Sounds good, don't it?"

"Yes, very good. Back from hell. Time to live again. You sure earned it, son."

"Amen to that."

* * * * *

The wedding took place in the Chapel at the Niagara Falls Air Corps Base and Reserve Center. It was the last thing Rawlins would do as a Marine.

Donning his dress blues with saber and piping and full decoration he looked more like a General than a Gunnery Sgt. His bride wore her Navy Reserve Lieutenant Junior Grade dress blue uniform. The ceremony was short and sweet and to the point. Typical military function. After the reception at the Base NCO Club they were gone. Sneaking off to Toronto for the honeymoon. What a surprise for Rawlins. The confirmed bachelor.

The happy couple rented an apartment in Buffalo because Rawlins had a promise of a job at Bethlehem Steel in Lackawanna, NY. The steel plant was on the outskirts of Buffalo on the Lake Erie shore.

Rawlins separation papers and DD214 honorable discharge from service were waiting for him at his parent's house. Also included were a substantial check, his mustering out pay with savings. Upon reading the papers he noticed a clause which stated that he was in the inactive Marine Corps Reserve until further notice. He shrugged it off, thinking: *What are they gonna do with an old bastard like me?* Little did he know that he would be heavily involved in the storm to come.

Taking some of the money he had received the ex-Marine and his new wife bought a forty one Chevy sedan. Then they went to a dealer and ordered a forty six model. As soon as post-war production geared up it would be delivered.

Eleanor shopped for new furniture. Not Rawlins' favorite thing to do.

* * * * *

The furnace room. Rawlin's new job. Shoveling coal. Hot as hell itself.

Shit, thought the ex-Marine, *what the hell did I get into this time. Well, at least the money is good. This place is like Iwo Jima. Hot as a bitch. Smelly, dirty, dark. Shit. I didn't expect this.*

After his shift he stopped at the bar across the street. Most of the crew from his shift were there. Sitting at a small table, he ordered a pitcher of beer and a shot of bourbon. As Rawlins drank and watched the lake through the picture window two fellow workers sat down with him. One of them offered a Camel. Rawlins accepted and they began to talk.

"How did it go, Rawlins?"

"OK. Hot, but I'm used to that."

"Why is that?"

"Marines, South Pacific. Hot as hell all the time."

"I was in the Second Division. My name is Joe Cardamon."

"Pleased to meet you, Joe. Semper phi."

"Semper phi, Rawlins. This guy was a sub Sailor. We let him buy us drinks 'cause we feel sorry for his underwater ass."

"Ted Robbins. Good to meet you, Rawlins."

"Likewise, Ted. I knew some of you guys when I was a Raider."

"No shit."

"No shit."

"We did a lot of work with subs. I remember. I was on the Cod. We hauled Raiders around some."

"Good boat and crew, the Cod. I remember her. She never ran from a fight. Even battle surface."

"Thanks, Rawlins. That's a compliment, coming from a Marine."

"You on Tarawa, Joe?"

"Yeah. What a cluster f**k."

"Yeah, I heard And Peliliu was as bad. They were all bad."

"F**king Japs. Ruined a lot of guys and families."

"Amen to that. Bastards. How about you, Rawlins?"

"Started as a Raider. Makin Island, Guadalcanal, to Bougainville. All through the Solomons. Then the Twenty Seventh of the Fifth Division."

"Iwo Jim?"

"Yeah. Bad ass place. Still having nightmares. Glad that shit's over. I would rather shovel coal. Ah, what the hell. It's no worse than digging rifle pits. And it pays better."

"Yeah, Joe, and nobody has shot at me yet."

They all joined in the laughter at that. The three veterans became fast friends. They happily got drunk swapping stories of women and war. They were relieved. Happy to be home. Happy to be alive. But an underlying sadness could be felt like an undertow in the lake currents they watched. Sadness for all their mates, buried in far off places. Sadness because they had killed their fellow man en masse. But it had had to be done and they knew it. And they had conquered a brutal enemy. A scourge on humanity that had had to be purged. And they, the young men of their countries military service, had done it, saving the free world in the process. But there was a price to be paid. So many of their brothers in arms were gone. They felt guilty for surviving. Why were they here at home when so many lay in their graves, far, far away.

* * * * *

Days turned into weeks and weeks into months. Rawlins was becoming an alcoholic. He couldn't deal with the day to day boredom of civilian life and going to a job he hated every day. And his wife was becoming disgusted with him and his drinking. Coming home drunk in the middle of the night was not her idea of proper behavior. Daddy had never done that. And Rawlins would say,

"Daddy can kiss my big ass. I don't see him paying the bills or shoveling coal all day and night."

Rawlins missed the Corps. There he had been someone. He had been respected. Now he was just a shovel. And he was tired of it. Men used to look up to him. Now they looked down their noses at him. The lowly steel worker. In the Corps he had had rank and privilege. Now he had blisters and heat rash and a constant cough from the dust. Finally he reached the breaking point. The foreman found him during his lunch break.

"Rawlins, you're slacking off. Production is down. You better get moving. A monkey could do better. Now get back on the line. Your break is over."

Rawlins didn't move.

"Did you hear me, mister?"

"I got ten more minutes."

"I said get off your ass now, you prima donna Jarhead."

Wham!! Rawlins hit him so hard it lifted him off his feet, breaking his jaw in the process. Good bye, job. Hello, lockup.

When the attorney spoke to him all he said was,

"F**k it. I should be dead anyway. I don't care what they do to me. That asshole shouldn't have made me mad."

Ninety days later Rawlins was out of the Erie County Holding Center, job gone, wife gone, no hope, and no future. Eleanor had gone home to mother. Wouldn't even talk to him. He rented a one room dive on Pearl Street and joined the rest of the lonely throwaways in the bars and cat houses in downtown Buffalo. His next job was as a body guard to a pimp. Big Louie had big connections. Prostitution, the rackets, gambling. Rawlins became his enforcer. Kicking ass for money. *Same old shit,* he thought. And Bettie Lou. A bar tender at the Northern Lights Club around the corner. She became his best friend among other past times. Also nurse, maid and cook. She was in love with the big tough. He could care less. If she as much as mentioned marriage she wouldn't see him for two weeks. Besides, he was already married and she knew it.

* * * * *

It was a good thing he still carried his beloved forty five pistol. One Saturday night he was jumped by three gang members who had been looking for some fun. Two had knives. One had a baseball bat. Rawlins deflected the first knife thrust and kicked its owner in the crotch, dropping him. Next the ball bat was laid across his back, knocking him down. Pulling his pistol, Rawlins cocked the hammer and fired twice into the knife wielders gut as he tried to stab him. The punk hit the ground dead, next to him. The other gang members ran for the hills not wanting to stop unexpected lead.

Staggering back to the Northern Lights, Betty grabbed him and took him down stairs to hide him from the police. Then she dressed and bandaged the cut on his arm and taped up his two cracked ribs.

The next day Louie came to see him.

"We gotta get you outta here, Ken. The heat is on. Coppers all over looking for you."

"I got friends in Chicago."

"We'll take you there."

* * * * *

"Ken. This is Vito Russo. He owns this part of Chicago since Big Al passed away. He said he would take care of you until the heat is off as a favor to me."

"Vito. This is Ken Rawlins. Kiss my ass, you ugly wop shitbird. I'm gonna take your broads and make you pay for it."

"Ken. Are you crazy? He's sorry, Vito. He ain't feeling right. Don't shoot him or anything. He's out of his head."

"I know the crazy bastard. We won the war together."

And Vito gave his long lost Sgt. a hug.

"Well, I'll be a son of a bitch. You still love me."

"What the hell happened, Ken?"

"I had to grease a dummy with a shiv. Now the heat is looking for me."

"Don't worry about it. I own the heat in this town."

"OK, Vito."

"Same old shit. I always gotta bail you out. When the hell are you gonna grow up? What happened to that job you had?"

"I punched out the foreman."

"Why?"

"He pissed me off."

"Shit. Now you sound like Junior."

"I got ninety days and lost my wife over it."

"You got married?"

"Yeah."

"The nurse?"

"Yeah. But she's gone."

"She'll be back."

"How do you know?"

"I know broads. Remember?"

Rawlins and Russo went to Russo's Club. Here Rawlins was given a room and anything he wanted. The two ex-Marines reminisced and got drunk at Russo's expense.

"So things ain't so good?"

"Things are shitty. I can't get used to this civilian shit. People messing with me. Wife messing with me. Just 'cause I drink a little.' Daddy said this, Daddy said that.' F**k Daddy. Pain in the ass. You would think I married him. She wants me to be like him. Mr. Perfect."

"I thought the old man liked you."

"He did. I doubt he does now though. Since his little princess is home. Shit. I'm probably enemy number one."

"Give it some time. She'll come around."

"It's been two years."

"Means nothing. This kind of shit can last for decades."

"What do I do if I see her?"

"Get her pregnant."

"Are you nuts?"

"I'm telling you, get her pregnant. Works every time."

"Whata you mean?"

"They get nutty when pregnant. All emotion. First she'll slap you, then hug you, then tell you she loves you, then call you a heartless bastard. When that happens you're in solid."

"You're nuts, Russo."

"Has my professional advice failed before?"

"Well, no."

"That's why they call me General. My tactics are fool proof."

"There's one problem with all this."

"What?"

"She might have a kid."

"Well, yeah, Ken. That usually happens when they're pregnant."

"Is there any way to make her think she's pregnant when she ain't?"

"Not that I know of."

"You sure?"

"I'm sure."

"Shit. I ain't ready for no kid."

"Who the hell is. But it's fool proof. Shit, Ken, you went through the war and survived. A kid ain't as bad as that."

"I ain't so sure. They throw up at you all the time. Yell and whine, bitch and moan, cry and get the old lady pissed off at you. And shit everywhere."

"See. You're already an expert."

"I've seen kids in action. They're worse than a three week boot with a sore ass. During the war I just got shot at. Big difference."

"You can handle it. I got confidence in you."

"Fine. Then you raise the kid. I ain't up to it. I raised enough of 'um during the war."

* * * * *

"Gunny. You big ugly bastard. How the hell are you?"

"Well, I'll be a sad Sailor in a cheap whorehouse. Junior. What the hell are you doing here?"

"I'm Vito's new enforcer. The old one got dead so I took the job."

"What about the farm?"

"We lost it. The back foreclosed on us and a lot of other farms. So Vito is helping me out."

"That's great. One big, happy family. You guys hear from Eyes or Ramirez?"

"Nothing from Eyes. Ramirez wrote and said he's healed up

and working his father's horse farm near El Paso."

"That's good. I figured he would be OK. He's one tough little Mex. He said when he got his papers they said he is in the inactive reserve."

" So did mine."

"Me too, Gunny."

"They planning on another war?"

"They're worried about the Commies. They're startin' shit all over the globe. They even got the atom bomb now."

"Son of a bitch. I had enough of that shit."

"We all have, Vito. We did our time in hell. I guess the government doesn't agree with us. Next time I'm in D.C. I'll have to look up Truman and tell him to knock off the bull shit."

* * * * *

As Rawlins healed from his latest combat he thought about his wife and what Russo had said. Maybe it wouldn't be so bad to have a kid. If it got her to stay with him it might be worth it.

When Rawlins was fully recovered he went out with Junior to collect money for Vito. First the whore houses, then the bars. As usual the bars had drunk stool polishers who became very possessive of their improvised homes. At one particularly seedy joint the opposition was met.

"You got your payment?"

"Kiss my ass, you ugly ape. Tell your boss I ain't paying no more."

The great ape grabbed the bar keep by the throat and whispered unmentionables in his ear. A local hood sitting at a nearby table decided to be the new kid on the block and muscle in on this action. He drew his switchblade and headed for the enforcer's back.

I'll cut this asshole deep, he thought. *Then I'll be top dog around here.* As he neared his unknowing target, Rawlins turned, saw him and grabbed the felon by the hair, placing his forty five in his left eye socket.

"Drop the knife, dummy, or your brains will decorate the wall."

Top Dog complied, then took a magic nap compliments of the butt of Rawlins' pistol. Junior polished the bar with the tightwads face. For some reason he paid without another word.

* * * * *

"Thanks, Gunny. I didn't see the shitbird with the shiv."

"Don't call me Gunny no more, Junior. I ain't a Marine any more. Just Ken."

"OK, Gunny."

Rawlins was thinking of calling his wife, wondering if she would even talk to him. During afternoon drinks at Vito's Club the question came up.

"Well, Vito, should I call"

"Are you ready for it?"

"I think so."

"What if she ain't interested?"

"No big deal. I've been through it before."

"Then call. You got nothing to lose at this point."

* * * * *

"Ken. My God, where are you?"

"Chicago. Staying with a war buddy."

"How are you?"

"OK. How about you?"

"Lonely."

"How lonely?"

"Why do you ask?"

"Just wondered. What's new?"

"I got a job at Memorial Hospital in the Falls."

"Like it?"

"It's OK."

"Seeing anybody?"

"Kind of. A doctor asked me out last week. We had dinner and went to the Club."

This burned through Rawlins like a lightning bolt.

"We're still married."

"Really. I almost forgot."

"You told me you love me."

"I forgot that too. All I remember is a bottle and bills from you, Ken."

"Is there anything else?"

"No, I guess not. Goodbye, Ken."

"Well, I'll be a sore assed son of a bitch. F**kin' Vito. 'Just call her. Are you ready. Dumbass wop. I shoulda known better. I ain't no good with real broads. Should just stay with whores, I guess. You don't have to make them happy."

* * * * *

"Well, how did it go?"

"Don't ask."

"That good, aye?"

"Yeah. She's seeing a doctor."

"Don't mean nothing."

"Like hell it don't."

"That's artillery."

"Whata you mean?"

"To make you jealous."

"Why?"

"'Cause you ain't been around. I feel sorry for the poor slob."

"Why? He's with my wife."

"No, he ain't. But he thinks he is. He's just a tool to make you jealous. And I see it worked. Women are the best strategists in the world. They should all be Generals."

"How did she know I would call?"

"They got special brains. They know shit that they don't know. It's like when a guy gets it in war. The mother always knows. Or when a guy runs around. They know. It's like when you went and saw Susan when the war ended. Your wife knew you would."

"How do you know about that. I never said anything."

"'Cause I think like a dame. I got the special sense. That's why I know what's going on. Just like I told you you weren't gonna die in the war. Remember?"

"Yeah, I remember. So what do I do now, General?"

"Get your ass to Niagara Falls and take what's yours. She's asking for it. And don't wipe out the doc. He's just a broad-struck dummy. Just a tool. Leave him be. He will hurt plenty when she dumps the poor slob."

* * * * *

Rawlins bought a new tweed suit and boarded the train for Niagara Falls. As he rode around Lake Erie he remembered making this trip before and stopping to see the Joker's wife in Pittsburgh. *Poor bastard. Dead a long time now. And I still miss him. Had it really been him on bloody Iwo or just his imagination. He didn't know. Some day he would ask him. On the other side. He missed a lot of friends. Too many. Some day he hoped they would all be together again.*

Then his family came into his thoughts. *He hadn't seen them in a long time. They probably preferred it that way. He was nothing but trouble for them. They had bailed him out one way or another too many times.*

When he reached his destination he rented a room at the Sheridan Inn near the Falls, then rented a forty eight Ford coupe with a V-eight engine. What a ride. Lots of power. Then back to the dance club to begin his assault. Vito had given him infiltration instruction and a call to Master Gunny Parker mustered similar tactics. Sitting in a dark corner the ex-Marine did his surveillance. He noticed friends of his wife. Then it happened. She came through the door with the doctor.

Shit, thought Rawlins, *he's an ugly, scrawny son of a bitch. Vito must be right. That crazy wop. She can do better than that.* He watched as they sat down. His wife looked detached, distant. The doc was stumbling and fumbling.

What an amateur, thought Rawlins. *Too nice. Looks like a high school kid working his first asset. He won't get far like that. She likes tough guys. This guy's a pansy. Probably wears women's underwear. Vito was right. Just a tool. I almost feel sorry for the jerk.*

She's gonna trim his ass but good. Poor dumb bastard.

Rawlins got up and walked to his wife's table. Sitting down, he said hello.

"Hi, Doc. Hi, Eleanor."

"Ken. What are you doing here?"

"Dancing like everybody else."

"Who is this, Eleanor?"

"My husband."

The doctor looked shocked.

"I thought he was in Chicago."

"I was, Doc. Thought I would visit and take in the sights. You look familiar, Doc. Were you in the Navy?"

"No. I missed the war. Probably in med school. Yes, that's right."

"Come to think of it, the doc I knew got his head blown off on Iwo Jima. He missed med school. Joined the Navy instead."

"How frightful."

"Yeah. Real shame. Lots of guys I knew got killed. They didn't go to med school either."

Rawlins lit a Camel and dropped the matchbook from the Sheridan Hotel on the table.

"Well, kids, gotta go. Got to make out my application for med school. See ya."

Rawlins left. Eleanor said nothing but her eyes told the story. They never left him. All the way out the door. The trap was set. Now the hunter had to wait. Master Guns was right. The hunt was far better than the kill. He hadn't even caved in the competition's head. Vito was right. Poor slob is gonna get his ass handed to him. Sure was dumb for a doctor.

Rawlins had a drink in the hotel bar and sat contemplating marriage and babies.

Shit, I don't know. Sounds pretty domestic. Don't know if I can handle it.

Back in his room, he waited. The knock on the door came at 2:00am.

"Go away. I'm sleeping."

The knock continued. Rawlins opened the door and there

stood his wife.

"You going to invite me in?"

"I dunno. Where's the doc?"

"Shut up, you big ape, and kiss your wife."

And he did so for the rest of the night.

* * * * *

The next day, Rawlins moved into Eleanor's apartment near the hospital on Ferry Avenue. She dismissed Horace and told him to find another nurse. Hubby was home.

Three weeks later Rawlins received a letter in his Post Office box. It was June 1950.

"Congratulations. You are hereby notified that you have been recalled to duty with the First Marine Division. Your rank has been upgraded to Master Gunnery Sgt. Report to First Division Replacement Depot at San Diego, California ASAP for transportation to the Republic of South Korea."

Chapter Ten

KOREA

Rawlins, now part of the First Provisional Marine Brigade, landed at Pusan, South Korea in late July, just in time for the Naktong River bulge battle. The Fifth Marine Regiment would fill holes around Army Twenty Fourth and First Cavalry Divisions.

The attack came suddenly and unexpectedly in this area of the Pusan perimeter. Rawlins and the Third Battalion were pushed into the gap on the river at midnight on August 2nd. As the Marines dug in they could hear the N.K.P.A. Fourth Division across the five hundred or so yards of the river. Only three to five foot deep in this spot, they would attack en masse with grenade and burp gun platoons. Then the "Russian T-34 tanks would come. Much larger than the Marine and Army M24 Pershing medium tanks and the only U.S. armor in the Pusan Naktong gap. But with their 90mm guns and armor piercing shells they would stall the tank advance, catching the Russian behemoths in the open, crossing the river. Also Army 155mm artillery would help. During daylight Marine F4U Corsairs made napalm runs on the surrounding hills, burning out the entrenched enemy.

Rawlins moved from hole to hole checking on his men.

"You guys got plenty of grenades?"

"Yeah, Master Guns."

"Lay out your ammo so you don't have to fumble for it. And keep quiet. Those slopes across the river can hear us."

"OK, Master Guns."

At the C.P. Rawlins briefed his squad leaders, trying not to insult the new Lieutenant.

"Ramirez, Russo, Junior. You guys know what to do. They're gonna hit us real soon. When you hear those people in the river call for illumination. Then mortars and arty.

"OK, Ken."

"And hold your ground. If we bug out they will flank the

Army and push Pusan into the sea. We're all that's here to fill this gap. Get back to your squads. Good luck."

Rawlins cocked his new M3 grease gun and headed for the line. He preferred his Thompson but this would do. At least it was in forty five caliber, his favorite. The night was dark and overcast. A perfect night for an attack. He could feel the enemy coming. His combat sixth sense was active.

Company mortars were ready with 81mm's and 42 inch heavy mortars. All zeroed on the river. Army arty would handle the tanks.

A parachute flare popped over the river and there they were. Ranks of North Korean Communist troops in the river. Some with Russian PPSH 41 burp guns, others with bags of grenades.

The half track mounted quad fifty opened fire; also the 30 cal. L1-A1 machine guns. The enemy fell in ranks. Still they came. Half crawling, half running. When the machine gun barrels grew so hot they had to be changed, the enemy rushed the line. Mortars fell in their midst, blowing them to pieces. Still they came. Now the riflemen opened fire. M1 rifles and B.A.R. automatic rifles mowed down the attackers. Then grenades. Somehow some of the Communists broke the line, mixing with the Marines. Fierce hand to hand fighting broke out. No time to reload rifles. Bayonets, knives, pistols, rifle butts were the weapons of choice.

Three N.K. Soldiers charged Rawlins. He mowed them down with his grease gun. Now with an empty magazine, attackers all around him, he dropped his sub machine gun and drew his forty five. A Commie bayonet slashed across his chest. Bam! He shot the bad guy in the face. A grenade detonated next to him. It blew off his helmet and knocked him down from the concussion. Another bayonet was plunged at him while he was down. He grabbed the end of the Russian Mosin Nagent rifle and kicked its owner in the crotch, dropping him. Then a struggle began over the weapon. A young Marine covered with blood stove in the N.K.'s head with the butt of his M1. Lights out for General Kim's lackey. Finally, the determined enemy retired for the night. Just the beginning probe of what was to come.

The next day the enemy brought up 82mm Russian mortars,

90mm captured Japanese mortars from the last war and 107mm
Russian howitzers. The bombardment lasted for hours. Then the
Russian T34 tanks tried to cross the river.

Marine Corsairs napalmed and bombed the tanks,
incinerating the occupants. And infantry with 157mm recoilless rifles
mounted on jeeps took care of the few that got through. This weapon
with armor piercing ammo proved very effective against Russian and
Chinese tanks.

Nightfall. Time for the infantry. Rawlins moved from hole to
hole getting his men ready, making sure they laid out ammo and
grenades and fixed bayonets. Then he returned to the Second Platoon
C.P. where young Lieutenant Williams listened to radio traffic.

As a favor to Captain Ashton, the Company Commander,
Rawlins was secretly watching the twenty one year old platoon
leader. The Captain was afraid the Lieutenant might crack under
pressure. All the companies NCOs were WW2 retreads like Rawlins.
They came in as replacements from the States or Japan.

Rawlins had reassured the Captain:

"Don't worry, Sir, I'll watch him. If he cracks I'll take over.
On Iwo with the Twenty Seventh I ran a company for a week after all
the officers were down."

"So I hear. That's why I requested you, Master Gunny. You
got a reputation."

"Gee, lucky me."

"A smartass too, I hear."

"Yes, Sir. Can't be helped, Sir."

"Yeah. I know. You mud Marines are all the same."

* * * * *

"Lieutenant. The gooks are coming, Sir."

"Yes, Master Gunny. I hear the traffic. They're probing all up
and down the line."

"Yes, Sir. Why don't you call Weapons platoon and get the
four two's on 'um."

"That's not necessary. It's just a probe. We can handle it."

Rawlins could hear bugles and whistles blowing off to the

east.

"Probe my ass, Sir. That's a full scale infantry attack. The Cavalry is getting the hell beat out of it. Get Second Bat up here to reinforce them."

"That will be all, Master Gunnery Sgt. The Cavalry can handle their part of the line."

"But, Sir, listen to the radio. They're being overrun. They're calling in artillery on their own position."

The young Second Luey looked stunned. Then perplexed.

"Master Guns. I don't know what to do."

"Get your carbine loaded, Sir, we're gonna get hit. And get outta the way."

Forty five in one hand, radio handset in the other, Rawlins took charge.

"Easy One calling Baker Five!!"

"Go ahead, Easy."

"Send Second Battalion into the Cavs rear. They're being overrun. Wait one. Easy One."

"Easy One. This is Colonel Samuel. What's the situation?"

"The First Cav is being overrun, Sir. They need our help, Sir."

"I'll send two companies, Easy One. That's all I can spare. The NKs are breaking through all over. Over and Out."

"Shit, Lieutenant. We're gonna be flanked."

Just then a Chicom grenade rolled into the tent. Rawlins hit the deck. Wham! Rawlins got up and met the infiltrators. Two enemies with Chicom Type 50 burp guns entered the tent. The Marine shot them both with his pistol before they could react. The Lieutenant didn't respond. He was still sitting in his chair, carbine across his lap, half his head blown away.

Shit. I gotta get outta here, thought Rawlins, *before they throw a bunch of grenades in here.*

Picking up his greaser, Rawlins headed outside and to the river, men locked in mortal combat all around him. Army illumination lit up the river.

Son of a bitch. It's crawlin' with 'um.

Locating a fifty cal. machine gun with a dead gunner and

loader, Rawlins took over. Finding an unattached Private, he set up the gun.

"Load me, kid "

"OK, Master Guns."

Rawlins cocked the bolt twice on the big gun, chambering a round, then pressed the twin thumb trigger. The weapon bucked as the 750 grain full metal jacket bullets left the barrel. The effect of the heavy machine gun was devastating. Bullets dismembered screaming, charging Communists. Some projectiles passed through two or three of the bunched up attackers. The river ran red with Commie blood. The Marine panned the weapon back and forth, cutting down swaths of would be killers. All around him grenades blew and men struggled in hand to hand combat. Now the bayonet being the weapon of choice, illuminated figures stabbed and slashed each other in the muzzle flashes of the big gun. Finally the enemy retired across the river, just as dawn broke.

The big machine gun's barrel smoked from the heat of firing. It needed to be changed. Rawlins tried to remember. Headspace – screw in barrel until it bottoms out; then two clicks out with spanner wrench. It had been a long time since he had operated a Browning 50 cal. M.G.

The scene of carnage was unreal. Like a medieval battle. Bodies everywhere. Dead men strangling or stabbing each other. The wounded sitting, waiting for a Corpsman. Smoking a Lucky. Bodies floating in the water which was red with blood.

The Marines had held their ground but at a high price. Thirty percent casualties. Rawlin's loader was shaking. It was his first combat.

"You OK, kid?"

"Shit, Master Gunny. Shit, shit, shit. I never seen anything like this before. They didn't tell me it was like this. Shit."

"Yeah, kid. They didn't tell you a lot of things."

Rawlins headed for the Company C.P. and reported to Captain Ashton.

"The Lieutenant is dead, Sir. Grenade got him, Sir."

"Can you handle the platoon, Rawlins?"

"Yes, Sir."

"You OK?"

"Yes, Sir."

"Good. One hell of a night."

"Aye, Sir.

"Reminded me of a night on Saipan. Same kind of shit."

"So I heard, Sir. Bad ass place, Sir."

"You there, Master Guns?"

"No, Sir. Missed that one. But a lot of my mates were."

"I'm surprised. I thought you won the war all by yourself the way I heard it."

"Yes, Sir. I don't like to brag, Sir."

"You're nuts, Rawlins."

"Yes, Sir."

"Thank God you're here."

"Aye, Sir."

"I want a recon in force across the river. Take two squads and keep in touch."

"Aye, Sir."

"I want to see why the NKPA bugged out."

* * * * *

Rawlins returned to Second Platoon.

"Ramirez, Russo. Mount up your squads. We're moving out. Junior. You're in reserve. Watch our asses. We may be back in a hurry. Be ready to lay down cover fire."

"OK, Master Guns."

* * * * *

It was early September. The sky was steel gray and overcast. The humidity was up. Men were wet with sweat as soon as they crossed the river. Ten o'clock in the morning and the heat was on. The men were as nervous as they were hot. After last night's attack they were waiting for the ambush they were sure would come.

Ramirez took point. As he passed burned out tanks, still smoking, and charred bodies he was feeling sick.

Son of a bitch. Just like Iwo Jima. I thought this shit was over. I was just starting to become a human being again and they start this asshole gook war. I did my time in hell. F**king Marine Corps. If you ain't dead you should be. That's their motto.

* * * * *

On a rock shelf on the side of a hill on the Nato side of the river laid a sniper and two ROK (Republic of Korea) Marines, watching the progress of the patrol. This particular sniper had been here from the day the war started. His job was to teach ROK Marines to scout and snipe. He worked independently of the Marine Corps Command and answered only to Colonel Min, ROK Marine Training Command O.I.C. As he watched through his twelve power German made Unertl telescopic sight mounted on his M1D Garand sniper rifle, he was surprised.

Ramirez on point and Rawlins behind him. Well, I'll be. I didn't expect to see them again. And it looks like Vito bringing up the rear with a bunch of boots in tow. They must have come in with the Provisional Brigade. I guess I'll cover their asses like old times.

Now six hundred odd yards from the shooter, Carlos rounded a bend in the trail, right into the sights of a Maxim light machine gun. Two NKs had stayed behind to ambush the patrol that was sure to follow the attack. Without a sound the back of the gunner's head blew out. Then his loader spun around and tried to run. Carlos cut him down with his full auto M2 Carbine. Rawlins ran up to the Staff Sergeant.

"Shit, Ken. That was close. Look at this old Maxim. These gooks don't have any good stuff. Not like our gooks. Look at that slope's head; or what's left of it. Sniper. I didn't even hear it. Must be a long way off."

"Good thing for you, Carlos."

"Yeah. I guess so. Lousy gooks. They gotta be sneaky bastards like the Japs."

"You notice something strange?"

"Yeah. They ain't here. Think it's an ambush?"

"Could be. Let's move out and see."

The Marines spread out, line abreast, in assault formation, and moved up the hill in front of them. Nothing. Just more charred bodies from the napalm strike. As they reached the crest of the hill and headed down the other side into the Naktong River valley it happened. Ambush. Heavy machine gun fire and mortars rained down. The enemy was dug in to a horse shoe defense perimeter on the high ground around the Marines.

"Hit the deck. Ambush. Dig in."

As Russian ordnance rained down the Marines dug for their lives. The only cover was to get below ground.

"Gimme that radio. Second Platoon six calling O.I.C. Over."

"Go ahead, Rawlins."

"Sir, the NKs are dug in on our flanks and forward. Possible battalion strength. Request air and artillery. Over. And more troops. Over."

"Arty on the way. Adjust fire. Over."

The Army heavy artillery sounded like a freight train on an express run coming in. Wham!! Boom!!

"Raise two hundred, right one hundred. Fire for affect."

The artillery rained down, blowing bunkers and trenches. Then the Corsairs came in so low the Marines could see their flying brethren in the cockpits.

"Give 'um hell, fly boys. Doc. How you doing? We got a lot of wounded. Better get 'um evacked. Baker six calling any Mash Transport Unit. We got wounded on Hill 76."

"The choppers are in the air, Baker six. They will be at your location in five. Over."

"Roger, Mash One."

The Corsairs dropped flaming death on the enemy, turning the landscape into burned dust.

"Master Gunny. There's our egg beaters."

"Baker one to Mash Medevak."

"We see you. Pop red smoke and direct us in, Baker one. I see red smoke. Coming in."

Two Sikorsky heloes landed and took the wounded men to the nearest Mash Unit. The firing from the enemy had stopped for the moment.

"Boy, Master Gunny. A lot better than the last war. Those guys have a good chance of making it. Those Mash Units are state of the art. Surgeons and everything."

"Good luck to 'um. They deserve it."

First Platoon was coming down the hill with Junior and his squad leading the way.

"Boy, I'm glad to see you, you big son of a bitch."

"What happened, Ken?"

"They ambushed us. They're dug in all around us on those ridges. They're quiet now but for how long. They're underground. Can't get to them."

"Why don't we pay them a visit tonight?"

"Good idea."

* * * * *

That night Rawlins picked his men for the patrol. They waited in the valley for an attack. It was strangely quiet. No mortars or artillery. No infiltrators. Nothing. Had the enemy left? Rawlins didn't think so.

"What do you think, Ken?"

"They're up there watching us. They're up to something new. Tired of throwing men away in frontal assaults. We'll find out later. Try to get some sleep. It's gonna be a long night."

Rawlins stood watch and thought about home.

Boy, this is some shit. Finally get back with my wife and the Corps comes calling. Like we're the only Marines in the world. A bunch of worn out retreads. We did our time. Ours is not to question why, but to do or die. I wonder what asshole said that. I'd like to choke him right now. "You are the Corps. You will always live in your brother's hearts." What bull shit. Dead is dead. I wonder what the old lady is up to. Must be getting lonely by now. I hope she's not hangin' around that dance hall. I gotta stop this. Every time she would get dolled up and go out somewhere I would start thinking bad shit. Gotta remember she ain't the whore from before. Whole different broad. Gotta try to trust her. Somehow.

"Hey, Ken. You OK?"

"Yeah Carlos. Just thinking about broads."

"Oh, shit. No wonder you look terrified. Old lady trouble again?"

"Naw. Just wondering. You know how it is."

"Yeah. You, me and a million other guys. I hooked up with this half Indian dame. Half Yaqui, half nuts. Hell of a body though. Every time I came home she had to know where, when and how much. Even when I was working. Told me her husband left her with a kid to raise. Just bailed out. So I feel sorry for her. Later I find out he got killed at Anzio. Bailed out my ass. So I'm raising her kid and she and the kid are calling me Dad. I don't give a shit. The kid was alright. I was taking her to the horse ranch and all. Taught her how to ride. My parents like the kid too. They were buying her stuff and treating her like a grandkid. So one day we go home and the broad is sitting there like Sitting Bull, ready to tomahawk me. So I ask her what's wrong. She looks at me with this nasty face look and says:

"You are trying to manipulate me with my child. Then she calls the sheriff's office and has me locked up and thrown out of my own house."

"No shit?"

"No shit. Tells the judge I abused them. Tells him I'm a crazy ex-Marine. So he says,"

"Don't go there for six months, Ramirez. So they have time to re-locate."

So I ask,

"Where do I stay, Judge?"

He says,

"The County jail. We have lots of room."

And I never did anything to this broad. So here I am in jail when I get the letter. And they escort me to the bus for Pendleton."

"Ah, don't worry about it. It was probably the wrong time of the month or something. They all go through that shit. I seen my mother give the old man all kinds of hell for no reason. It's when they ignore you completely that you got a real problem. As long as they're messing with you they still want you around. When they stop and just go along with everything is when you got a real problem."

"Why, Ken?"

"Cause they're broads. They're supposed to drive a Joe nuts. God made 'um that way."

"No shit?"

"No shit. Have you heard from her?"

"Yeah. Got a letter three days ago. Says she loves me and she's sorry and they miss me. Wants me to come home now that I can't."

"See. I told ya. She just took a fit. Don't mean a thing."

"Where did you learn this shit, Ken?"

"Vito. He knows about broads. That's why they call him the General."

* * * * *

0200 HOURS:

"Alright. Listen up. No packs, no helmets, just ammo. And fill your canteens so they don't slosh. Boot black on face and hands. Tape your tags. No talking. Hand signals only. We move out in ten."

The patrol moved up the mountain, Rawlins in the lead. Very slowly, very quietly. The ground was rocky with sparse vegetation. Very little cover. Near the top of the ridge Rawlins heard talking in Korean. He made the signal to fix bayonets. This would be close work. The Team bellied forward up the slope. Rawlins spotted a sentry, half asleep, leaning on his rifle. Slinging his grease gun over his back he crawled up to the NK. Slipping behind him, he grabbed the enemy around the neck with his right arm and gave it a vicious jerk and slammed him down hard on the dusty ground, then gave his head another twist to make sure the sentry's neck was broken and he was off to Commie never, never land.

Rawlins looked around and made the all clear sign, then jumped in the trench on the crest of the ridge, forty five in one hand, and grenade in the other. This reminded him of his father's stories about night raids of the German trenches in France during the Great War. His Team rolled in the trench behind him, then advanced toward the bunker where the voices were coming from. Low crawling on the trench floor, they approached the sandbagged revetment. Inside they saw five NKs looking at a map and talking. Rawlins flipped an M2 frag through the firing port of the bunker. At the detonation, he charged through the door, kicking it open, and shot the Koreans that tried to respond. The Team poured through the door, ready to fire. But there was no need. The NKs were all finished.

"Hey, Ken. Look at this map."

The topo map showed the river, the valley, and surrounding hills. On a plastic overlay there were red grease pencil arrows in half circles on the crest of the ridges overlooking the valley. Then more lines into the Pusan perimeter beyond.

"Well, boys. There's the answer. Classic pincer movement. They drew us in, hoping to encircle us in the valley, then roll up our flanks and wipe us out, then hit the perimeter at the two weakest points and break through to Pusan and the sea. Radioman."

"Right here, Master Gunny."

"Call this in to Regiment. And tell them to be ready for the biggest assault yet."

"Hey, Master Gunny. Look at this hatch in the deck. I bet they're underground. They didn't bug out. They're under us."

"Let's find out."

Rawlins grabbed the map and stuffed it in his grenade bag, then opened the hatch. No firing. He dropped a frag in the tunnel entrance. At the detonation the Team entered the unknown cavern. Lighting the way with flash lights, they followed the corridor, ready to fire. So far there was nothing but dirt and unlit torches protruding from the walls.

Farther along they heard voices. Enemy voices. Rawlins held up his fist (halt), then crawled up to a lit room, forty five in hand. Hospital. Two doctors and three badly wounded comrades. The Marine stepped into the lit room, pistol in hand, and took the doctors prisoner. The wounded were ignored. Too injured to be a threat.

"Junior. Get back to your squad in the bunker and get these two love birds back to Regiment. Russo. You're on me."

The two vets and two of Russo's squad mates pressed on.

Next they found an armory.

"Shit. Look at this stuff. Springfields, M1s, Mausers, Enfields, Arisakas, Nagants, Lugers, Smith and Wessons, Colts, Brownings. It's like the ultimate war surplus store. Shit from all over the world. They don't make their own stuff, Ken. Other than burp gun copies. They just use everybody else's stuff. It must be a logistical nightmare for their supply people. Even a Jap Nambu woodpecker. Shit. I thought we'd seen the last of them. These slope heads are real scavengers. They even have Russian tanks and arty."

"Let's get out of here."

As the pair of Marines rounded a bend they ran right into a squad of NKs. Opening up with their forty fives they mowed down half of them. The rest ran back where they had come from.

"C'mon, Ken. Let's get the hell outta here."

Half way back to the hatch they set grenade traps. Something to slow down any pursuers. Then back to the bunker. The rest of Russo's squad were waiting for them.

"Let's move out. The slopes are right behind us."

Muffled explosions were heard from the grenades left behind.

"That should slow them down. Let's move outta here."

The Marines moved fast down the trench and down the hill, back to their positions in the valley. Then they waited for the enemy they knew was coming.

× * * * *

Back at Regiment the two doctors were being interrogated. They gave information freely, claiming that they had been forced by the Communists to serve them. The Forty Second People's Army Regiment was going to storm the entire front at any time and push the Americans into the sea.

Rawlins had given the map to Junior, who gave it to Regimental S2 (Intelligence).

Artillery was being massed to fire on the ridges the enemy would attack from. Naval and Marine Air was coordinated to bomb and strafe the enemy.

Same old shit, thought Rawlins. *Ass out in the wind. Thousands of screaming gooks in those hills and here we are in the middle of them. One little recon platoon.*

* * * * *

The old vet set up the L1A6 Browning on one end of the perimeter and the B.A.R. Team on the other. Riflemen stretched out in two manholes in between. It was the best he could do with what he had. He gave strict orders not to fire until they were within twenty yards. Maybe they would miss them on their way to attack the perimeter. All positions were camouflaged with brush. No smoking, no talking. Grenades first if they get close. Don't give away your position with muzzle flashes.

It was deathly quiet. Insects buzzing was the only sound. It was also dark. Rawlins could barely make out the hills on this overcast night. He was being lulled into complacency by the heat and fatigue. He was getting old. He was tired and sick of war. As he began to nod off he was jolted awake by a strange sound in their forward.

I don't believe it. Some asshole is blowing a whistle .Next came a bugle. *Assembly call. Gotta be. They're gonna attack.*

Rawlins called for illumination. Much to his surprise the hills were alive with NKPA.

"Shit. Fire mission, over."

"Go ahead, Recon."

"There's hundreds of 'um all around us. And they're headed for the river. Give 'um hell. Everything you got."

As the rounds came in, Rawlins opened the bolt cover on his grease gun and cocked it. The 155mm rounds sounded like freight cars on a midnight express. The 105mm rounds and 4.2 inch heavy mortars whistled as they came over. Then the crash of impact and detonation. The ground shook as Rawlins lay in his hole, directing fire.

"Raise two hundred, left three hundred. Walk 'um back and forth. Fire for effect."

The fire storm was devastating. Men were blown apart as they ran. Squads and platoons wiped out. There was no escape. They could only run forward into the American guns.

Rawlins heard the heavy Browning fifty cal. mg's. open up behind him. Then the smaller thirty cals. and 81mm and 60mm mortars from Weapons Platoon. All firing on the flanking attack in recon's rear. They were cut off now. Surrounded. Fight or die. No

way out. First the 11A6 opened fire. Then the B.A.R. , then the line
erupted with rifle fire and grenades.

Three NKs headed for Rawlins position with Chicom
grenades. Two were shot by the B.A.R. gunner but the third kept
coming. He threw his grenade at Rawlins. The detonation blew off the
Marine's helmet and knocked him down. He lost his weapon in the
process. The Grenadier jumped on his prostrate form and tried to stab
him with a long curved blade. Rawlins grabbed his wrist and grabbed
a rock with his other hand, pounding the Communist in the side of the
head with it. The attacker fell off Rawlins, stunned. The Marine
grabbed his face in a rage and beat his head into the rocky ground
until his brains leaked out. End of attacker.

Then one of the enemy's comrades tried to bayonet the old
Marine. Rawlins deflected the thrust and kicked the Commie hard in
the crotch. Commie's eyes crossed and he went down. Rawlins cut his
throat with his Ka-Bar. Now he recovered his greaser and headed
down the line. Close fights had broken out all the way to the end.
Rawlins cut down infiltrators as he went. Reloading the grease gun,
he took a position on the flank. A squad of NKs tried to take the
platoon from the rear as he had expected. Rawlins picked up a 57mm
Bazooka anti-tank weapon. Its dead gunner had no further use for it.
Firing into the center of the infiltrators broke up the attack. He
followed up with grenades, then charged them with the grease gun.
Russo and his squad saw what was happening and attacked them on
the flank, cutting them down with rifle and carbine fire. Rawlins fired
the full thirty round stick into the fleeing Comrades of labor. He
burned his hand on the hot barrel of the M1A3 sub gun in the process.
With no fore end like the Thompson had to protect the shooter from
barrel burns, this was a problem on full auto.

Russo's M2 carbine came up empty after burning a thirty
round clip of the 110 grain thirty carbine ammo into the enemy. Its
barrel was smoking from the heat.

Sunrise came a half hour later. The attack was over. The
NKPA gone. Their regiment destroyed. Marine Corsairs came in and
strafed and napalmed the retiring troops in the hills to the north,
where they were heading for Inchon.

Navy F9F Pumas bombed the remaining armor, moving on

the roads north. The Forty Second Regiment was no longer a fighting unit; just a decomposing remnant of the proud unit it had been before the Naktong River battle.

"We beat 'um, Master Gunny."

"Yeah, kid. We beat 'um alright," he answered an exuberant private.

"Look at 'um go, Master Gunny. They're running away. We kicked their gook asses. They weren't ready for us Marines. Dumb bastards."

Going through the remains of the dead, many weapons were found. Lots of souvenir pistols. Tokarevs, Makarovs, Smith and Wessons, even two broom handle Mausers with Chinese markings. Cheap copies of the original C96 Peter Paul Mauser version.

* * * * *

"Hey, Ken. I got a present for you."

"Whatta you got, Vito?"

"Take a look."

"Well, I'll be a son of a bitch. Where did you find that?"

"That slope Sergeant over there gave it to me. He don't need it anymore."

"What will you take for it? How about this greaser?"

"Naw. I'll keep the carbine. I don't like those pipe guns. Here, Ken, just take it. You don't look right without a Thompson."

Russo handed the older weapon and the six magazine pouch web gear to his friend.

"This son of a bitch has Chinese markings. Looks real enough though. Must be a lend lease gun from the U.S. to Chang Kai Shek's Army during the last war. That slope must have picked it up during the 1948 Civil War. Their Commie brothers liberated a lot of U.S. and British equipment during that fracas."

Rawlins fired two bursts from the captured weapon.

"Works OK. I think I'll keep it."

Rawlins slung the grease gun over his back.

"Thanks, Vito."

"Ramirez. You got rear guard. Russo take point. We're movin' outta here. Back to our position on the river."

Carrying their wounded with them, they went back the way they had come in the day before. Back through the valley of death, as the Marines were calling it. The stench of bodies was growing with the heat. Flies and maggots everywhere. Men vomiting as they walked.

"Shit, Sarge, this is disgusting. They don't even bury their dead."

"This is nothing, kid. You should have seen Iwo Jima. Piles of dead Nips. Stinking like hell. Hot as a bastard. Up to your ass in flies. Couldn't even eat your rations. I was glad when I got hit."

"Really, Sarge?"

"Yeah, really. And here I am again. Some Navy Surgeon who didn't even look at me decided I'm fit for duty. Holes and all."

" What a bunch of shit. He probably heard about your horse ranch."

"Yeah. Could be. Who knows. The bastards seem to know everything about a Joe."

No one shot at the recon patrol as they went to their position. The enemy was gone, moving north to Inchon and Seoul. The flyboys were having a great time bombing and strafing their columns. The Pusan perimeter was safe for now.

*****

After reporting in to Company and making his After Action Report, Rawlins found a bottle of hooch and relaxed by the river. Firing up a Lucky and pulling on the slope juice he began to unwind. His men were cleaning equipment and washing their dungarees in the river. Some were even swimming. His three squad leaders gathered around. Junior with a bottle of Scotch he had found back at Regiment.

"What you got there, Junior?"

"Just what you need, Ken. American gut rot."

"Gimme that stuff. This gook shit is terrible. Rice and rotten fish juice, I think. It burns like hell. Well, here we are again, boys. Gotta win another war for the politicians and General MacArthur, the biggest politician of all. Truman thinks he's running this war. What a dummy. MacArthur will break him in just like he did Roosevelt. Did you know he told Chesty Puller that we're his Marine Corps. I'm surprised Chesty didn't shoot him. Don't like the Army much. I suppose we'll be moving out soon. The gooks are headed north. I guess we'll be after their asses. Gonna be a long walk to the thirty-eighth parallel."

"Heard from your wife, Ken?"

"Yeah. She's telling me she loves me all the time. Funny she didn't do that before."

"That's 'cause you're gone. The best way to get along with a broad is to stay the hell away from them. They always love you when you ain't around."

"OK, General. Any more advice?"

"That's your lesson for today.

"I'm getting the same shit."

"Wadda you mean, Carlos?

"The Yaqui broad. Now she can't live without me. Loves me. And such shit. When I was home she tried to stab me and the Judge gave me a year in the County pen 'cause she missed. All my fault, you know. Now she's rubbing her ass and calling my name. The General here says that's normal."

"Yeah, well, he ain't normal."

"Now, now, we musn't upset our General. He may stop counseling us. How about you, Junior?"

"You guys won't believe it."

"What happened?"

"I ain't telling. You guys will think I'm a bull shitter."

"We're all bull shitters, Junior. What happened?"

"She sent me a letter."

"Who?"

"The New Zealand dame."

"You're kidding."

"See. I told you."

"Are you for real, Junior?"

"Yeah, Ken. She really did."

"What did it say?"

"She love me, misses me, and wants me back."

"No shit."

"No shit."

"What about hubby?"

"She said he changed after Italy. He's mean and unpredictable now. So she left him."

"You going back?"

"I dunno. Don't know if I can trust her. She told me to bring my parents and we can buy a farm together. But I dunno. She said her old man was dead. Remember?"

"Yeah, Junior, I remember."

"Well, he ain't no more. And what if he comes back? I'll get dumped in a foreign country with no friends."

"You got a good point, Junior. Could be a rough deal. There's plenty a broads in Chicago. Don't worry about it."

"Not like her. She was different."

"That's 'cause she was the first. They're all the same."

"Yer fulla shit, Gunny. If they're all the same how come you gave up Miss Hollywood for the nurse?"

"You got a good point, Junior. When I figure it out I'll let you know."

* * * * *

A runner from Battalion found Rawlins and told him to move the Company to Pusan Harbor and stand by to board ship. The Army would fill their position on the line.

"What's up, Master Gunny?"

"Listen up. We been ordered to Pusan to board ship. That's all I know. Grab your gear and mount up in those trucks. We got a ride for once."

* * * * *

The sniper and his ROK spotters lay high on a ridge above the retiring NKPA. Wearing ghillie suits made from local vegetation, they were nearly invisible. The passing enemy, moving at night to avoid air strikes, didn't have a clue that there was a sniper nest above them.

Eyes was testing a brand new Starlight Scope mounted on his M1D sniper rifle. It was designed to pick up moonlight and intensify it in the mirror, magnifying chamber. The huge objective lens helped in gathering any ambient light. Targets had an eerie green glow. Six hundred yards away NKs toiled up the steep Korean hills. All heading north. Back the way they came. Back to the thirty eighth parallel and beyond.

This was the first time in combat for the Starlight M1D combo. He had been chosen to test the unit by Army Ordnance because of his location and ability. He was well known in military circles as a leading scout sniper. While the final Naktong battle had been going on the night before he had slipped around the enemy's flank and found this position in their rear.

The three men lay motionless all day as NKs walked by, hoping they would retreat through the pass in the mountains. Good guess. A whole company lay before them. And of particular interest was an officer mounted on a white horse, wearing a dark green uniform with red trim and a red star on his high peaked hat. When the officer turned to spur on his lagging troops, Eyes noticed a large silver buckle on his belt with a red star in the center. He also wore knee high polished leather riding boots and matching officers riding crop. Chinese royal family officer.

What the hell was he doing here with these peasant NKs. Below the parallel. Were the Chinese getting directly involved? So far they had only supplied weapons and support along with the Russians. He had heard stories of Russian Mig 15 pilots being spotted up north. Now he wondered if it was true. Was this the beginning of World War three?

* * * * *

"See the officer? Range him. The ROK spotter looked at the Chicom Captain through the spotter scope. Six hundred twenty seven yards. Eyes made the adjustment on the scope, then settled the crosshairs on the middle of the Captain's back. At the shot the

Chicom pitched forward off his white horse and hit the ground dead. His lackeys fired wildly into the air at the surrounding hills. But to no effect. They had no idea where the shot had come from.

"Let's get the hell outta here and report this to Regiment. They should be real interested in the Chicom Captain."

* * * * *

Rawlins and his company waited on the Pusan piers to load on the ships heading north.

MAIL CALL:
A Jeep pulled up with the latest mail drop. Standing in the rear of the Jeep the driver passed it out.

"Russo, you got three. Evans, one, Ramirez, one."

And so on for the company.

"Damn, Vito. Your mail smells like a whorehouse."

"That's probably because it's from a whorehouse. Mine, remember?"

"Yeah. How could I forget. All those nice motherly types you got working there."

"They tell me things are getting tough. The cops have been harassing them since we've been gone. Expecting free service.   Me and Junior will have to end this skirmish soon and get home. Put those cops in their place. Hey, Junior, listen to this: 'How is my big protector. The guy you call Junior. He's so cute and so big. I just love big. Tell him I'm waiting. No one else measures up.' Now you got two broads to worry about, Junior. You're a regular Casanova. What are you gonna do now?"

"What broad is it, Vito?"

"Candy. Remember her?"

"Yeah. She's the one with the big things."

"What things, Junior?"

"You know, the front things."

"You mean breasts?"

"I ain't supposed to say them kinda words but, yeah."

"It's OK, Junior. We don't mind."

"She showed 'um to me once but I don't know why."

"What happened?"

"She caught me lookin' at 'um once in the back room. And she said, 'you want a good look, Junior? Get a load of these.' And she pulled them out in front of me. Just like that."

"Well, what did you do?"

"I was embarrassed, so I looked away and she laughed at me 'cause I got red."

"Then what?"

"Then I left. I didn't know what to do. So I left. I guess she ain't mad no more."

"No, Junior, I guess not."

Everyone was trying not to laugh at this spectacle. Afraid of the Junior smash. You shouldn't make him mad. Everyone but Rawlins. He was sitting there, staring at his letter from Eleanor in disbelief.

"Ken. What's the matter?"

"You won't believe it."

"What?"

"I'm pregnant."

"What?"

"You know, gonna have a kid."

"How did that happen?"

"I dunno. Wasn't supposed to. Shit. I can't have no baby."

"Why not?"

"'Cause I'm over here. And they're too small. And they cry and yell all the time. And shit everywhere. And get sick."

"Just like big people."

"Yeah, but they can't tell you nothing. Just scream and shit. Then you gotta wash their little ass and they still scream. Pain in the ass. Then their mother gets weird. 'You don't love me. You think I'm ugly. Don't touch me; I'm married. We can't. The baby.' Shit. I'm better off here. Maybe the kid will be grown before I get home."

"Yaqui punta!!"

"Carlos. What's wrong?"

"That lousy whore. She's pregnant too but not sure it's my kid. She says I gotta send her my pay in case it is. When I get home

I'm gonna cut her throat. Rotten son of a bitch. She says I left her alone too much, being in jail and now Korea. She had to find companionship somewhere else. So the baby might not be mine. Dirty whore. I'll settle this once and for all when I get home. "

"Junior. How did you make out?"

"Got another letter from New Zealand. The broad says her husband is coming to Korea with Nato forces. Wants me to be nice to him if I run into him. She says they're friends now. He comes over sometimes to discuss their on-going co-habitation and mutually agreed intimacies. What the hell does that mean, Vito?"

"It means he's still screwing her. But she wants you to join the party."

"You shouldn't talk dirty like that, Vito. She's a nice girl."

"Like Mom and apple pie, right?"

"Yeah. Kinda. She wouldn't do dirty things like that."

"Junior, you're hopeless"

"At least I don't do bad things with dirty girls like you do."

"What are you, Junior? Twelve years old. When the hell you gonna grow up?"

"Knock it off, Vito. He's getting mad. His head is beginning to swell. I can't stop him if he decides to smash you."

"Sorry, Junior. I'm just sick of the bull shit, that's all."

"Just don't talk dirty, Vito."

"OK, big guy."

Chapter Eleven

INCHON TO CHOSIN

Rawlins and the recon platoon got the word about the invasion that would take place one hundred miles north of their last location. Inchon Harbor. Ten miles from Seoul on the Han River. They would land on Red Beach, then push inland following the river, to Seoul, the South Korean capital, now occupied by the Communists. Their mission was to report enemy positions and strength on the road to Seoul. They would infiltrate along the river while the rest of the battalion would secure the beachhead.

Rawlins' men were very quiet. Like before Iwo Jima. They knew that some of them would be killed, a hard thing to face at twenty years old. They spent their time cleaning and preparing equipment, loading ammo clips and magazines and writing last letters home. Rawlins wrote to the nurse telling her how happy he was that they were pregnant and how he missed her. In reality he felt lousy. He didn't like kids or pregnant women. Both were a pain in the ass in his mind. Always whining and crying for no apparent reason like a bunch of first week boots at Parris Island.

"Hey, Master Gunny. What's it like when you hit the beach,?" asked a nineteen year old Marine.

"Loud, noisy, confusing. Just stick close to your Sergeant. Let him do the thinking."

"What if I get hit?"

"The Corpsman will be there. Don't worry about it." *That is if the Corpsman doesn't get killed first,* thought Rawlins.

"Just put on your sulfa and bandage like you were taught. Then your morphine syrette if it's bad enough."

"You ever been wounded, Master Gunny?"

"Yeah. Couple of times."

"What's it feel like?"

"You just go numb. No big deal." *After you pass out,* thought Rawlins.

"Then you get to swap bull shit with the nurses on the hospital ship, sleep in a real rack with sheets, eat hot food, and use real toilet paper. It's a good deal."

Watch friends die, get in trouble with officers, get cut open. Really fun.

"Shouldn't be as bad as the Naktong and you got through that OK. Don't worry so much."

* * * * *

That night Rawlins got hold of a bottle of Scotch from the black gang in the engine room. Two Tokarev pistols did the job. The Marine got drunk as usual before an invasion. Or any other time he could. And of course, the singing began.

"Kiss my ass on the main mast. Ha, ha, ha."

"I'm a Gyrene and my balls are green. Ha, ha, ha, ha. "

"My ass is blue and my feet are too. My Momma told me never to lie, so kiss my ass until you die. Ha, ha, ha."

"You're so ugly you look like a gook. A slope head Momma with a big line of drama."

"Truman and MacArthur are both full of shit. Leave the whole thing to the U.S. Marines. Ha, ha, ha."

"He's at it again, Vito."

"Don't worry about it. It's tradition. He'll be OK tomorrow. He loves landings. Wouldn't miss it for the world."

* * * * *

The next day, September 15th, invasion day. After Wolmi-Do Island was taken in the harbor entrance the invasion had to wait until late afternoon because of the tide. It rose and fell thirty two to thirty six feet. At Red Beach the Fifth Marines carried scaling ladders in their landing craft to breach the sea wall.

It was nearly dark when they landed and scaled the wall, then attacked the bunkers guarding the harbor and the road to Seoul. As darkness fell the recon platoon headed up the Han River as ordered and the battalion dug in.

"Hey, Ken, where we going?"

"Up the river. We gotta find the gook hard sights for the battalion. When they come up the road to Seoul they don't want any surprises. Ramirez and Russo, dig in here. You're in reserve. We're going up the river bank. You hear, fire, get your asses up to our position. Assess the situation and flank the enemy if necessary. And don't fire on the enemy here unless there's no choice, even if they're close. Let 'um go by. We don't want to reveal our position out front like this. See you in the morning."

The two squads dug in and set up for the night. Rawlins took Junior's squad with him. The big farm boy dwarfed the rest of the Team. As total darkness fell they moved up the river, moving fast and quiet. The firing in the town of Inchon had ceased. Only the occasional rifle shot was heard.

Second Battalion was dug in for the night, waiting for the attack that never came. The NKPA was on the move, heading for Seoul, ten miles to the northeast.

The regiments near the Pusan perimeter were cut off. No supplies, no retreat. They would be destroyed piecemeal by the Army and ROC forces in the weeks to come.

Operation Chromite was a huge success. One more battle honor for Commanding General MacArthur and General O.P. Smith of the First Marine Division .

* * * * *

Rawlins dropped to one knee and held up his fist. Junior crawled up to the Team Leader. The rest of the men hit the ground and froze.

"I hear something, Junior."

"Yeah. I hear it too. Sounds like digging."

"I bet they're mining the road. They know our tanks will be coming through here. Let's have a look see."

The two ex-Raiders crawled through the tall grass to the road. Sure enough, a squad of NK were planting Chicom anti tank mines in the road.

"What do we do, Gunny?"

"Let's hit 'um with granades, then beat it."

The two Marines threw M2 frags at the miners. At the detonation they got up and ran back to the river. The mining operation was devastated. Eight men killed or wounded. Their bodies and unplanted mines would tell the advancing infantry the story. Engineers would then sweep the road with mine detectors. End of problem.

The squad moved out, heading for Seoul. A mile up the river they heard engines idling. Rawlins checked it out. Two trucks with infantry, digging in, at least a reinforced platoon on both sides of the road. Hidden under some trees was a Russian T34 tank.

Ambush, thought Rawlins. *Gotta break this up. The lead platoon of the advance will be slaughtered.*

Rawlins returned to the Team. In low whispers, he said:

"Listen up. This is what we got. A reinforced platoon is digging in on both sides of the road. I'll call up the other two squads to hit the other side. Gimme that radio. Drop your packs and check your weapons. Baker six calling two six. Over."

"Go ahead, six."

"Ambush two miles upriver on Main Road. Advance to our position. Over."

"Roger, six. Out."

Fifteen minutes later, First and Second Squads walked up on Third Squad's rear guard.

"Halt and be recognized. Password?"

"Bug-Jitter."

"Come ahead."

"Alright, you guys. There's a tank in those trees across the road and half a platoon of infantry. Fall back two hundred yards so you're around the bend. Then slip across the road and don't make any noise. Crawl up to their position and blow the tank with the Bazooka. Then wipe out the infantry. Set up the A6 Browning and B.A.R. before you attack. We'll hit this side when you blow the tank. Got it? OK. Move out and good luck."

A half hour later all was ready. Rawlins' Team was in position, ready to throw grenades, watching from the tall grass as the enemy dug in. The other squads were ready. Machine guns were emplaced two hundred yards from the ambush site. The Bazooka Team was ready. Russo gave the gunner the thumbs up. The 107mm rocket hit the tank right at the turret ring. Ammo in the tank exploded, sending flame a hundred feet into the night sky and incinerating the crew. In a blinding flash of light the machine guns opened fire. Red tracers resembled laser beams from some future battle as they streaked toward the enemy position. Green Chicom tracers replied from Dashika 12.7mm guns. Riflemen poured 30 cal. M1 fire into the enemy ambush.

"Throw grenades," bellowed Rawlins. At the detonations he yelled,

"Give 'um hell."

The squad fired everything they had until their weapons came up empty.

"Reload. Let's go. Up and at 'um."

The Marines charged the position. Some of the Communists got up to run. Rawlins cut down two with his Chinese Thompson. The rest were eliminated by other Marines. Some kept fighting. Rawlins blasted through the firing port of a log bunker, then dropped in a grenade. At the detonation he dropped his empty Thompson gun and pulled out his forty five. Cocking the hammer, he shot two gunners as they staggered out of the revetment. The rest were all down. The fight was over. The ambush had turned into flaming hell for the aggressors.

Two men had been killed, three wounded. But the lead elements of the regiment wound not be ambushed or blown up with mines.

"Good job, boys. They never knew what hit them. Amateurs. They didn't figure on Marines coming to call. Let's dig in and wait for Battalion."

* * * * *

The next morning the Battalion pushed out of Inchon. Resistance was light but steady. Dug in enemy troops were encountered along the road to Seoul and dealt with, either by Naval gun fire or Marine Air. The enemy was fighting a delaying action on the main route to their stronghold; Seoul. At the same time the recon platoon moved off the road and into the countryside, fearing a larger force than they could handle might attack on the road from Seoul. They moved inland a mile and dug in in a grove of trees. From a ridge above their position they watched the road.

* * * * *

"Hey, Master Gunny. There's a patrol coming down the road."

"Ours or theirs?"

"Gooks."

"Any armor?"

"No. Just troops. Platoon strength."

"They're looking for the dead we left for them."

:Now they're starting to bury them. Should we go down there and get 'um?"

"No. That's what they're looking for. Us. There's probably a company down the road just waiting for us to attack. That platoon is bait to draw us out."

" How about we shell them?"

" Let's wait for a bigger fish. Like the whole company."

"Ramirez."

"Yo?"

"Take your squad up the road until you see something interesting, then report back here."

"OK, Ken."

As the sun rose Ramirez headed up the road on its northern flank, staying a mile out. His squad stayed in the trees and tall grass and moved slowly, keeping ten yard intervals, knowing they could run into enemy troops any time.

"Hey, Sarge."

"What?"

"What are we looking for? The gooks are back there."

"More gooks. They ain't enough to bother with. They're no threat to the battalion."

"But, Sarge, they were right there in front of us."

"You gotta learn to think big, Haskins. The big picture. If we wipe out that platoon their company is sure to come and find us. And that's too many for us to handle. But if we see them first we can call in fires on them and wipe them out at long range. Tactics, my boy. It's called recon by fire. We did it in the big war many times."

"OK, Sarge."

Rawlins was getting nervous. Full sun and Ramirez out front with just a squad in Indian country. And they had been gone for an hour. But there was no firing. Must be OK. He needed a drink bad. His nerves were getting jumpy.

"Russo. You got anything?"

"Got some gook juice in my left canteen."

"Gimme that shit."

Rawlins took a long pull on the fiery liquid. It tasted like rotten fish and rubbing alcohol but it was working. The old timer fired up a Camel and drank some more. His hands stopped shaking and he was getting numb all over. His nerves were shot. Too much war. Too much shit. He was getting too old for this shit.

"Here, Vito. Thanks."

"Keep it, I brought it for you anyway. And it's better than morphine if you get hit. Must be two hundred proof. Good for cleaning a rifle too.

* * * * *

Ramirez held up his fist. The men behind him froze. The point man crawled back to him.

"Sarge. They're everywhere."

"Reinforced company. Dug in on those low hills. Did they see you?"

"I don't think so. I was in the trees. Real careful like."

"OK. Good job, Rooster. Take me up there and show me."

The little red headed Marine called Rooster crawled ahead, Ramirez right behind him through the trees. They crawled right into a Communist taking a nap. The sleeping sentry awoke just in time to grab Rooster, dragging the little Marine to the ground. Now a scuffle ensued, fists flying. Both men had lost their weapons. They were punching, kicking, scratching, biting each other. Finally the NK got on top of Rooster and began choking him. Ramirez, now with a clear target, clubbed the enemy with his M1 rifle.

"Shit, Sarge, you didn't have to do that. I was taking him prisoner. Now his brain ain't working."

"Yeah, Rooster. I saw how you convinced him to surrender while he was strangling you. Must be a new tactic I haven't learned yet."

"Well, thanks anyway, Sarge. I can see how you could become confused by my superior tactics."

At the edge of the tree line the two Marines saw the enemy digging in, still exposed. Still above ground. Digging holes and cutting wood for bunkers.

"This is a job for the Navy. Let's get back to the squad. Gimme the radio. Baker two calling U.S.S. Missouri, fire mission. Over."

"Go ahead, Baker two."

"Coordinates delta tango Charlie, two four niner, Infantry concentration. Fiire eight inch, proximity fuse ten feet air burst h.e. Will adjust. Over."

"Roger, Baker two. Mail on the way."

Three shells came in with a roar and a crash, sending flame and broken trees into the air.

"Right on the money, Missouri. Fire for affect. Walk 'um back and forth."

The barrage was devastating. The huge Naval shells shook the ground when they hit. The enemy bivouac looked like the moon on a clear night. Destroyed bodies and equipment lay everywhere. The few survivors headed to Seoul and safety. The people's No. Twenty Seven Worker's Rifle Company no longer existed, compliments of the U.S. Navy.

"Let's get the hell outta here."

Ramirez and company headed back to the recon platoon. Upon arriving they found their comrades nervous.

"Where the hell you guys been? We thought you got cut off."

"Sorry, boys. Had to take time to wipe out a reinforced slope head company, thanks to the Navy."

"We heard the chatter on the radio. We thought you were

making a run for it.

"Used the barrage for cover. They never knew we were there. Now they ain't there. How about that platoon on the road?"

"They beat it back up the road when the barrage started. Must have gone right past you."

"We didn't see them. Maybe they crossed the river."

"Probably. They didn't want the same medicine. I'll call it in to Battalion. That should make 'um happy. And maybe a silver star for you, Carlos."

"Gee, I could hang it on my cover and give the slopes a good target. Or mail it home to the princess so she can pawn it like she did the rest of them."

"It's gonna be dark soon. Russo. Put out a double guard tonight. We might get a visit. Junior, take your squad down to the ambush site and find something to eat. And any booze lying around. Those gooks left in a hurry. They must have left something behind."

* * * * *

"Hey, Sarge. Look at all this stuff. All Chinese. Grenades, mortars, burp guns, rations and gook juice."

"Gather up all the shit you can carry. We may need it later."

Back at the night defense position (NDP) the platoon looked over the resources Sgt. Evans had brought them.

"Gunny. I got two bottles here for you."

"Thanks, Junior. I can use it. You guys divi up the grenades and rations. Henshaw. Set up this 60mm mortar in the middle of the NDP."

"OK, Master Guns."

"And set the fuses now. Don't wait till we need it."

"OK, Master Guns."

"Hey, Junior."

"What, Carlos?"

"Can I take this Russian PPSH?"

"Go ahead. I don't like those little burp guns. I'll stay with my M1."

"Thanks, big guy."

"Watta you got there, Carlos?"

"Burp gun. New toy. I figure it's better than a rifle when they get close. It's no Thompson but it will do."

As it grew dark a mortar team set up on the reverse slope of a large hill three hundred yards to the left. They knew that a company of infantry was moving in their direction, looking for revenge for their brother company having been destroyed.

A sniper watched as the mortar crew dialed in the tube and set fuses. The starlight scope held the green images in the sighting aperture long enough for target acquisition. As they prepared to fire on the Marines the sniper, lying on a ridge two hundred yards away, fired. The first bullet hit the Corporal behind the left ear, killing him instantly. The next round slammed into the loader's chest, flattening him. The third hit the ammo bearer between the eyes, emptying out his skull.

"That was an M1."

"Yeah. And everybody's here. It must be that sniper again. He's on our flank."

"Get ready, people. We're gonna get hit any time."

* * * * *

The enemy company deployed into three separate platoons. Their Captain, a student of Military History and Tactics at Cambridge University in England, decided on the Zulu tactic that had been used to wipe out a British regiment a hundred years before. Shaka Zulu, their Chief, had deployed his warriors in the horn of the buffalo formation. One frontal assault unit; two flanking units in the hills above the British. A classic pincer movement. Not unlike General Piepers attack on Bastogne with his SS Panzers in WW2. The enemy soldiers filed onto the hills surrounding the Marine position and the flat land on their right flank, adjacent to the road and river. It was hoped by their Commander that they would be too close when discovered to suffer an artillery attack like the one that had destroyed their brother company. The Americans would have to fight man to man tonight.

"Sarge. I hear something!"

"Yeah, me too. Call for illumination."

As the star shells burst and parachute flares drifted on their chutes, the enemy's plan was revealed. In the stark white phosphorous light the enemy troops stood out like demons on Halloween, all staring down at the Marines a hundred yards away.

"Shit. They're all around us. We have been flanked."

Bugles and whistles began to blow. Party time.

"First and Second Squad, echelon right and left. Form a triangle with Third Squad at the base, facing forward. Move. They're attacking."

Two men set up a German Spandau MG42 machine gun gleaned from some weapons dealer after the last war. Probably a Russian. Thousands of German arms were captured in Stalingrad when General Paulus surrendered the German Sixth Army to Russian Field Marshal Zhukov. These weapons were put into service by the Russian Army. After the war the arms were sold as surplus to the highest bidder or given to Communist China after the 1948 Revolution.

The sniper, one hundred fifty yards to their right, zeroed in on the M.G. Team. At the shot they both dropped. The gunner had been shot through the head, the loader catching the spent round in the neck. Like being hit with a sledge hammer. Lights out. His second shot was directed at the gun. Hitting the receiver tray, he caused enough damage to the thin sheet metal to put the gun out of action.

These people had a habit of picking up weapons from their dead and wounded. And this one was a formidable example.

"Here they come! Open fire."

The barrage was intense. The sniper was reminded of Civil War battles his grandfather had seen. The rattle of musketry. The smoke of spent gun powder. The roar of artillery. Both exhilarating and terrifying at the same time. The old man had spoken of it until he died. The addiction to battle. The unspoken reason some men can never live without war after being in one. The mercenary. To be a civilian is unfulfilling. To be a warrior and survive. Gratifying. Some truths are never to be spoken. Only acted on.

Eyes was directed to an officer talking into a radio handset.

His South Korean spotter student was given the shot. Eyes gave him the rifle. The little Soldier placed the crosshairs on the Captain's open mouth while he talked. At the shot the handset blew out of his hand and his brain blew out of his head. All that strategic knowledge, learned from the English, lying on the muddy ground. His aide, a Sergeant, stood up with a Type 50 Chicom burp gun and sprayed the area. His Korean Advisory placed a 150 grain, full metal jacket, thirty cal. distraction in his chest, driving him to the ground. He tried to get up, blood pouring from his mouth, then fell over dead before another round could dispatch him. The L1A6 Browning MG grew hot from firing and was down to its last ammo belt. The bar was smoking and cooking off rounds it was so hot. The gunners' hands were burning. Riflemen fired clip after clip, listening to the familiar ping when an empty ammo clip discharged from the M1 receiver, then instinctively reloading the rifle.

Russo's carbine overheated and jammed. He picked up the dead Marine's M1 that lay next to him and fired on the closing enemy. He had no ammo for this weapon but it didn't matter; the enemy was closing. Time for the bayonet.

Rawlins fired in short bursts at the mutable targets, not wanting to run dry or jam the gook Thompson. But there were too many. They were in the perimeter. The fighting was hand to hand. Two determined enemies bent on destroying each other. Medieval.

Three NKs came at Rawlins. The Tommy gun fired three rounds and jammed.

Lousy gook oversize ammo. Always jams a hot automatic.

One enemy fell with his chest torn out. The other two closed on the Marine. Rawlins clubbed the first one with his useless weapon. The second attacker disarmed him with a butt stroke, then tried to bayonet him. Rawlins deflected the thrust and pulled his Ka-Bar. The gook slashed and missed. The Marine grabbed the Chicom rifle and pulled the enemy close then stabbed him twice in the gut. The Soldier fell to his knees, grabbing his leaking abdomen. Rawlins kicked him in the face, knocking him down, then stomped on his throat. Goodbye, gook.

The Rooster rose to the occasion by bayoneting a Commie for Mommy. The dumb lackey of the People's Revolt tried to get in his hole with him. Rooster made him eligible for his own. Six by six.

Henshaw used his entrenching tool to nearly decapitate a burp gunner that fell in his hole with him. Then he grabbed the Chicom's T.fifty and killed three of the headless horseman's followers, not ten yards away. His 30 cal. ammo gone, he would adapt and overcome as he had been taught. The enemy weapon might be junk by a Marine's standards, but effective.

Ramirez fired away at the enemy with his forty five pistol. Walking the line, directing the fire, shooting enemy infiltrators as he went. His squad said he was nuts the way he exposed himself. They may have been right.

Russo teamed up with Junior near the end of the fight. They led their squads in a counter attack on the left flank as the enemy quit the field. Junior had a broken M1 with half the stock missing. Russo had his forty five. His carbine was hopelessly jammed. Most of their men had empty weapons but they threw their last grenades at the fleeing enemy.

Midnight. The fight was over. The leaderless enemy in full retreat, not knowing what to do with their Comrade Captain just lost for words.

The Corpsmen did what they could for the wounded.

The remaining ammo was collected and re-distributed, two clips per man. Luckily the enemy had had enough for the night. Another attack could have been fatal for the recon platoon.

Rawlins made the decision to stay put instead of bugging out, afraid of another ambush. At least here he could call in fires on his own position if necessary. They did fall back four hundred yards into a wood lot and dug in; the logic being that the enemy knew their position and could mortar them.

It was a long night. No talking, no smoking. Absolute noise and light discipline. The enemy could have a recon team looking for them right now. And the NKPA had Russian 107mm howitzers. Very nasty surprise for infantry.

The Corpsmen kept the wounded doped up with morphine. For once they had enough.

The sniper moved into a position two hundred yards from his mates and waited for dawn.

Rawlins was edgy all night. He was sure they would be probed at the least. And their ammo situation was critical. But nothing happened. Just some artillery fire behind their position between them and Inchon.

The Third Battalion was breaking through. Sunrise and no attack. Third Battalion with Army tanks was heard moving up on their rear, engineers checking the road for mines slowing their progress.

* * * * *

"Master Gunny. What the hell is that?"

"That's our sniper team dressed in ghillie suits. And they're coming in. Hold your fire. Those are Marines."

"Damn, Master Guns, they look like swamp beasties from Arkansas."

"What are you talking about, Carter?"

"My granddaddy told a story about big furry critters way back in the swamps back home. Said he saw one once. Scared the hell out of him. Everybody thought he was drunk as usual. Then one day my daddy was squirrel hunting way back in the woods on the other side of a big bog and saw one. Said it walked out of the bog and stopped in front of him, then just stood there staring at him. It was eight feet tall and covered with long hair. It started growling and huffing at him, then threw rocks and sticks at him. Finally the old man shot at it and it ran back into the bog. He never went into the woods again even with a gun."

"Well, these critters are Marines so don't shoot at 'um."

Poor kid, thought Rawlins. *Been in combat too long.*

Eyes and Company walked into the perimeter and shed their suits.

"Well, I'll be a son of a bitch. Eyes. How the hell are you? I thought that might be you out there."

"I'm still saving your ass, you jarhead son of a bitch."

"How long you been here, Eyes?"

"A year. Been teaching the ROK Marines. They love me. Got my own hooch, maid, hot chow and all the free booze I can handle.

These little fellas are my spotters. They're good shooters too. We took out a mortar crew last night during the attack. And their Captain. That broke 'um up good."

"Were you at the Naktong covering our asses?"

"Yeah. That was us. Saw you through the scope and figured I better dog you as usual. Keep you out of trouble."

" I see you got another stripe."

"Yeah. They made me a Staff Sergeant. But don't get no ideas. I'm on my own. Don't answer to anybody but their Major. So hands off."

"OK, Eyes. You gonna hang around?"

"No. Gotta go. Gotta scout that sector over where the gooks came from last night. See if there are any officers out in the open. These guys need some long range practice."

"Good luck, Eyes. See ya later."

"OK, Ken. We'll be around."

* * * * *

Two hours later the Battalion reached their position. Rawlins made his After Action Report. Then the recon platoon moved to the rear for a day to re-arm and re-supply.

Ten Corps engaged the NKPA west of Seoul with the First Marine Division and Seventh U.S. Infantry. They engaged Russian built T34 tanks and massed infantry. The M24 Sheridan tanks with their 90mm guns evened the score, doing well against the T34 tanks. ROK Marines took part in the battle, also in the re-taking of Seoul. After pushing the Communist forces north and east Ten Corps entered the city. Fierce street and house to house fighting erupted, reminiscent of the battle of Aachen in Germany during the last war. There the Tiger tank outclassed the M4 Sherman medium tanks the U.S. and Britain were using at the time. Its 76mm gun could only penetrate the Tiger from the rear where its armor was thin. The German 88mm gun could completely penetrate a Sherman with its tungsten core armor piercing round.

* * * * *

"Alright, ladies. Grab your gear. We're moving out."

"Where to, Master Gunny?"

"Seoul. We gotta clear the way for the tanks."

"Oh, that's just great. We gotta protect armor plated tanks. What's gonna protect us?"

"Your dungaree blouse. They're bullet proof. Now get your asses movin.' Let's go."

The platoon loaded into a truck and two jeeps and headed into Seoul where they were immediately taken under fire from nearby houses. The tanks machine guns silenced the snipers.

"Alright, people. Gather around the tanks and advance."

As they moved into the city they fired into doorways and windows. Wherever a rocket team might be lurking. Whenever enemy troops ran into a building the tanks would blast them through the walls. Then the Marines would clean them out.

Rawlins and Russo took one squad into a hotel. They could hear the NKs above them on the next floor.

"Ken. You hear 'um?"

"Yeah. Right above us. Sounds like they're settin' up some kinda gun. Must be in the window."

Rawlins grabbed the B.A.R. man.

"Hear those gooks up there."

"Yeah. I hear 'um."

"Give 'um a burst through the floor."

"OK, Master Guns."

The Browning automatic rifle made a terrible muzzle blast in this confined area. Ten rounds of 30 cal. M2 ball tore through the thin floor. Three NK gunners fell dead on the floor, riddled with high velocity death. Two others shot down through the floor with their burp gun. Rawlins answered with a burst from his Thompson. Silence. He pointed to two Marines and then pointed up. They ran up the huge mahogany stair case and threw grenades into the room, then ran inside at the ready. But there was no need. Seven dead NK lay on the floor of two adjoining rooms and the 107mm recoilless rifle sat in the window waiting to kill an American tank. The gun was rendered inoperative by removing the breech block and the fuses on its ammo. The squad moved on. House after house; kick in the door, throw in a grenade, spray the room. Finally darkness fell and they secured for the day, staying in the last house they cleared for the night.

A young Marine made the fatal mistake of lighting a cigarette near an open window. A bullet entered his head just above his mouth. Sniper; using the glowing butt for a target. Everyone in the room emptied their weapons into the house across the street. But to no avail. The sniper was already gone. One more dead Marine. One more foolish mistake. He should have known better.

The next three days were the same. Tanks would draw fire, the Marines would clean out the enemy nest. Monotonous, boring, deadly. The worst kind of fighting for the infantry Soldier. Hidden death.

"Master Gunny, I got the creeps. The gooks are watching us. They're all around us and they're watching."

"Relax, kid. The ROKs cleared this area yesterday. All we gotta do is walk through. No big deal."

Grenade!!

The squad hit the deck. Wham! Chicom grenade from a window. Two men down.

Son of a bitch. Rotten gooks.

The entire squad opened fire on the small house. Then a tank shell blew it apart. No more grenades.

"I thought this area was cleared yesterday."

"It was."

That night on the northern edge of town the squad slept in a house with the enemy. The squad was on the upper floor, the enemy was in the cellar. The Marines were so exhausted and so low on ammo they left the NKs alone. The NKs slipped away in the middle of the night, escaping through a cellar window.

The next day, October 7, the battle was declared over. Seoul was officially in NATO hands. The Army and the ROKs remained to occupy and secure the city. NKPA units were heading north from Pusan after hearing about Inchon, in fear of being cut off and destroyed.

The First Marine Division moved back to Inchon and was taken to the east coast at Wonsan in late October. There they landed again but this time were unopposed. Then began the drive north to the

Yalu River and the border of China. The Fifth Marines held the ground at Hagaru-ri at the south tip of the Chosin Reservoir when they were deployed there on November 15th. A deadly surprise waited for them just above the Yalu River. Eight full divisions of Chinese Communist People's Liberation Army waited to strike the depleted Marines. Their goal – to wipe out the entire First Marine Division.

* * * * *

"Master Guns, I'm freezing."

"Relax. It's only ten below. Wait until it gets cold. You got your gear on from the Army?"

"Yeah, but I'm still freezing. I ain't used to this shit."

"Who the hell is. Two months ago we were sweating our asses off. Make sure you guys dig in deep. We're gonna get hit soon."

"I thought the NKs were finished, Master Guns."

"They are. But I got a feeling."

"Shit, Ramirez, he's got feelings."

" Son of a bitch. We're in for it now."

"Waddaya mean, Master Guns?"

"I mean there's people out there and they don't like us. And they're gonna come and tell us all about it."

"But you said the NKs are finished."

"They are."

"Then who's out there?"

"People."

"What people?"

"Bad ass people."

"How do you know, Master Guns?"

"'Cause I'm the Master Gunny."

* * * * *

"Hey, Sarge."

"What, Rooster?"

"The Master Gunny said there's people out there. What do

you think?"

"He's right."

"How do you know?"

"He's having feelings."

"So what?"

"He always has feelings before bad shit."

"Why?"

"'Cause he knows shit we don't know."

"How come?"

"'Cause he's the Master Gunny. Now shut up and dig. We're gonna get hit soon."

The weather was turning colder and it was snowing; always snowing." At night it would fall to thirty below. Trench foot and frostbite were becoming major problems.

"Master Guns. The Major wants to see you pronto."

"OK, Corporal. Tell him I'm on my way."

* * * * *

"Master Gunnery Sgt. Rawlins reporting, Sir."

"Come in Rawlins. Have a seat. Like a drink?"

"Yes, Sir."

"So would I. Too bad we're all out. Have some bad coffee instead. Sorry we haven't got you a new Lieutenant yet. They're hard to come by lately. Get hit right away and sent out."

"It's OK, Sir. I can hardle the platoon."

"Yes, I can see that, Rawlins. You're doing a good job. The Seventh Infantry boys on our flank lost a patrol. Gone two days. No contact. They asked us if we would send out you recon boys to help find them."

"Aye, Sir."

"Don't go out too far, Rawlins. We don't know what we're dealing with here. There's rumors of Red Chinese slipping across the Yalu. So watch your ass."

"Aye, Sir."

Rawlins noticed the cold when he left the warm tent. The temperature was dropping rapicly.

*Shit, this is different. I'm used to just the opposite. Sweating
my ass off.*

The platoon was just finishing up their holes when he
returned.

"Playtime's over, ladies. Gear up. We got a patrol. No packs.
Just weapons and ammo. First and Third Squads, let's go."

"Where we going, Ken?"

"Northwest, Vito. The Army lost some of their children. We
gotta find them."

The going was tough. Deep snow, rocky uneven ground, low
visibility, still snowing. After a mile they halted.

"Gee, Master Guns, just like Buffalo."

"Yeah. Pretty close. Only in Buffalo it would be up to our
necks by now."

"Man, this shit is all new to me. I'm from Miami. Never seen
this before. Pain in the ass, ain't it?"

"Not to the slopes. They love this shit. Like to hide in it. You
can't see 'um ten feet away. The snow is stopping. Let's move out.
I'll take point."

Rawlins moved north and west. Slow and deliberate.
Something wasn't right. He felt it. Every hundred yards or so he
stopped and scanned their forward. His Navy 10x50 binoculars
worked will for this. After a mile of this slow progress he spotted
something in the distance. O.D. green sticking out of the snow. An
arm. Attached to a body buried beneath the snow. Then a leg.
Remnants of a platoon lay dead in the snow. He walked back to the
patrol.

"We found them. They're a hundred yards ahead. All dead."

"Son of a bitch. How?"

"Ambushed. They didn't have a chance."

Twelve men lay in close order where they had fallen. Killed
with automatic weapons.

"Shit. Where's the rest of them?"

"I dunno. The slopes must have taken them prisoner. It was a
full platoon. Gather up their tags and personal affects and let's get the
hell outta here. Whoever did this may still be around."

The remainder of the platoon had been herded over the Yalu

River the night before and taken to a prison gulag for interrogation and containment, then eventual execution as war criminals.

Rawlins marked the site on his map for later burial, then led his people out of the killing zone, hoping they wouldn't suffer the same fate before returning to their position.

Back at Company Rawlins reported to the Major.

"We found them, Sir. Here's their tags and affects, Sir."

"All dead, Rawlins?"

"Twelve of them, Sir. They were ambushed. Killed with automatic weapons, Sir. Lots of brass all around their position, Sir."

"What about the rest?"

"Taken prisoner, Sir. Gone."

" Across the Yalu, I presume."

"Yes, Sir. That's where their prints headed."

"Any dead enemy?"

"None, Sir.:

"They must have taken their dead with them. Sounds like the rumors are right, Master Guns."

"Sir?"

"Red Chinese infiltrating and ambushing patrols. Then back across the Yalu where we can't go."

"Yes, Sir."

"Tell your men to be ready for infiltrators tonight. Dismissed."

"Aye, Sir."

* * * * *

Rawlins returned to his men and gave them the word. Double guard tonight. They were so cold they couldn't sleep anyway. A squad at a time was rotating to the rear for hot chow and a spell in a warming tent. A kerosene stove and a wood burner helped to take the chill off.

"This shit is crazy. One mortar round could take us all out."

"Go outside where it's safe, dummy. And freeze to death instead."

Back on the line it was dark and overcast. The surrounding

hills looked like ominous mounds of evil carnivores ready to cascade upon the Marines.

"Hey, Sarge."

"I'm not here."

"It's too quiet. There ain't noboby out there.

"Shaddup and keep watchin'. They're out there."

"How do you know?"

"'Cause I'm the Sergeant and you're the dummy. Now shut the hell up before I club you or send you out there to find 'um."

"Shit, Master Guns. What the hell was that?"

"Bugles. They want us to know they're out there."

"Why?"

"So you get nervous and don't sleep."

"Sleep. Who the hell can sleep."

Wham! 82mm mortars. A ten round barrage in the perimeter.

"Hold your fire. Don't give away your position. They're trying to bait us into firing."

Then the infiltration began. First grenades. Then the Marines countered with grenades. The grenade contest lasted for fifteen minutes. Then the enemy crawled into the perimeter and tried to kill the Marines hand to hand. Junior dragged one into his hole and his partner clubbed the Red with his rifle. A satchel charge dropped in a log bunker by a sapper killed the two machine gunners inside. Then Ramirez shot him with his burp gun from ten feet away, stitching the Red up the middle.

Russo found himself in a bayonet duel with a Chinese Corporal using a Russian Mosin-Nagant rifle. Russo discovered the Russian rifle was better suited for this use than his stubby carbine. All he was able to do was block the Red's thrusts. Finally he dropped his weapon and grabbed the Red's rifle. A tug of war ensued. It ended when Russo caved in the enemy's head with his steel helmet. The Chinese pleated cap was no match for the steel pot.

Rooster took a knife in the gut but shot his attacker with a Russian Tokarev pistol liberated from a dead NK officer weeks before. Rooster was on his way to Kobe, Japan the next day. The war was over for him.

Rawlins got out of his hole and walked the line. Between the

CP and the mortar batteries he spotted two sappers trying to crawl to the mortar ammo. He killed them both with a burst of his Chinese Tommy gun.

White ghosts bayoneted each other in this winter hell. The only color distinguishable in all this white was the red of blood on the snow.

At dawn the enemy was gone. Rawlins found out later at the Senior NCO briefing that it had been just a probe, not an attack. The Reds did the same thing up and down the line, looking for weak spots. The major attack would come on the twenty seventh of November. Eight Chinese divisions would swarm out of the hills and descend upon the First Marine Division.

The recon platoon was pulled off the line for a day and a night. Mail, hot chow and hot water was their reward for fighting and freezing for the previous week. Rawlins found a bottle and he and his squad leaders soaked their frozen feet and got drunk while sitting around a kerosene stove. The fifty degree tent was like Miami Beach compared to the line. And hot water like champagne to a wedding virgin. They shaved for the first time in a week, washed their socks and their feet.

"Hey, Junior. You hear from the crumpet queen?"

"Yeah. She's right here."

"What did she say?"

"She says her husband's dead again."

"No shit."

"Got killed on the Naktong."

"Boy, this guy don't get along with rivers. First he gets it on some river crossing in Italy, then comes back to life and gets it on the Naktong. Amazing."

"What are you saying, Vito?"

"I'm saying don't believe it. What else does she say?"

"She wants me to come to Wellington and marry her."

"You gonna?"

"Maybe."

"What if you get there and hubby's alive again."

"Then I'll smash 'um both and be done with it."

"Ramirez. What's wrong? You look white."

"The Yaqui broad bought a new Crestliner and says I'm responsible for the payments. Wants me to send my pay to her for the future and the car. She says I got to change my will so her and her kid are bennies. She can kiss my Mexican ass. I don't owe that broad shit. I was just being nice. Now she thinks we're married."

"Ken. What's a matter. You look sick."

"You won't believe it."

"What?"

"She did it."

"What?"

"She had the kid."

"No shit."

"No shit."

"What kind?"

"A boy. Named it Ken."

"Congratulations. How big?"

"Nine pounds. Big like me, she says."

"So why are you upset?"

"I can't have a kid."

"Why not? Millions of people have kids."

"Not me. I don't know anything about 'um. Just that they yell and shit all the time."

"Yeah, Ken. Just like Marines. You're already used to it."

"Yeah, but they're little. They might break easy."

"Well, you can't play football with 'um. At least not for a while. Don't worry about it. Your old lady will take care of it. They like that kind of shit. All you gotta do is sit there and pretend you're enjoying the whole thing."

"What if I gotta feed the kid or change shitty pants. I'll throw up."

"So throw up like a million other guys. You kill me. You can kill a man with your bare hands but you're afraid of a baby."

"What if I break it?"

"You ain't gonna break it. They don't break so easy. You just got to be careful. Don't drop it or toss it around. Your old lady will train you. It's just like combat for the first time. Once you get through that it gets easier. You'll get the hang of it."

"Shit. I ain't ready for this. She didn't tell me she was gonna have kids. Son of a bitch."

* * * * *

The next day they were back on the line. Back to freezing hell. Back to living in an empty grave in the frozen earth.

"Shit. I hate this. I'm so cold I can't feel my ass any more."

"Don't worry about it. When you get killed you won't need it anyway."

"Thanks a lot, shitbird."

"Don't mention it."

"Hey, Master Guns. You hear that?"

"B29 raid on the bridges at Koto-ri. They must expect Chinese armor to cross there."

"Son of a bitch. Look at those ridges to the north west. They're crawlin' with Reds. Look at 'um all."

"They must be staging for an attack. Better call Regiment and get some air power up here."

* * * * *

The Navy F9F Puma fighter bombers streak in from ten miles off Wonsan Harbor, dropping tank after tank of napalm on the enemy concentrations. Then the Marine F4U Corsairs dropped to the deck and made strafing runs until their ammo was depleted.

"That broke up the bastards. They're either dead or underground now. Better get ready for a major attack tonight or tomorrow."

Rawlins made the rounds, checking each man in the platoon. Extra ammo and grenades were brought up and two Browning fifty cal. heavy machine guns were borrowed from the Army next door. Tonight would be the first of the classic Chinese human wave assault and the two Brownings would play a big part in repelling them.

"Rawlins, Master Gunny Rawlins."

"Over here, Corporal."

"The Colonel wants to see you ASAP. He's at Battalion with

the Major."

"OK. Tell them I'm on my way."

"Master Gunnery Sgt. Rawlins reporting, Sir."

"Come in, Rawlins. This is Colonel Puller. He would like a word with you."

"Yes, Sir."

"So you're the son of a bitch we heard about."

"Yes, Sir."

"All balls, no brains."

"Yes, Sir."

"I got a job for you if you think you can handle it."

"Sir?"

"There's at least six Chinese Red divisions out there, Master Guns. Maybe more. We can't stop them alone. And I'm not ready to sacrifice the regiment or the division. I've been ordered to activate a fighting withdrawal. Attacking in a different direction."

"Yes, Sir."

"We're going back to Wonsan and board ships there for deployment to Pusan. As you can imagine, we need a rear guard action to slow these people down so we can get our wounded and equipment out. You understand?"

"Yes, Sir."

"Your company and platoon will be that rear guard if you agree to stand alone to protect your mates. You will probably be over-run. Is that clear?"

"Yes, Sir."

"The lives you save will offset your casualties. Do you accept this mission?"

"Yes, Sir."

"Good man, Rawlins."

Chesty Puller shook his hand.

"I'll see you on board ship."

"Aye, sir."

Rawlins returned to the recon platoon. The point of the spear, they were called. He lit a cigarette and wrote a letter to his wife and son. He assumed it would be the last letter he would ever write.

As the newly promoted General Puller made his First Division ready to pull out and head for Wonsan Harbor, Rawlins readied his men for the onslaught to come. He called a squad leader meeting.

"Alright, you guys. Listen up. The Division is pulling out. And we're the rear guard. There are at least six divisions of Red Chinese out there and they don't like us. We're gonna slow them down enough for the Division to get to Wonsan for evacuation. We'll pull out at the last minute and execute a fighting withdrawal. The Seventh Infantry, as part of Ten Corps, is leaving too. They have a rear guard also. They will remain on our flank. We will mutually support each other. We will have Naval gunfire and air plus heavy arty from Army at Wonsan. When we pull out we'll call in fires behind us. I know this is a shitty deal but somebody has got to slow the bastards down or the Division will be over-run and cut off. There's just too many of them. Every night they come across the Yalu by the hundreds and we have no way to stop them. So tell your people the deal and have them grab as much ammo and rations as they can carry. We're on our own."

* * * * *

As the sun began to set Navy jets made napalm runs on the surrounding hills, burned black by jellied gasoline. A stark contrast to the white ground around them. Trees looked like skeletal remains from a battle fought long ago.

Rawlins thought:

We may look like that before long.

He was having feelings of dread again. Feeling trapped. The call of duty on one side, cold raw fear on the other. He knew the chance of survival was slim. It reminded him of Iwo Jima. He had thought he would die without question there but he had survived. Like a young Marine told him:

"You ain't gonna die in this war, Gunny; or the next."

Now he wasn't so sure. He imagined his dead Raider buddy, Joker, coming to get him and take him to the place where dead Marines go. Like he had thought on Iwo when Joker had appeared in front of him. He got up and checked the line, watching vehicles moving down the road to the sea below him.

"Now remember boys, conserve your ammo. Don't fire until they're close. One shot, one kill. Use grenades first. Try to break 'um up."

Finally darkness fell. Every few minutes star shells illuminated the torn, burned landscape. Rawlins cradles his Tommy gun. Two thirty round magazines taped back to back for a fast re-load. Nothing. Just rocks and snow.

Where are the bastards.

He knew they were out there. He knew they would come to kill him and his men. But when.

"Master Guns, I hear something. A scraping sound like metal on a rock."

Dark now. Flares popping over the Seventh Infantry next door. Another scraping sound.

"Master Guns, there's something out there."

"Yeah. I hear it now. Shuman. Fire a para flare."

At the pop stark white light lit the landscape.

"Shit! They're everywhere. They're wearing white camouflage."

Twenty yards away the Chinese jumped up and charged the Marines.

"Open fire! "

The heavy and light Browning machine guns opened up, cutting huge swaths out of the enemy advance. Still they came. Riflemen fired their M1 rifles at point blank range. Clip after clip until they grew hot. No time for grenades. The Chinese dead were piling up in front of their positions. More troops crawled up the ridge in standard issue uniforms. No need for white now. Many had no weapon. They picked up one from a dead comrade. Four Commies rushed the line in front of Rawlins hole. He stood up and mowed them down, expending a whole magazine. Quickly changing sticks, he shot two more behind him. The enemy were all around the Marines. Hand to hand fighting had broken out. Bayonets flashed in the frozen moonlight. Blood ran into the snow as men beat and stabbed one another. Rawlins found Clark, the radioman and grabbed the handset. The operator was dead, killed by a Type Fifty burp gun. He had been nearly cut in half. Rawlins called in artillery. The valley was hit with saturation fire, anti-personnel 155mm. The Army was happy to help the Marines dispose of the enemy. Their attack broke the back of the Commies and they melted away.

As two Navy Corpsmen tended to the wounded the dead were stripped of ammo and weapons. Even the Chinese were stripped of anything useful.

Just before dawn they struck again. Hordes of Chinese, screaming like demons from hell, came across the valley, bugles blowing. No stealth this time. Human wave assault. One of many to come. The first attack had been just skirmishers. This was the real thing. A full reinforced battalion. Six infantry companies on line.

The Marines opened up, machine guns cutting them down. Rawlins called in Naval fire support. Eight inch Naval rifles turned the valley into an inferno. Hot steel tore into the invaders, tearing them apart. The dead were in piles, the living crawling under them and up the hill to the ridge. Weapons overheated and jammed. Rawlins fired his Thompson until it was empty. No time to reload. He dropped it and pulled out his forty five. A Chicom reached the top of the ridge and fired at him with a burp gun, missing him, tearing up the ground behind him. The Marine shot the enemy between the eyes.

Junior was bayoneted climbing out of the hole. This enraged the giant Marine. Using his rifle for a club he smashed Chinese after Chinese. He was shot with a burp gun but got up and killed the gunner with his forty five. Another gook stabbed him in the back. The big Marine swung around with a huge fist and broke the neck of the small Asian with one blow. Finally, he collapsed in the snow, bleeding uncontrollably.

The fight was over. The Chinese still alive walked down the hill into the valley of death unopposed. The Marines didn't even fire at them. They had had enough. Most were out of ammo anyway.

* * * * *

The Corpsman found Rawlins.

"Master Gunny, Sgt. Evans is asking for you. He's hurt pretty bad."

"Junior, you big son of a bitch. If you die on me, I'll kill ya."

"Gunny, I can't feel nothing. And it's getting dark. Everything is blurry. Where the hell am I?"

"What happened?"

"I don't feel good, Gunny."

"Hang on, Junior. We'll get you outta here."

"Gunny. I gotta go now. Corporal Johnson is here, smiling at me. Holding out his hand. I gotta go, Gunny."

And Junior was gone. Off with a dead Raider buddy killed on Bougainville long ago. Rawlins was crying like a baby, holding the dead Marine like a child.

"Don't die, dammit. Come back. You're just a kid. Don't leave like this."

The Marines around the spectacle were shocked. No one said a word. The hadn't thought the old hard ass Marine had any feelings and here he was crying over a dead man. Just another dead Marine.

Rawlins sat in his hole stunned. As it grew light he was overtaken with grief. He fell apart, finally broken by the horror of war. Unable to think or move. He just shook all over and wept like a child. So many dead friends. Two wars and no end in sight. They were all going to die. There would be no life without war for them. The sacrifices of freedom. The U.S. Marines.

Junior's body was wrapped in a shelter half and taken to the rear with the rest of the dead. He would be buried in Hungnam in the First Division cemetery.

Ramirez was next to pay the ultimate price. At 0700 hours an artillery barrage commenced. Russian 150mm cannon and 107mm pack howitzers pounded the ridge which the Marines held. They walked the rounds back and forth, trying to clear a path for the infantry to break through. They Commies were in the valley once more massing for another human wave assault. Ramirez received a direct hit in his hole. He disappeared in a sheet of dirty flame and debris. Nothing left. Vaporized. The Yaqui would receive her ten thousand dollars insurance money. Carlos had changed his will at the last minute before moving back to the line.

The artillery lifted and they came; hundreds of them. Marine Corsairs came in low and strafed them. Still they came. Navy air bombed and napalmed the surrounding hills, trying to stem the human tide. There were just too many. The Marines fired their weapons until they were cooking off rounds in their overheated barrels. Then grenades and mortars. There was no stopping them, an irresistible human tsunami. A full regiment of the People's Forty Second Division. As they over-ran the hilltop, Rawlins knew it was over.

Goodbye, little nurse. Goodbye, kid. This is it. The end for us.

Determined to go out fighting, the Marines jumped out of their holes, screaming like banshees, and charged the overwhelming enemy. They would not die easily. A vicious hand to hand battle ensued. Fists, rocks, knives, bayonets, gun butts. No quarter was given. No prisoners taken. Only life or death.

Rawlins charged the Chicoms, screaming like the devil. He heard nothing. Everything was in slow motion. He had tunnel vision. He felt his Thompson bucking in his hands but did not hear it. Mowing down gook after gook he finally came up empty. He used the weapon for a club. A Commie hit him in the side with a burp gun, the rounds feeling like hammers striking him, knocking him down. He rolled and got back up, pulling his pistol. As the burp gunner tried to reload, Rawlins put two slugs in his chest. A bayonet came at him. He deflected it but still caught it in the shoulder. He killed the attacker with a shot to the face. Growing weak now from blood loss and shock the big Marine was beginning to pass out. He pointed the forty five at a gaggle of Commies coming over the top of the ridge and pulled the trigger until it was empty. Dropping the empty pistol in the snow, he pulled out his Ka-Bar, determined to fight to the end. Suddenly he was lifted off the ground by an unseen force and slammed into the ground. The last thought in his mind was of the young Marine on Iwo Jima who had told him he wasn't going to die in a war.

The Chicom grenade nearly severed his left leg. Luckily, the Corpsman tied it off with a tourniquet before he bled to death.

The Chinese withdrew as a battalion of ROK Marines stormed the hill. They were the mobile reserve for the delaying force and they saved Rawlins' life. One of them gave blood for a transfusion on the spot where he was wounded. The Corpsmen sewed him up the best they could, then an Army chopper came in from Pusan and medevaced him out. His left leg was amputated below the knee. Too damaged to save. Then he was shipped to Kobe, Japan to the big Army Hospital there. Now in a coma, as much steel as possible was removed from his broken body along with two crushed ribs. He lay in this hospital for three weeks before waking up. He was on the "not expected to live" list for a month.

* * * * *

"Well, Master Gunnery Sgt. Welcome back."

"Thanks, Miss Nurse. Where the hell am I?"

"Kobe, Japan. You were seriously wounded. We gave you up for dead twice. We can't believe you're still here."

"I ain't your average bear, Nursey."

"Yes. I can see that."

Rawlins was shipped to Pearl Harbor for another round of surgery, then Bethesda Naval Hospital in Maryland. The war was over for him.

Vito Russo was lucky. As always the smart operator, he saw the horde coming over the ridge top and fired into them, emptying his carbine. Then he grabbed a convenient dead gook, dragged him into his hole and hid under him. He was eventually wounded with grenade fragments and evacuated. The two surviving NCOs would remain friends for the rest of their lives.

Staff Sgt. Fisher, alias Eyes, would remain in country with the ROK Marines until the treaty was signed in 1953 and hostilities ended. He never knew the fate of his ex-Raider buddies until ten years later at a Raider reunion when the story of the bloody ridge came out and he learned that his ROK Marines had saved the day.

Chapter Twelve

RECOVERY

Bethesda Naval Hospital, Maryland, January 1951

"You big ape. Why did you get shot and blown up again?"
" So I could see you again? Works every time."
"Stop it."
"Stop what?"
"You're making me cry."
"Why?"
"Because you're here."
"I thought you wanted me to come home."
"I did. But not like this. You almost died. Twice."
"Yes, dear."
"It's not funny. You're always doing this and I hate it."
"Doing what?"
"Shot, stabbed, blown up. Why can't you be normal?"
"I am, for a Marine."
"You're hopeless."
"How's the kid?"
"Big and loud like his father. Already acts like a Marine. Do you know you lost a leg?"
"I still have the other two."
"Don't talk dirty. Just stop it right now. We're not in a barracks."
"OK."
"How are you going to handle it?"
"I've seen lots of guys lose their heads or worse. They handled it."
"How?"
"Usually by dying."
"Stop trying to be funny. It's not funny."
"What do you want me to do. Whine and moan like a boot? I

can handle it as long as you can."

"It doesn't matter to me as long as you're here. Maybe it'll be a good thing. Finally, no more Marine Corps and deployments. By the way, you won the Medal of Honor."

"What? You're kidding me."

"No. I'm serious. We have to go to the White House. President Truman is going to decorate you."

"For what?"

"General Puller of the First Division claims your company saved the division from the Reds. Without your rearguard action the division would have been decimated. And since you were in charge and were severely wounded you get the medal."

"What about Junior" He got severely dead."

"He gets the Navy Cross. Posthumously."

"How about Ramirez?"

"Him too."

"Shit. The whole company was almost wiped out. There were thousands of them. We just couldn't stop them all."

"I know, Ken. We saw it in the news reels. Terrible."

"How's Mom and Dad and Sis?"

"Very happy their hero is alive. They can't wait to see you."

"Shit. I shouldn't be here. I should be on that mountain buried with my men. This ain't right. Why does everybody die but me?"

"It's not your time, Ken. And only God knows when that is."

* * * * *

After three months of therapy and learning to walk with a wooden leg, Rawlins boarded the train for Buffalo. His wife had gone home two months before to take care of the baby at her parent's home. The Marine pulled out a fifth of scotch a friendly nurse had given him and fired up a Lucky. Trying to relax, he watched the countryside in rural Pennsylvania slide by. His leg that wasn't there any more hurt like hell. Memory pains, they called it. Shit. What the hell were real pains like. It was hard to believe it was really over. He had seen the world in the last ten years, fought in two major wars and survived. So many of his friends had not. They were buried in some far distant jungle or volcanic island never to be seen again. Semper phi. And now even more. Some were resting forever on a mountain covered with snow in a distant, strange land. And for what. Politics. Democracy. Buddy buddy bullshit. The politicians and generals that start wars should have to fight them. Shit. That would be the end of war.

What would he do now? He would have his disability pension but it wouldn't be enough. Maybe he should write a book. He sure had plenty to say. Maybe even make a Hollywood movie. Errol Flynn looked like him. He could play the lead role.

People on the train were staring at him. They always stared at him when he was in uniform.

More ribbons than a general's general, he thought. *And three up and three hangers with hash marks to his wrist below that. What a spectacle. They probably think I won the war all by myself. If only they knew.*

Finally, the Buffalo Terminal and home. As he exited the cab his parents came out of the house. They stared as he walked up the front steps and made the ascend, trying not to help the wounded Marine, knowing he had to master this alone. Then they grabbed him and held him for a long time, tears streaming down their anguished faces.

"Welcome home, son. Semper phi."

The wounded Marine called his wife at her parents' home and asked her to come to his parent's house. He was too fatigued to travel any further and in too much pain.

His father came up with a bottle and a six pack; their favorite medicine. They talked about Korea and how most people hadn't even known there was a war going on. Popular opinion was that it had been a police action. No big deal.

"Like hell," Rawlins told his family.

"It was just as bad as the last war. Especially when the Reds got involved. A lot of good men are buried there; a lot of my men. Guys that made it through the last war. They ain't coming back this time. Forever more they ain't coming back. Lousy Commies. We helped 'um out in the last war. Now they want to destroy us. No favor goes unpunished. My Tommy gun came from a dead slope head. It had Chinese and American markings. A lend lease gun from Chang Kai Shek's Army. Captured by the Reds in forty-eight, now being used against us. They have all kinds of U.S. stuff. It's disgusting. And Russian. Even Jap and German surplus. Some of my guys were cut down with a German Spandau MG42 machine gun."

Eleanor walked in with Rawlin's son and put him down in the Marine's lap. Rawlins stared in stunned silence, just looking at the baby. Big with blue eyes and blonde hair.

"And a big mouth just like his Dad's," uttered his wife.

"He's kinda little, ain't he?"

"Not for a baby."

"Vito was right. It's different when it's yours."

"How does he know?"

"He's Italian. They know about family stuff."

Rawlins looked down at his son smiling at him and began to shake all over and cry.

"Ken. What's wrong?"

"When the gooks came over the ridge and over-ran us I said goodbye to you and the kid. I knew I was gonna die but here I am. I don't understand. Men dying all around me. Hundreds of Reds bearing down on us. And I'm alive. And here's my son. I never thought I would get to see him."

Now the whole family was crying.

"It wasn't your time, Ken. God has other plans for you."

* * * * *

The next day the new family went to Eleanor's apartment in the Falls. Rawlins had a rough time with the stairs but he made it, his wife fighting back tears the whole time. Rawlins was a wreck. Drinking again. Nightmares every night. Depression. Anxiety. He went to counseling at the local Veteran's Affairs Office but it didn't help. All he could think about was:

What the hell does this college boy know about war. He can't even wipe his own ass without the manual.

Back to the bars and the war stories with other counseling drop-outs. They formed their own group of ex-military anti-socialites.

Eleanor took the baby to her parent's house, afraid of what her husband might do in a drunken rage. She no longer trusted him. He was returning to his "between wars" pattern of drinking and fighting. She had decided the last time she had bailed him out of jail that that was it. No more. He had broken the jaw of a young punk for calling him an old cripple. But it had to stop. So she told Rawlins:

"Make your choice. Either the bars or me and the baby. I have had enough of this."

To everyone's amazement, he stopped. Just quit. The night before he had had a dream of Bloody Ridge. He was sitting in his hole holding his son when Johnson, Joker, Junior and Ramirez appeared in front of him, all with stern looks on their blackened faces, still in their combat dungarees. They looked at him; then at the baby. Then they pointed to the baby like they were going to take him. Then Ramirez pulled his ever present bottle out of his pack, held it up and shook his head "no." Then he smashed it on a rock. Then the four men smiled and disappeared.

I'll be a son of a bitch, thought Rawlins. *They want me to stop 'cause of the kid. Or I'm gonna lose him.*

Rawlins never took another drink. He told his wife about the dream a week later. All she said was, "I know. I had the same dream."

* * * * *

The plane ride to D.C. was long and boring. A Douglas DC10 out of Buffalo International served the purpose. Rawlins was nervous. He hated planes. When they sank you can't get out and swim. You fry. He didn't even have a parachute. This was worse than combat. Of course they probably wouldn't get shot at. He hadn't seen too many Zero or Messerschmitt fighters lately.

"What's wrong, Ken?"

"Don't like planes. They crash."

"Not always."

"Sooner or later they all go down."

"The wars over, Ken. Remember?"

"Don't matter. They still crash."

"Have you been in a plane crash?"

"No. I always jumped out of them first."

"Well, don't jump out today. You will miss your appointment at the White House. The President doesn't like being kept waiting for his guests. Remember what happened to MacArthur?"

"Yeah, I remember. And the General was right. We shoulda nuked 'um. We're gonna have to fight 'um again sooner or later. It would have saved a lot of American lives. Truman is a coward. Typical politician. 'I'm from Missouri. Show me.' What a bunch of bull shit. The General showed him twenty Red Chinese divisions across the Yalu waiting to destroy us and Truman fired him for it. And we got our asses kicked because of it. Wait until I see that hard headed son of a bitch."

"Ken. You're not going to give the President hell."

"Why not? He deserves it."

"Because he's the President. The Commander in Chief. Remember, Marine?"

"I ain't a Marine any more."

"You are today. That's why our uniforms are with us. You're still in."

"I'm out."

"Not today you're not. You're a Marine for a day. So don't insult or hit the President or you will be in the brig for eternity."

* * * * *

Master Gunnery Sgt. Rawlins and Lieut. Commander Rawlins.

"It's an honor to meet you both. Sit down. The Commandant of the Corps is here, Rawlins."

"Rawlins. Why you sea dog son of a bitch. I thought you got killed on that ridge I put you on."

Rawlins saluted.

"No, Sir, General Puller. Almost, but not quite. It was a close run thing, Sir."

"I heard you were over-run twice, Rawlins."

"Yes, Sir. Lost most of my men, Sir. The ROK Marines and the Army Seventh Infantry helped us out, Sir, or we would have been wiped out , Sir."

"Well, Rawlins, it turned out that your people and a few others saved the First Division from annihilation. There were more Reds than we knew about."

"Yes, Sir. Thousands, Sir. When they attacked in battalion and regimental strength we were surprised, Sir. Didn't expect that, Sir."

"Well, Rawlins, you and your men did an outstanding job saving their mates. Outstanding. I wish I could decorate them all."

"I wish they were here, Sir. Instead of buried on some stinking hill in Korea."

"Semper phi, Marine."

"Aye, Sir."

"And who is the lady you didn't tell me about in Korea?" Eleanor spoke up.

"Lieut. Commander Eleanor Rawlins, U.S. Navy Reserve, Sir." And the little nurse saluted the General.

"How does it feel to be married to a Marine Corps hero, Commander?"

"Tiring, Sir. Hard to keep up with his green behind, Sir." (laughs)

"Well, Rawlins, maybe you better slow down and let her catch up. After all she is an officer. She should lead the charge."

"Aye, Sir."

(more laughs)

Then the President spoke up.

"Tell me, Rawlins. What do you think of MacArthur?"

"Finest combat General the country has ever produced, Sir."

"Really?"

"Yes, Sir. He beat hell out of the undefeated Japs, Sir, with almost nothing and he could have beaten the Reds in Korea, Sir."

Eleanor cringed at that statement.

You just had to do it, didn't you, you big ape)

General Puller looked at her and winked, almost laughing.

"Well, Rawlins, I guess that means you didn't approve of my firing of your beloved General."

"No, Sir. We could have won, Sir. He had a great plan, Sir.

And good men under him."

"Well, son of a bitch. I expected that from a Marine that was there. Every man has a right to his opinion. That's what democracy is all about. Right, Rawlins?"

"Yes, Sir."

"I have an awful feeling that prima donna Hollywood General is going to beat me in the next election. He's too damn popular with the military and civilians alike."

"Yes, Sir."

"Would you vote for him, Rawlins?"

"Yes, Sir."

""Well, I guess that's to be expected from a bunch of heroes. They stick together."

(laughs)

"Yes, Sir."

* * * * *

The ceremony was conducted on the east lawn. Rawlins and his wife stood at rigid attention as the Commander in Chief said the words. Cameras snapped away and the press corps copied the speech.

"For heroism and gallantry above and beyond the call of duty, during the battle of the Chosin Reservoir in Korea, for maintaining command of a rear guard action while wounded and never leaving his post until he was incapacitated, his actions playing a major role in allowing the First Marine Division to withdraw and be evacuated, I hereby present , by the powers vested in me as Commander and Chief of all United States military forces, the Congressional Medal of Honor."

The President placed the medal, suspended by a blue ribbon, around the Marine's neck. Rawlins snapped a perfect salute, then shook his Commander and Chief's hand, then went to parade rest. He spotted his parents and sister on the lawn, all crying with pride and emotion. He fought back the tears and waved to them. The President had had them flown in for the ceremony.

* * * * *

Later, during dinner, the President asked the senior Rawlins about his C.M.O. He explained his part in the battle of Belleau Wood as a young Marine and how he eliminated three German machine gun nests with grenades and a pistol.

"I was in your war, Mr. Rawlins. Battery B of the Missouri Volunteer Artillery."

"Army artillery saved a lot of Marines in the war, Mr. President. Just like in the two wars my son has fought in."

"Good of you to say that, Rawlins. I had always hoped that I did my part in that fracas."

"I'm sure you did, Sir."

"Now I see where this warrior came from," said General Puller. "Family tradition."

"I was in your war too, Mr. Rawlins. A young lieutenant. I know how bad those trenches were. The artillery, machine guns, then bayonets. Pretty rough."

"Semper phi, Sir."

Puller raised his glass to the old man.

"Semper phi, Marine."

Then the President stood and raised his glass in a salute to the warriors in his company.

"I have never been in the company of such heroic men and I fear I never will be again. Thank you, gentlemen for protecting our beloved country."

The men said nothing, the ladies cried. It was very emotional.

* * * * *

The Rawlins family returned to Buffalo by train. Neither of the men liked to fly. It was like a small vacation; a family reunion. The Rawlins' hadn't seen much of each other lately.

The old man was getting to know his grandson. The son was getting to know his wife. They had been separated more than together. That would change now. What did the future hold? Time would tell, but the conflicts they faced would be shared as they faced each day together.

Epilogue

Rawlins would become a writer, recalling his war experiences and his time in the Marines. He would also travel the lecture circuit, teaching WW2 Pacific history to college students. He would be the advisor for two movies about the Korean War.

His son would become a Force Recon Marine in the Vietnam War, and would be subjected to drinking and marital problems after the war as his father had been before him.

His grandson would become a Force Recon Scout Sniper and lead a NATO Team in the middle east conflict of the new century. Finding and eliminating terrorists all over the world would be his war.

Able Team, his comrades, would rely on tactics developed by Marine Raiders long ago to survive and wage war as a small unit in an international conflict.